The
Cuban
Daughter

BOOKS BY SORAYA LANE

THE LOST DAUGHTERS

The Italian Daughter

The Cuban Daughter

Soraya
LANE

The
Cuban
Daughter

Bookouture

Published by Bookouture in 2023

An imprint of Storyfire Ltd.
Carmelite House
50 Victoria Embankment
London EC4Y 0DZ

www.bookouture.com

ISBN: 978-1-83790-003-9
eBook ISBN: 978-1-83790-002-2

For Richard King
Thank you for believing in this series and telling the world
about it.

PROLOGUE

Esmeralda had her arm linked through her sister María's as they walked into the sitting room to join their father. Their maid had come dashing upstairs in a hurry to tell them there was a visitor, and that they were expected to come down immediately, but it wasn't an unusual request. Her father liked to show his daughters off; they were his pride and joy. Before, when her mother was alive, her parents would have likely entertained guests without need for their daughters to do more than whisk in and out of the room for show, but now her father preferred his girls by his side. He liked nothing more than to see them smile and entertain his business associates and friends, his eyes always lighting up when they entered a room, never more content than when he was with his daughters.

But today was different. Today, for the very first time, Esmeralda lost her perfectly practised composure, her feet stopping of their own accord even though María kept walking and tried to tug her along, even as Gisele glided into the room behind them and bumped her shoulder on the way past, eager to see who the unexpected guest was.

Because there, sitting on their opulent gold-edged sofa,

rising slightly as she and her sisters entered the room, was Christopher.

My Christopher is here. Her heart skipped a beat and her mouth went dry. *It can't be. How is Christopher here, in Cuba?*

'Esmeralda, you remember Mr Christopher Dutton, from London?' Her father beamed at her, a cigar in hand as he waved her into the room. 'And these are my daughters, María and Gisele.'

Esmeralda forced her feet to move, not wanting her father to know how affected she was by Christopher's presence, and she was grateful for the way his eyes only fleetingly met hers, his composure impeccable. Had she imagined what had happened between them? The looks he'd given her when she'd been in London, the way their hands had brushed, their little fingers just touching as she'd walked away from him that very last time?

'It's so lovely to see you again, Esmeralda,' Christopher said, standing and nodding, before gently taking first María's hand and then Gisele's. Her cheeks heated as she watched him, as María glanced over her shoulder at her, eyebrows raised when he pressed a kiss to the back of her hand. Of course Esmeralda had told her sister all about the handsome Englishman, her thoughts had been consumed by him since she'd returned from London, but never in a million years had she imagined he'd come to Cuba to visit. When it came to her turn, Christopher kept hold of her hand just a second too long, his lips lingering against her skin, his eyes locked on hers.

'What, ah, what,' Esmeralda quickly corrected herself, clearing her throat as he dropped her hand. 'What brings you all the way to Havana, Mr Dutton?'

'Your father was most insistent that someone from the company come here to see the production first-hand,' Christopher said, sitting back down as her father gestured for them all to sit, although his eyes barely left hers. 'I have to say, he's a very hard man to say no to, and I couldn't resist the opportunity to come to Cuba myself, especially after all the stories you regaled me with of Havana. You certainly painted a beautiful picture of your exotic country.'

One of their maids rushed into the room then, and, with her father's attention diverted, she indulged in truly looking at Christopher, the knot in her stomach dispersing when he smiled, his eyes telling her that he was as relieved to see her as she was him.

Perhaps I didn't imagine his feelings towards me after all.

'A bottle of our finest champagne,' her father announced as he lit his cigar, puffing the pungent smoke into the room as their maid scurried off to fulfil his request.

When Esmeralda moved past Christopher, her breath stilled in her throat as she brushed so closely to him that the fabric of her dress must have touched his knee, and he caught her finger in his. It was only a split-second, their fingers intertwined in a hold so brief that no one could have possibly noticed, but it told her everything she needed to know.

He didn't just come to see Cuba.

He travelled all this way to see me.

1

LONDON, PRESENT DAY

Claudia had the music blaring loud, paintbrush in hand as she touched up the white windowsill. She'd spent the past six months working on the flat, breathing life into the once-dated interior, and she only had a few days of renovation work left before it was finished.

She stood back and looked around at what she'd created, nostalgic about having to part with the place despite never having intended on keeping it. *This is a business*, she told herself. *No falling in love with the project. This is not home.*

It was the second flat in Chelsea that she'd renovated in the past year, and she'd loved every second of it. The design, the painting, the styling—it was so far removed from her previous job, yet it bought her a level of satisfaction that her first career had always failed to provide.

The music stopped then and was replaced with the ringing of her phone, and she set down her brush and wiped her hands on her overalls before picking it up. She knew it was likely to be one of her parents before she even saw the screen; the only people who actually called her these days were her family or telemarketers.

The caller ID told her she was correct. 'Hey Mum.'

'Hi darling, how are you?'

'Great. I'm just finishing up some painting but I'm almost done here.'

'Wonderful, we're so looking forward to seeing it when we're up next.'

Claudia knew how hard the transition had been for her mother. She'd been so proud of her only daughter when she'd been studying business at university, and even prouder when she'd landed an impressive job in finance, just like her father. Her brother was a lawyer, which they'd been equally happy about, but her mother had never gone to university or had a career of her own, and Claudia often felt as if she were living vicariously through her daughter. Or at least she had been, until Claudia had quit her fancy job and announced she was going to start renovating real estate for a living instead.

'Is it still okay for me to come and stay this weekend?' Claudia asked.

'Of course! We're so looking forward to seeing you, but that wasn't why I called.'

Claudia waited, absently starting to clean the paintbrush while she waited for her mother to continue.

'I was actually wondering if you could attend a meeting for me, on Friday.'

'This Friday? Sure. What's the meeting about?'

Her mum cleared her throat. 'Look, it's going to sound strange, but we received a letter to your grandmother's estate recently, and although your father thinks it could be a hoax, I believe it's worth going, if not just to see what it's all about.'

'Okay,' Claudia said, walking through to the kitchen to make coffee while she listened to her mum. *What type of appointment could it be that her father wouldn't approve of?*

'I'll send the letter through to you when we get off the phone, but it would mean a lot to me if you could go. I'd hate to disrespect your grandmother by not making the effort, just in case.'

Claudia nodded. Her mother rarely asked her to do anything, so she didn't mind, but the fact her father thought it could be a hoax, whatever it was, did alarm her. His instincts were usually right.

'Mum, if you want me to go, I'll go. Just send the details through.'

'Thank you, darling. I knew you'd say yes.'

They chatted a few minutes longer before Claudia said goodbye, and shortly after the call ended, the promised email arrived. She opened it, quickly scanning the message.

TO WHOM IT MAY CONCERN,

IN REGARD TO THE ESTATE OF CATHERINE BLACK. YOUR PRESENCE IS REQUESTED AT THE OFFICES OF WILLIAMSON, CLARK & DUNCAN IN PADDINGTON, LONDON, ON FRIDAY 26TH AUGUST AT 9 A.M., TO RECEIVE AN ITEM LEFT TO THE ESTATE. PLEASE MAKE CONTACT WITH OUR OFFICES TO CONFIRM RECEIPT OF THIS LETTER.

Claudia reread it, puzzled. No wonder her father thought it was a scam. But if her mother wanted her to find out what it was all about, then she would go. It had been hard on all of them when Grandma had passed, most especially because it was her grandmother who'd been the great cook in the family and had always had them all for Sunday lunches—a tradition that had waned and then eventually fizzled out after her passing the previous year. Perhaps it was still too soon for her mum to deal with her estate; perhaps there were some things that hadn't been taken care of, although her dad was usually very particular about paperwork and loose ends.

Claudia turned the music back up again and spun around in the flat, not wanting to think about how difficult the last year had been. She'd lost her grandmother and her best friend within months of each other, and one of the reasons she loved her new job was because it had no links to her past.

She looked around, smiling as she admired her work. The interior looked amazing; the walls were now a soft white, the kitchen was almost finished and beneath the drop sheets the wooden floor was the most perfect shade. It was going to look gorgeous once it was all staged with furniture.

She might have traded a suit for overalls, her hair in a messy bun instead of styled, but in truth she'd never been happier. She couldn't have stayed in her old job, not after what had happened, and this work made her feel good instead of twisting her into knots each day.

Now I just have to sell the place and try to make a profit.

2

Claudia walked the estate agent through the flat, showing her the recently tiled en suite bathrooms and admiring the newly installed furniture as they made their way back to the open-plan kitchen and living area. The sun was shining and she had the doors to the terrace thrown open—it was the kind of day that made it impossible not to feel good.

'It's stunning, absolutely stunning,' the agent said, running her hands across the stone bench in the kitchen. 'I'm sure we'll sell it quickly. When do you want to list it?'

'I'll be making a decision this week,' Claudia said, looking at the outdoor sofa and once again seeing herself staying there. But if she stayed, she'd have to find another line of work; there was no way she could afford to buy another project if she didn't sell. She turned her attention back to the agent. Perhaps she shouldn't have lived in the house while renovating; that way she wouldn't have become so attached.

'Well, let me know what you want to do. I know we'll have clients ready to look through even before we advertise it.'

Claudia's phone buzzed in her pocket and she took it out. *Meeting with lawyer.* 'I'm so sorry but I've just realised I'm running late for a meeting,' she said. 'I'll be in touch very soon. Thank you so much for coming!'

She quickly showed the agent out and ran to her bedroom, rummaging through her clothes and pulling out a blazer, which she put on over her white T-shirt. She found a pair of jeans and tidy trainers and wriggled her feet in, grabbing her bag and dashing to the door. She looked at her watch.

The tube from Sloane Square to Paddington ran every ten minutes, which meant she should easily make it from home to the offices in time. If she didn't, her mum was going to be furious with her.

Claudia ended up arriving at the glass-fronted offices of Williamson, Clark & Duncan with ten minutes to spare, and after speaking with the receptionist she found a seat and caught her breath. She hated being late, which meant she'd run the distance from the station to the offices, but it hadn't been necessary. As she sat she noticed the other people in the waiting room, who were surprisingly almost all female and of a similar age to her. Several were flicking through magazines, and a few more were sitting as she was, bag on her lap and surveying the room.

She hadn't had time to think much about the meeting, but now that she was here she was leaning towards agreeing with her mother; it certainly seemed legitimate. The offices alone were enough to convince her.

Before she had time to think about it anymore, the friendly young receptionist rose from behind the desk and addressed the room. Claudia was surprised to hear her call a handful of female names, not just hers.

Some of the women exchanged glances with her, and Claudia stood back to let two of them go ahead of her. She heard one of them mention something about an inheritance, and her ears pricked up.

Hmm, I hadn't even thought about an inheritance. It would be just like her grandmother to ensure they were all taken care of.

The chatter around her stopped abruptly when they stepped into a large conference room and were ushered to seats, with a well-dressed man positioned at the head of the table. To his left was a woman in her mid-thirties, her eyes wide as she seemed to consider everyone in the room. She was impeccably dressed in a silk blouse and high-waisted black trousers; she actually reminded Claudia of herself, when she'd still been in finance. She almost missed her old wardrobe just from looking at her.

Claudia took the piece of paper handed to her and sat back, casting her eyes over it as the man began to speak. She wasn't surprised when he acknowledged how strange it was to have summoned them all in as a group.

She glanced around the room, curious as to whether any of the other women knew why they were there, or whether they all felt like her and didn't have the faintest clue what it was all about. Claudia sat back in her seat as the lawyer took a few paces forward, one hand casually slipped into his pocket as he smiled and spoke.

'I'm John Williamson, and this is my client, Mia Jones. It was her suggestion that I summon you all here today, as she's following the wishes of her aunt, Hope Berenson. Our firm also represented her aunt many years ago.'

Claudia reached for the glass of water in front of her and took a sip, wondering who on earth Hope Berenson was.

'Mia, would you like to take over now and explain further?' he said.

Mia nodded and stood, and Claudia sat back in her chair to

listen, noticing how uncomfortable Mia suddenly looked, or perhaps she was simply nervous speaking to a group.

'As you've just heard, my aunt's name was Hope Berenson, and for many years she ran a private home here in London called Hope's House, for unmarried mothers and their babies. She was very well known for her discretion, as well as her kindness, despite the times.' Mia laughed, looking nervous as she glanced around the room. 'I'm sure you're wondering why on earth I'm telling you all this, but trust me, it will make sense soon.'

Hope's House? What connection could her grandmother have to a house for unmarried mothers? Was she insinuating her grandmother had an illegitimate child? Was that what this was all about? Her mother was going to be speechless if that was the case!

'What exactly does this old house have to do with us?' Claudia asked.

'Sorry, I should have started with that!' Mia said, looking embarrassed as she moved out from her chair and crossed the room. 'My aunt had a large office there, where she kept records and such, and I remembered how much my own mother had liked the rug in that particular room. So, I decided to roll it up and see if I couldn't use it somewhere instead of it being thrown out, only I saw something between two of the boards when I pulled it up. And, me being me, well I had to come back with something to prise them up and see what was down there.'

Claudia shook her head and sat back in her seat. *Unbelievable.* Although she still couldn't quite figure out her grandmother's connection.

'When I lifted the first board, I could see two dusty little boxes, and when I pulled back the second, there were more, all in a line and with matching handwritten tags. I couldn't believe what I'd discovered, but as soon as I saw there was a name on each box, I knew they weren't mine to open, no matter how badly I wanted to see what was inside.' Mia smiled as she glanced up, looking at each one of them before continuing. 'I brought those boxes here with me today, to show you all. I can't believe that my curiosity brought you all together.'

Mia carefully placed one box after the other on the table as she watched, and Claudia sat forward, eagerly looking to see. And that's when she saw her grandmother's name, written by hand, on a tag attached to a small box. Catherine Black. *Why is my grandmother's name on one of those boxes?* She couldn't take her eyes off the tag as the lawyer began to speak again, wondering just how long it had been hidden.

Claudia looked up. She desperately wanted to reach for the box and pull the string to see what had been left behind for her grandmother, but instead she stayed still, listening intently to the lawyer as he spoke again.

'What we don't know,' the lawyer said, planting his hands on the table as he slowly rose from his chair, 'is whether there were other boxes that were given out over the years. Either Hope chose not to give these seven out for some reason, or they weren't claimed.'

'In which case I may have uncovered something that was supposed to stay buried,' Mia finished for him.

One of the women stood, but Claudia didn't even listen to what she was saying, barely registering when she left the room. *My grandmother was adopted, and I didn't even know. Did she even know?* Surely if her grandma had known, she would have told her daughter, who would in turn have told Claudia. But perhaps it was one of those family secrets that simply wasn't talked about?

Claudia signed the documents when the lawyer put hers in front of her, before eagerly reaching for her box. It was made of wood, with string tied tightly around it, a name tag clearly identifying the recipient. Claudia traced her eyes slowly over her grandmother's name again, the letters all linked together in the most perfect handwriting, clearly labelled by the same person. *Hope.* The woman named Hope must have done this when her grandmother was born.

'Thank you,' Claudia said to Mia as she put her bag over her shoulder, the box still clasped in her hand. 'You've made such an effort to reunite all these boxes with their rightful owners.'

'You're welcome,' Mia said, reaching out and touching Claudia's arm, her smile warm. 'Thank you for coming to claim it.'

As she left, Claudia noticed one box was still sitting there with no one there to take it. Her curiosity piqued, she hurried out into the sunshine and decided to find the closest café. There was no chance she was waiting until she got home to pull the string to find out what clues awaited her in the little box.

3

HAVANA, CUBA, MID-1950

Esmeralda stood with two of her sisters near the foot of the sweeping staircase and surveyed the room. Waiters stood with silver trays held high, offering champagne to anyone who passed, a string quartet played in the far corner, and couples danced across the marble as the girls watched on. All the women wore their finest dresses, necks adorned with jewels, as were their earlobes and wrists—the room was full of the richest families in Havana, but all eyes still landed on the Diaz sisters when they arrived at the party.

'If it isn't the most beautiful girls in Cuba!' Esmeralda laughed and swatted at her cousin Alejandro when he called out. He never failed to make her laugh, *or* to make a spectacle of himself.

'Alejandro, leave us alone,' her sister, María, lamented. 'You always scare all the boys away!'

Esmeralda laughed and tucked her arm through Alejandro's, happy to leave her sisters and stroll the room with him. She knew all the boys there and she held no interest in any of them, so she was thankful to have him as a distraction; she

certainly wasn't going to complain about him scaring them all
away.

'I was lying before,' he said. '*You* are the most beautiful girl
in Cuba, Es.'

She dropped her head to his shoulder. 'You don't need to
flatter me, Alejandro. Just keep me busy so no one can ask me to
dance.'

'You know I will. It keeps all the mothers from showing off
their daughters to me.' He laughed. 'You'd think they were
prized chickens the way they parade them in front of me, it's
disgraceful.'

They both giggled. Alejandro was presently in love with a girl
who lived in Santa Clara, and Esmeralda wasn't interested in
marrying for the sake of it. She much preferred her role as her
father's favourite, learning everything she could about his sugar
business and being on *his* arm at parties, fulfilling her duty to her
family. If her mother had been alive, she'd have been like any
other Cuban mamá, determined to find the perfect matches for all
of her daughters, starting with her eldest. But her papá was far
more interested in keeping his daughters close; she was certain he
wanted to keep them under his roof for as long as he possibly
could, preferring his home filled with their presence and laughter.

'You know you'll have to take a husband one day, Esmeralda. You can't cling to my arm for the rest of your life.'

She sighed. 'I know. But I want a man to sweep me off my
feet. I want a man who listens to me and doesn't just want me to
sit meekly and smile, with no opinion of my own.' She laughed.
'I already know all the men here, there's no one I'm interested
in.' She tucked closer to him. 'Other than you, of course. You're
the highlight of my evening.'

Alejandro laughed when the band burst into song, clasping
her hand as they joined in with the dancing, as couples twirled
around them. She preferred dancing with her cousin than with

any other young men; her sisters couldn't understand it because they were desperate to fall in love and couldn't understand her reluctance, but being with Alejandro scared off any suitors who might otherwise have asked her to dance. He was her father's second in command, well respected in business despite his young age. *If a man is brave enough to approach me when I'm with him, he'd be worthy of saying yes to.*

'Whoever steals your heart is a lucky man, Es. Don't you forget it.'

She just smiled. 'I could say the same about the girl who's already stolen yours.'

Esmeralda often had her breakfast in bed, bought to her on a tray so she could sit and indulge, but each Sunday her father liked them to eat together late in the morning. It was the one day he didn't leave early for work—his life revolved around his business, his every thought consumed by his sugar empire. She'd heard rumours that he was the richest man in Cuba, but she'd never been brave enough to ask him directly about their finances. All she knew was that his generosity knew no bounds when it came to his daughters—he indulged their every whim in a way that would never have been allowed if her mamá were alive.

Marisol appeared in the hallway at the same time as Esmeralda so she held her baby sister's hand as they walked down the sweeping staircase. A nanny followed, but Marisol always preferred her big sisters to look after her.

'Come on, cariño,' she whispered as Marisol looked up at her. 'You can sit with me this morning.'

Marisol was only three years old, the sweetest child Esmeralda had ever known, despite not being raised by her mother, who'd died during childbirth. But she was lucky, because all three sisters adored her and she was doted on despite what had happened.

Esmeralda walked into the dining room and smiled when she saw her father already seated. 'Good morning, Papá,' she said, brushing a kiss to his cheek as she passed and waiting for Marisol to do the same. Her little sister ended up climbing onto her father's lap, which only made his smile grow.

As usual, their breakfast feast was lavish, and Esmeralda indulged in fresh mango and papaya, as well as freshly baked bread topped with their cook's famous guava jam. She noticed Marisol reach for the sweet pastries straight away, and she sighed without reprimanding her and took one for herself as their maid poured her a strong cup of coffee.

'Esmeralda, I'm planning a trip to London next month,' her papá said, folding away the paper he'd been looking at and gesturing for another cup of his favourite café Cubano.

'Will you be home in time for María's quince party?' she asked, seeing from her sister's desperate gaze that she needed to ask. It was the biggest moment in a Cuban girl's life—the day she turned fifteen and became a woman, celebrated with an extravagant party that often took months to prepare for.

'Of course! I wouldn't miss seeing my little quinceañera for anything,' he assured them, wiping his thick moustache with his napkin. 'María, do you think you could spare your sister for two weeks though? I trust the preparations for the celebration have been completed?'

'Papá, no!' Esmeralda gasped, dropping the piece of pastry she'd been holding. 'To London? You're inviting me to travel with you for two weeks?'

He smiled at her across the table. 'Esmeralda, I would very much like to take you with me,' he said. 'I need to impress a very important British firm, to convince them that our sugar is the best. We will have the most lucrative sugar business in the world if this is successful, and I'd like my beautiful eldest daughter by my side.'

Esmeralda folded her hands in her lap despite her excitement. Her three sisters were all silent as she spoke. 'It would be my honour, Papá,' she said. 'I know Mamá would be travelling with you if she were here, but it's a privilege to go in her place. Thank you.'

'Come to the office tomorrow so I can tell you more about my plans for expansion,' he said. 'I need you to understand how important this trip is, and I want you well informed on business matters so you can make conversation there.'

'Si, Papá, I will.' She could barely contain her excitement, her smile radiant.

As her sisters started gossiping about the night before, more interested in their own lives than what had just been announced, Esmeralda closed her eyes for a moment and imagined herself travelling to England, wondering what clothes she should pack, who they would see there, where they would stay. This was a dream come true for her.

She was nineteen years old, and that meant there were only so many years left before she would be forced to think about her future, or before one of her aunts implored her father to start marrying off his girls. She had been lucky so far, but there was only so long she and her father could delay the inevitable; he knew it as well as she did, although it was never something they spoke of openly.

Going to London would be the adventure of her lifetime, and she couldn't wait.

When she opened her eyes, her father was watching her, and she mouthed 'thank you' to him. He responded by touching his hand to his heart.

4

LONDON, PRESENT DAY

Claudia tugged at the string, not surprised when nothing happened. It was so old that fibres started to come away, and she used her nails to prise the knot apart. She took a deep breath as she opened the box, not sure what she expected to find. Perhaps she thought it would be a jewel nestled on tissue paper, or a photo, but instead she found an old business card and what appeared to be a hand-drawn sketch of a crest.

She held the card first, turning it over in her hand and noticing the Capel Court address. It was vaguely familiar to her, due to it being the former premises of the London Stock Exchange, and she immediately took out her phone and googled the name 'Christopher Dutton,' which was printed on it in gold letters. She didn't find anything connected with his name or the address when she entered it, but then she guessed the card had to be over seventy years old, given that her grandmother was born in 1951. The firm listed was Fisher, Lyall & Dutton, nothing stood out to her when she searched that name, either. Curious, Claudia lifted the sketch of the crest out of the box, tipping it and looking inside, half expecting there to be something else. But there was nothing, just the crest.

Her coffee arrived and she thanked the waitress, reaching for a sugar and stirring it in, careful not to spill anything on to the precious items. How would she find out what the crest meant? Or who it belonged to? She hadn't expected such a mystery.

Claudia turned it over, but there was nothing written there, nothing at all that could point her in the direction of who it might have belonged to.

How are these clues supposed to help me find out my grand-mother's past? She set the paper down and sipped her coffee, still staring at them as she pondered what they could mean, what they were supposed to tell her, but there was certainly nothing obvious standing out to her.

Out of ideas, she took a photo of both and emailed them to her father. He was an avid history buff, and now that he was retired he loved nothing more than reading about the past and discovering items of historic value. If there was anyone who could make head or tail of the clues, it was him.

She finished her coffee and put the clues back in the box, dropping it into her handbag as she stood. *I wish you were here to talk to about all this, Grandma.* Although perhaps her grand-mother wouldn't have wanted to know, perhaps it would have raised questions about the past that would have made her uncomfortable?

All Claudia knew for sure was that she liked to know everything, she craved facts and information, and if there was truly a hidden heritage that her mother's side of the family knew nothing about, then she was going to do everything within her power to discover it.

Claudia stepped off the train and walked through the station, excitedly waving to her father who was waiting for her in his car. She always felt like a young girl again when she arrived back home to Surrey; it was as if she was coming for the weekend from school or university all over again, desperate to get back home.

'Hello my love,' her father greeted her with a hug and a kiss. 'How are you?'

'I'm great,' she said, passing him her overnight bag. 'It's so good to see you.'

They got in the car, and she'd barely done her belt up before he was excitedly bringing up the clues. 'I've made progress,' he said. 'An old friend of mine is looking into the name Christopher Dutton for me, but I've almost figured out the crest myself. It's absolutely consumed me since you sent it through yesterday.'

'Really? I honestly thought it would turn into nothing.' She laughed. 'What happened to you thinking this was all a hoax, anyway?'

'Well, let's just say that these clues piqued my interest,' he said, glancing at her as he drove. 'Would you believe that the crest appears to be Cuban?'

'Cuban?' Claudia shook her head. 'Unbelievable.'

'My thoughts exactly. I couldn't believe it and neither could your mother when I told her. To be honest, I think it's all come as quite a shock to her, it's so unexpected.'

Claudia nodded and looked out the window. To think there had been a secret like this in their family for so many years was certainly unsettling—she could only imagine how her mother must feel.

Within minutes they were turning into the driveway, and Claudia had the same feeling she always did when she arrived home; absolute contentment. As a teenager she'd been desperate to spread her wings and leave, finding Surrey far too quiet for her pace of life and all the things she wanted to achieve, but as soon as she'd moved to the city, she'd missed it terribly. *I still do.*

'Your mother's busy in the garden,' her father said when he pulled up outside the two-storey house. She looked up at the familiar dormer windows and green Venetian shutters, smiling as she noticed the wisteria that seemed to cover even more of the house now than it had when she'd lived there. 'How about you go and find her, and I'll take your bag in and get back to work. I'm only waiting on one email to confirm what I've discovered about the crest, and I want to see it the moment it comes through.'

She leaned over and kissed his cheek, before stepping out into the sunshine and going to find her mother, who was around the back of the property, on her knees in the flower bed. The garden had once been more overgrown than manicured, but since retirement both her parents had become keen gardeners.

'Hello?' she called out, not wanting to alarm her by appearing around the corner without warning.

'Claudia!' Within seconds she was being wrapped in her mother's arms, gardening gloves and all. 'Let me go and get myself cleaned up.'

'No, you're fine as you are,' Claudia said, sitting on the grass near to where her mother had been kneeling. 'It's lovely to get some fresh air, I'm happy to stay outside.' She sighed. 'I think it's exactly what I need.'

Her mum smiled, but instead of going back to her gardening she sat nearby, taking off her gloves and dropping them to the grass. 'You're right, it's lovely to soak up the sun when we have it.' She leaned back on one elbow as Claudia faced her. 'Now, tell me what you think of all this business about Grandma? Do you really believe it all? Do you think it's all true, what they told you?'

Claudia nodded. 'It was a shock, but it's definitely legitimate. All they wanted yesterday was to reunite the estates with the boxes left behind, so I can't see any reason *not* to believe it.'

'Do you think she knew and didn't tell me? I keep wondering if it was a secret she held in all those years, not wanting anyone to know, or whether she was never even told she was adopted. Did my grandparents keep it a secret, for fear of anyone finding out she wasn't their natural born child at the time?'

'I don't think she knew, honestly Mum, I don't,' Claudia said, hating the tears shining in her mother's eyes, knowing how much she'd struggled since her passing. 'If Grandma knew, she would have told you. There's no way she'd have kept it a secret, you two were so close, and if you think about it, why would she? There's no shame in being adopted, certainly not in this genera-tion, so I think it would have come up.'

'I suppose you're right.' Her mother wiped her eyes with the back of her fingers. 'It's just so hard when she's not here to ask, and this has only made me miss her all the more.'

Claudia was about to reply when her father burst around the corner of the house, triumphantly holding a piece of paper in the air.

'Mystery solved,' he announced.

Claudia laughed, he looked so comically triumphant. 'What did you discover, Dad?' she asked. 'Was it Cuban after all?'

'This crest,' he said, folding his arms over his chest and wearing a smile befitting a cat with the cream, 'is indeed Cuban. It belonged to the Diaz family,' he said. 'Look how different it looks printed in colour, though? It's rather impressive.'

She took the paper and held it so her mother could see it, too. The crest was now a bright blue, with touches of yellow and white; coming to life on the page compared to the black-and-white rendition that had been more crudely drawn.

'Cuba?' Claudia's mother asked in disbelief. 'This clue is definitely from Cuba? You're absolutely certain?'

Her father nodded. 'It's from Cuba. It's a popular surname, but from what I've been able to find out so far, this Diaz crest is from a prominent sugar family who lived in Havana. It's going to take me a while to find out more, and unfortunately we still don't have much on the name from the card, but this is progress.'

'What link could a business card from London have with a family in Havana?' Claudia thought out loud. 'I mean, is it plausible they could have been doing business together, this London firm and the sugar family? Is that what the link could be?'

Her father shrugged. 'Perhaps, although I don't think it's going to be the easiest puzzle to solve.'

'Should we,' she paused, looking between her parents, 'consider hiring a personal investigator?'

Her mother paled, but her father seemed more thoughtful, staring down at the crest. 'Give me a few weeks to see what I can learn, Claudia,' he said. 'Then if I keep hitting dead ends, we can reconsider our options.'

'Mum?' Claudia asked, realising how quiet she'd been, which was highly unusual. 'How do you feel about it all?'

'I want to know,' her mother said as she picked up her gardening gloves and stood, dusting her trousers off. 'If there's a story to be told about Grandma's past, then I think we owe it to her to find out. I don't like loose ends, and this is about family. It's something we should both know, if it's part of our past.'

Claudia exchanged glances with her father. 'We're in agreement then,' she said. 'We let Dad see what he can uncover, and if it leads to nothing, we find an investigator to locate this Christopher Dutton. He can't have just disappeared into thin air.'

'There must be someone who knows her story,' her mother said. 'I just hope that whatever secrets there are, they haven't been lost to the past. It's been a long time.'

Claudia helped her mother pack up her gardening things

and followed her inside. It was a mystery how they were linked to the clues, and the more she thought about them, the more her interest grew. But Cuba? She almost wondered if she'd been given the wrong set of clues. *Surely we'd know if we were of Cuban heritage, wouldn't we?* How could it have been kept a secret for so long?

5

Claudia sat outside on the terrace of her flat on Sunday night, a blanket over her legs, which were tucked up beneath her on the sofa. It was almost too cold to be out, but she loved the view and she wasn't ready to go in yet.

She stared at the diamond ring on the table in front of her. *Just like I haven't been ready to let go of my past.* Her mother had asked her about Max while she was there, as she always did, and this time Claudia hadn't bristled as per usual. It had been time to tackle her mother's questions head on instead of being evasive, because as loving and supportive as her mum was, somehow she hadn't been able to understand the decision her daughter had made.

'You two always looked so happy together,' her mum had said. 'He was such a lovely young man. Are you sure you weren't too hasty in calling things off?'

'Mum, he *was* lovely, but we weren't right together. He couldn't understand how I could walk away from my career, and he didn't make any effort to try to understand what I was going through.' She paused. 'Our marriage would have been destined to fail.'

Her mother went silent, and she knew why. Claudia's ex-fiancé wasn't the only one who couldn't understand why she'd given up something she'd worked so hard for, despite what had happened, despite what she'd lost. She'd given up her job and her engagement in the same week.

'Mum, I'm happy now, truly I am. I'm finally living my life, on my terms. Before I left my job, I was so stressed that my hair was starting to fall out in clumps.' She took a deep breath, not wanting to remember what those final months had been like, what she'd been through. 'Some days it was as if I couldn't breathe, the pressure on my chest made me feel like I was going to have a heart attack. I couldn't stop wondering what it was all for, wondering why I had to pretend that my life was so wonderful when in fact I was miserable. You know why I did this, Mum, but it's time you tried to understand. After what happened to Lisa, how could I have stayed?'

Her mother reached for her hand. 'I'm not trying to trivialise what happened, I just didn't realise it was so bad for you. I kept thinking that if you'd only stuck with it for longer, you'd have come out the other side and had a career you loved. That it was just a knee-jerk reaction to what had happened, I suppose.'

'I was good at hiding how I was feeling,' she replied. 'I didn't want you or anyone else to see that I wasn't coping at the time, but what I do need you to see is how happy I am now. That I made the right decision for me.'

They sat together in silence, at the table, until her mother finally spoke again, reaching for Claudia's hands.

'I'm sorry I wasn't more sympathetic. I should have been, I mean I saw your father work himself to the bone for most of our marriage, yet somehow I thought it was different for you. Somehow I thought things had changed for your generation. I was worried that once you'd grieved your friend, you might have wished you'd stayed.'

She shook her head. 'Nothing has changed, Mum. In fact, I

think it's only become more competitive, and it was almost like we had to work harder than the boys to prove ourselves, which is ridiculous in this day and age.' But it was Lisa, too. Claudia felt she owed it to her friend to live both their lives now, and that certainly didn't include staying on at the firm that had effectively killed her.

Claudia reached for the diamond ring as she pushed her thoughts away and slid it onto her finger, wanting to feel the weight of it one last time. It was perfect; everything about Max had seemed perfect, though. That was until she'd been honest with him about how she felt, and he'd looked at her with the kind of horrified gaze one might receive upon announcing a truly awful secret. He'd wanted a modern-day Stepford wife, the kind of woman who could work a sixty-hour week, as well as run a household and pop out 2.5 perfect children along the way. As soon as she'd tried to change the narrative, as soon as she'd tried to explain to him why their life wasn't working for her, he'd packed his things and told her to have a hard think about what she wanted from life. Which was precisely what she'd done.

She took the ring off and put it back in the velvet box, blinking away tears. In the morning, she was going to have it couriered back to him. If she was truly turning her back on that life, there was no need for a reminder of the past, and she certainly had no intention of taking back up with him or selling it. He'd bought it for her, and that meant he could do with it as he saw fit. She should have done it months ago.

Claudia reached for her iPhone, which was sitting beside her glass of wine. If it wasn't so late she would have called her friend, Charlotte, but a quick glance showed it was almost ten. She wasn't going to wake her pregnant friend to talk about Max —they'd already talked him to death since the break-up. She clicked on Instagram and then Facebook, absently scrolling for a few minutes before finding herself searching for British

Airways, her mind drifting back to the clues. Her father had been so excited about his discovery, and she had to admit it had piqued her curiosity too.

I wonder how expensive flights to Cuba are?

She scrolled down and selected Havana as her destination, clicking through to search for flights before putting in her dates, which meant it automatically showed her the next available flights. *Tomorrow?* She smiled to herself. Imagine actually doing it. Actually just booking a flight and getting out of London for a week.

Claudia glanced back inside, her phone in one hand. The flat was finished, the furniture had all arrived, and she'd decided to give the listing to the agent she'd met earlier in the week. Her work was finished, but she couldn't buy another property until she'd sold this one, which meant her schedule over the next few weeks, if not months, was clear. There was essentially nothing keeping her in London.

She opened her phone up again and checked the day after tomorrow. There was a seat to Havana, departing late morning. Claudia reached for her wine and took a large gulp. *I can't just go overseas on a whim. I can't.*

Her finger hovered.

Oh, but I can. And just like that she clicked the button to purchase the seat, before promptly bursting into laughter.

I'm going to Havana!

She'd spent almost all her life being a super planner, making a pros and cons list for every decision she'd ever made and following every step from school to university and beyond as if life had been prescribed to her with a set of rules. But this was her living life on her own terms, and from the moment she'd seen that crest in colour, she'd known she wanted to know more.

If that's where your story begins, Grandma, then it's exactly where I'm supposed to be. And what better place to discover more about the Diaz crest than in Cuba itself?

She wasn't going to get the answers she needed in London, but at least in Havana someone might be able to point her in the right direction. Maybe someone would know how she could find out more about the family the crest belonged to.

She finished her wine and decided it wasn't too late to text Charlotte after all. Her friend was never going to believe what an impromptu decision she'd made, although they had made a promise to each other when their lives had been turned upside down. *Carpe diem.*

I'm seizing the day, Lisa, just like I promised you I would.
Carpe bloody diem.

MIRABELLE RESTAURANT, LONDON, 1950

Esmeralda walked down the stairs into the restaurant on the arm of her father, holding her head high despite the hush that fell over the room when they entered. As they moved through the dining room, heads turned their way, but she refused to feel self-conscious. That was until a young man standing at the farthest corner met her gaze, his smile sending a shiver through her body.

She knew why she was here; her father wanted to impress his business contacts, and bringing his eldest daughter, of whom he was so proud, was his way of doing that. Esmeralda only wished she'd known how much she would stand out in London, her finest dresses more low-cut than anything she'd seen, her waists cinched in more tightly, and her jewellery far more extravagant. She certainly wished she'd had some warning about what to expect. Not to mention her raven-black hair, styled to tumble down her back and over her shoulders, making her look different from every other woman in the room who seemed to have either updos or much shorter styles.

'Mr Diaz, it's a pleasure to see you,' the young man said,

holding out his hand to her father. 'Thank you for travelling all this way.'

'The pleasure is all mine, but please, if we're going to be doing business together, call me Julio,' her father replied, before standing back and sweeping his hand towards her. 'And this is my eldest daughter, Esmeralda.'

The man held out his hand and she lifted hers for him, watching as he gently clasped it, keeping hold for a few seconds. His bright blue eyes met hers for a moment, and she couldn't help but stare into them. He was much younger than she'd expected her father's business associate to be. 'It's lovely to meet you, Miss Diaz. I'm Christopher Dutton,' he said, pulling out a chair and gesturing for her to sit. 'May I order you champagne?'

Her father nodded on her behalf, and she sat, excited when Christopher took the seat beside her and flashed her a quick smile. He didn't look like the men she knew in Cuba; his hair was cut shorter, his cheeks freshly razored and not sporting a moustache or short beard that so many young Cuban men favoured. Not to mention his accent, which was making her want to giggle; she couldn't wait to write home and tell her sisters all about him. He sounded so formal, yet when she smiled at him, his confidence seemed to wane as his cheeks turned a deep shade of pink, which only made him all the more endearing. So many men she met back home seemed to expect her to swoon at their feet, which never failed to amuse her, their confidence unwavering no matter how little interest she gave them.

She took a sip of her champagne when it arrived, smiling politely to her father as she half-listened to their conversation, her eyes dancing constantly over Christopher. *Perhaps shopping isn't going to be the only thing I fall in love with in London.*

'Esmeralda, Christopher works for the firm I was telling you about, Fisher, Lyall & Dutton,' her father said. 'His father started the business thirty years ago, and now the younger Dutton is making his mark.'

She nodded. 'We are both children of successful businessmen, then.'

Christopher smiled. 'Yes, we are. And I'm hoping to close this deal with your father personally, to convince my own father it's time for me to run the firm.'

They all laughed, but Esmeralda kept her gaze firmly on Christopher as he lifted his glass of champagne.

'To new acquaintances,' he said, his eyes briefly meeting hers.

'To brokering the most successful sugar deal ever made,' her father added.

They all held their glasses high, clinking them gently together before taking a sip. Only it wasn't the sugar deal on Esmeralda's mind as the bubbles from the champagne tickled her throat.

I think I've finally met a man who could hold my interest for longer than one dance.

7

HAVANA, CUBA, PRESENT DAY

Claudia stood, bags in hand, unable to believe what she was seeing. *It's like stepping back in time.* Cars that would have once been the height of luxury were now ghosts of their former glory despite their still-gleaming paintwork, and as she looked at the buildings around her with their pretty pastel colour schemes, it was obvious they too were merely shadows of what they'd once been. It was expected of course, she'd read plenty about Cuba and had looked up endless travel blogs about the country as she'd lain awake in bed the night before, but it still came as a shock to see it first-hand. Cuba was completely stuck in the past, or at least it appeared to be.

The people around her spoke the kind of fast-paced Spanish that a tourist would never have a hope of deciphering as she gazed at the scene before her and listened, but they also looked friendly. She loved their brightly coloured clothes, and the few Cuban people she'd encountered so far, including her taxi driver, had been quick to smile. She wasn't sure if that was because they were grateful to have tourists in the country spending money, or if it was simply their way.

Claudia had decided to stay in Old Havana, and as she was

making her way in the direction of the hotel she'd booked into, she noticed someone waving out to her. She looked over her shoulder, wondering if there was perhaps someone behind her, but when she looked back at the man, he was still waving and nodding encouragingly to her. He stood beside a baby-blue vintage car that was absolutely gleaming, and Claudia hesitantly made her way over to him.

'You look lost,' he said in heavily accented English.

Claudia grinned. 'I'm heading to the Hotel Saratoga,' she said. 'I wouldn't say lost so much as enjoying the sights on the way.'

'Ahh, what a shame,' he said with a dramatic sigh.

She frowned. 'What's a shame? That I'm not lost?'

'That you're staying at a hotel instead of a casa particular.'

'You think I should be staying in someone's home instead?' she asked, recognising the term. She'd considered it, apparently it was the best way to discover the Cuban culture, but travelling on her own she hadn't been sure it was the most sensible option, not when she wasn't familiar with the country.

'It's the only way to truly experience Cuba,' he said with a shrug. 'But I'm sure the hotel will be very pleasant.'

Claudia's eyebrows lifted. 'Pleasant?' she laughed, deciding to indulge him. 'Well, I didn't come all this way for *pleasant*. Where exactly should I be staying?'

His skin was sun-kissed and leathery, a contrast against his white singlet, open white shirt and white hat. 'A few streets away, that way. I can take you there.'

She nodded as he stood almost too close. 'You can take me there?'

'It's my grandmother's house,' he said. 'You stay there?' He smacked his lips together. 'You'll be eating roasted pork and fried plantains for dinner, and her version of rice and black beans. Nothing ever tasted so good.'

She considered him, looking at the man and then his car. Or at least she presumed it was his car. 'You're a driver?'

He nodded. 'Sí.'

Claudia took a moment, glancing back up in the direction of the hotel she'd been heading towards. *I didn't come here to hide away in some fancy hotel, I came to learn about Cuba, to discover my heritage.* The little box she had tucked away in her bag was the reason she was here, and maybe in a local house she'd be able to ask questions and find out more.

But she also didn't know whether to trust a stranger, especially a man. It was all very well for him to tell her to climb into his car, but her instincts weren't to take the word of just anyone.

She looked around, to the handful of other men leaning against cars, or polishing paintwork that was already gleaming.

'You're all drivers?' she called out. 'Can I trust this man?'

The response was universal; they all either laughed or nodded and called out yes.

'Fine, take me to your grandmother's house,' Claudia said, for which she received a big grin from the man. 'I'm Claudia.'

'Carlos,' he said, tipping his hat.

'Well, Carlos, how about you put my bags in the car and we get going before I change my mind?'

So much for being mindful about travelling alone. Claudia got into the back seat of the car and pulled her phone out of her handbag, disappointed to see she didn't have any coverage. She would need to cancel her hotel room sooner rather than later, but she'd have to see if she could either get her phone to work or use a telephone at Carlos's grandmother's house.

'Tell me, why Cuba?' Carlos asked as he slipped his sunglasses on and started the car.

Claudia wasn't sure how much to tell him, but then on the other hand if she didn't tell the locals she encountered, she was unlikely to discover anything that might help her to make sense of her clues.

'I believe my grandmother may have been Cuban,' she said, hesitantly. 'I've come to see if I can find out more, about her heritage.'

He slipped his glasses down his nose and looked at her in the rearview mirror, and it took all her efforts not to laugh, he looked so comical.

'Why do you think that?'

She took a deep breath. 'I was recently given some information, and I'm trying to make sense of it. All I know is that she has a connection to a family here, only I don't know how.'

Carlos nodded and sped up, but it wasn't long before he was parking outside a house that reminded Claudia of a set from a Dr Seuss movie. The two-storey house was canary yellow with a blue handrail stretching up the side and matching blue fretwork. There were areas of exposed brick, contrasting against the yellow, and pots full of flowers positioned along the upper-level balcony. She opened her door and stepped out onto the pavement, admiring the stained-glass windows.

'What do you think?' he asked

'I think,' she said, 'that I've never seen anything quite like it in my life before. It's beautiful.' And it was, in a completely unexpected kind of way that was so different to the architecture she was used to.

As if she'd known to expect them, a woman with grey hair and an apron tied around her middle opened the door, her face softening when she saw Carlos. Claudia guessed it was his grandma when he hurried to embrace her, kissing both her cheeks, and she wasn't wrong.

'Abuela, this is Claudia,' he said. 'Claudia, this is my abuela, Rosa. Please tell me you have room for her?'

Claudia held up a hand in a wave, but the woman stepped forward and smiled, reaching for her hands and then kissing her cheeks in greeting instead.

'Of course I have room,' she said. 'I'll need half an hour to make the bed and air out your room, but my grandson will entertain you, won't you, Carlos?'

'I don't want to be an imposition,' Claudia said.

Carlos shook his head. 'Tourists mean everything to us, we welcome you into our homes.'

She nodded, understanding. Presumably his grandmother would be grateful for the business, and she was certain it would cost less than a hotel.

'Claudia's grandmother was Cuban,' Carlos said as he carried her bags inside. The interior wasn't as vibrant as the outside of the building, but it was still quirky in a way that Claudia hadn't expected. It was also clean as could be, freshly swept and dusted, and she loved how the doors opened to a little courtyard in the back.

'Where was she from? Your grandmother?'

'I'm not sure yet if she was Cuban, that's what I'm trying to find out,' she replied as she followed the pair. 'But I do have a clue about my past that might help to point me in the right direction.'

'What is this clue?' Carlos asked.

She opened her bag and took out the little box, unfolding the piece of paper that bore the family crest and passing it to him as his grandmother looked on.

Carlos looked up at her, his smile gone and replaced with a look of surprise, as his grandmother crossed herself and muttered something under her breath.

'This the Diaz family crest,' Carlos said.

'You know the family?' she asked hopefully.

'Buen senôr,' his grandmother muttered. 'Take Claudia to the courtyard, Carlos.'

'If there's something you know, I—'

Carlos gently took her arm and led her outside as his grandmother continued to mutter under her breath.

'Have I upset her?' Claudia asked. 'Should I not have shown you that?'

'The Diaz family were once the most powerful, wealthiest family in all of Havana, if not Cuba,' he said quietly. 'And if I'm not mistaken, my grandmother's mother used to work as a maid at their mansion.'

'She knew the Diaz family?'

Carlos laughed. 'Cariño mío, *everybody* in Havana knew the Diaz family.'

8

Claudia sat down when Carlos's grandmother returned with fresh juice in a jug for them all. *Perhaps information on the Diaz family won't be so hard to find after all.*

'May I ask why everyone in Havana knew the Diaz family?' Claudia asked. 'Was it because of their wealth? Did they have a reputation?'

Carlos sat back. 'Abuela, tell her. It's better to come from you than me.'

'The Diaz family were like royalty in Havana,' Rosa said, a faraway look in her eyes as she leaned back in her chair, resting her hands on her thighs. 'The father, Julio Diaz, was known as the sugar king of Havana before the revolution. He was well liked, even though he was the wealthiest man in all of Cuba, and his daughters were so beautiful they could take your breath away. They would glide into a room, the three eldest, and no one could steal their eyes from them. I think every girl in Cuba dreamed of being a Diaz at some time in their life.'

Claudia smiled, creating an image of them in her mind. The opulence of Havana in its heyday must have been quite something to experience, and she wished she could have seen it, even for a moment.

'I was a similar age to the eldest daughter, I still remember wishing I could live her life, that I could wear her fine dresses and have her jewels dripping from my lobes and wrists. I went to bed some nights dreaming of what their life must be like.'

'They sound like quite the family.'

'They were. They were the family everyone wished they were part of, even after the tragedy.'

'Tragedy?' Claudia asked, glancing at Carlos. 'There was a tragedy?'

'There was more than one,' he said.

His grandmother made a tutting sound, but he only replied with a shrug, which piqued Claudia's interest all the more.

'Julio's wife died in childbirth. The three eldest girls were very close in age, almost young women when their mother passed, and they became like little mothers to their baby sister. She was a darling little girl, as pretty as her sisters and with beautiful big brown eyes like saucers.'

'Are they still here?' Claudia asked. 'In Havana?'

'No, they are long gone, they left along with almost every other wealthy Cuban when our country changed,' she said, wiping at her eyes. 'We all stayed here with nowhere to go, but anyone who could fled, many to Florida to try to make their fortune in America.'

Claudia tried not to be too disappointed. After all, she hadn't expected her journey to be easy, not when it came to discovering the past. But hearing about the Diaz family, even just that little taste of information, had whet her appetite for more.

'And have you ever heard of them in recent years? Does anyone still talk of the family, or do they ever return to visit?'

'Most Cubans who left did so believing they'd be returning within years, if not months,' Carlos said. 'They never thought they were leaving for good, they expected to come back to reclaim their homes and the country they loved. Many hid their jewels, some covered their furniture with sheets as if they were leaving for the summer. But none of those families ever came back.' He sighed. 'The Cuba they loved was gone.'

'Were their homes given to members of the communist party?' Claudia asked.

'Sí. And left to decay over the years because there wasn't the money to keep them.'

Claudia sat back in her chair, sipping her juice as she thought about what Cuba must once have been, about what it must have been like to walk away from not only your home but also your country.

'Was everyone sad about those families leaving or did they welcome their departure?' she asked. 'I'm guessing there was a divide between the extremely wealthy families and the working class?'

Carlos's eyes widened at the same time as his grandmother's clouded over.

'Many of the poorer families supported Castro, believing that change was what Cuba needed,' she said. 'There was a fire among the people to see Batista's government overturned, but in the end, perhaps Batista was the better option? All of the change we'd expected? It wasn't worth it, not for all the losses, not for what we became.' She took a long, deep breath. 'But in answer to your question, I think many people resented what the wealthy had, without taking the time to consider what a contribution they made to our country. Without those wealthy businessmen, Cuba struggled to prosper.'

'Our country is a time warp from what some would describe as Cuba's best years, only so many of the people who made Cuba what she once was are long gone,' Carlos said as his grandmother rose. 'Perhaps we should all stand up and fight for what we believe in again!'

'They are words of a young man who hasn't seen what his abuela has.' His grandmother placed a hand over his shoulder as she stood beside him, her words firm. 'No good ever comes from losing our men to war.'

Claudia watched as she turned, wishing she could ask her more. She would sit all night and listen to her speak about Cuba if she could—it was fascinating.

'Carlos, why don't you take Claudia to Mateo's food truck tonight? If anyone can answer her questions about the Diaz family, he can.'

'Mateo?' she asked, at the same time as Carlos groaned.

'But your pork and beans,' he moaned. 'I can already taste them!'

'There's always tomorrow night, nieto,' she said with a laugh. 'Besides, I don't have enough for you, anyway.'

Claudia couldn't help but laugh at the scene before her, with Carlos dramatically clutching his stomach as if he couldn't stand not to eat his grandmother's cooking for another moment.

'Rosa,' she suddenly called. 'You never did say what the other tragedy was. For the Diaz family?'

Rosa crossed herself and made a tutting sound under her breath. 'The eldest daughter, Esmeralda, she disappeared one night.'

'Disappeared? Was she ever found?'

'All I know is that the family never spoke of her ever again, and neither did anyone else, unless they were whispering behind closed doors. It was as if she'd just disappeared into thin air.' Rosa sighed. 'Some said she was the most beautiful girl in Cuba, the apple of her father's eye from the moment of her birth, but after her disappearance her sisters were married off quickly, and soon after that they moved to Florida. Julio stayed behind, right until the bitter end, until he had no choice but to leave.'

Rosa disappeared into the house then, their conversation at

an end, but Claudia couldn't stop thinking about the daughter who'd disappeared. *Esmeralda.* Could she somehow be the missing link to her grandmother's past? And if she was, then how?

'I'll return at five,' Carlos said, rising and smiling down at her.

'Who is this Mateo?' Claudia asked. 'He has a food truck?'

Carlos grinned. 'Mateo cooks the best street food in Havana. You'll love it.'

'But what connection does he have to the Diaz family?' she asked. 'Why does your grandmother want me to meet him?'

'His grandfather was the Diaz family's personal chef until the very end.'

Her eyebrows shot up as Carlos raised his hand in a wave. 'I'll see you soon.'

Claudia stayed seated as Carlos left, taking the box from her bag again and placing the piece of paper and the business card side by side on the table. *How does the Diaz family relate to a firm in London?* She was still staring at the family crest when Rosa came back out and told her that her room was ready, the sun starting to lower in the sky as the temperature cooled ever so slightly.

If only you were here to ask, Grandma. If only I wasn't having to do this on my own.

She put her things away and followed Rosa through the house, stopping only to collect her bags as they went outside and then walked up the steps that led to the upper level of the home.

'This is your room,' Rosa said, her smile kindly. 'But you are welcome to come downstairs whenever you want. My home is your home while you're here.'

Claudia thanked her, walking over to the window and looking out over Old Havana, wondering if it was a view her grandmother had ever enjoyed. Had she ever come to visit? Had her family ever brought her here? And if she had, why would she have kept it a secret?

'Claudia?'

She turned.

'If your grandmother was a Diaz, you'll find your answers while you're here. Secrets always have a way of being discovered, there's only so long the past can stay hidden.'

She nodded, grateful for the older woman's hospitality. Only she couldn't help but think about what Rosa had said about the family's tragedy.

If the eldest Diaz sister had truly disappeared without a trace, either it was a mystery, or the family had buried a secret. If she'd truly gone missing, a family with that kind of wealth would have stopped at nothing to find her, which told her that they'd instead used their influence to stop anyone from looking into her disappearance. Which only made Claudia more interested to find out what had happened.

9

THE SAVOY HOTEL, LONDON, 1950

Esmeralda looped her arm through her papá's as they strolled through the foyer of The Savoy. She looked around her, well used to luxury, but still in awe of the beautiful hotel they were staying in as they walked towards the elevators. Esmeralda held only her purse and a small blue bag from her visit to Tiffany's, and she glanced over her shoulder at the two porters carrying the evidence of her afternoon shopping trip. Despite her papá's protests, she knew he secretly loved spoiling her and her sisters, and she'd taken great pride in buying things for Marisol, already imagining her little face when she saw her new clothes.

'Excuse me, Mr Diaz!'

She stopped when her father did, her fingers still lightly against his arm.

'There was a letter hand delivered for you,' the concierge said, coming out from behind the desk to pass a thick cream envelope to her father.

'Thank you,' her father replied, sliding his finger beneath the seal and taking out an embossed card that matched the envelope.

Esmeralda leaned in closer to him, tucking her head to his

shoulder as she tried to read what was written. But she needn't have bothered, for he read it out aloud anyway.

'Dear Mr Diaz, I would be honoured if you and your daughter could join me tomorrow evening at The Ritz, at seven p.m. Please advise Miss Diaz that it is a formal occasion, and there shall be dinner and dancing afterwards. Best regards, Christopher Dutton.'

Esmeralda gasped as her father looked down at her. She quickly regained her composure, not wanting to appear too excited.

'What do you say, my darling? Shall we go to The Ritz tomorrow evening?'

She nodded, looping her hand more tightly around his arm. 'I would love nothing more than to see The Ritz, Papá. I've heard the architecture is simply breathtaking.'

'And where, my dear, have you heard that?'

Esmeralda fixed her smile, not about to be caught off guard. She had to make her father believe she was excited about the destination, not the company. 'I found a book in your library before our departure about English architecture,' she said evenly. 'It was very complimentary about both The Ritz and The Savoy.'

His nod told her that he was impressed, and she waited while he instructed the concierge to contact Christopher and confirm their attendance. As they stepped into the elevator, Esmeralda could barely contain her excitement; it welled up inside of her, tickling her throat like the bubbles from champagne.

When they reached their floor, Esmeralda waited for one of the porters to open the large double doors to the Royal Suite. She crossed the room as they brought all the bags in, lining them up on the floor, and she looked out of the window, leaning against the sill.

'You're looking out at the South Bank,' her father said as he came to stand beside her. 'It's quite the view, isn't it?'

'Yes, Papá, it is.' She sighed as she spoke, mesmerised by London and how different it was to Havana.

'I have some business to attend to, but shall I see you for dinner at six?'

She nodded and stood on tiptoe to kiss her father's cheek. 'I shall look forward to it.'

Esmeralda waited a moment, until he'd left the room, her breath catching in her throat as she saw the cream envelope discarded on the coffee table. She quickly reached for it, taking it with her to her room and shutting the large doors, before falling backwards onto the four-poster canopy bed with the envelope clutched to her chest.

I only have to wait until tomorrow night to see him again. Twenty-seven torturous hours until we will be having dinner together. She wondered if he might ask her to dance.

Esmeralda rose and went to the closet, throwing the doors open and studying the dresses she'd brought with her. She'd have someone sent up to hang her new items from Harrods so she could consider them all.

Her heart raced as she abandoned her clothes and decided to run a bath instead. That was what she needed to calm herself, a long soak in the beautiful clawfoot tub.

Although as she stood and watched the water filling the bath, she knew that ridding her mind of the charismatic Christopher Dutton was easier said than done.

10

HAVANA, CUBA, PRESENT DAY

Claudia wasn't sure what to expect when Carlos arrived to pick her up later that day, all she knew was that somehow everything about what had happened since she'd arrived in Cuba felt right. Rosa had waved her goodbye and told her she looked lovely before she stepped outside to wait for Carlos, which had reassured her that she'd dressed appropriately in her simple dress and flat sandals.

She'd tied her hair up—the humidity in Cuba was truly something else—but as she reached up to touch it she could feel tendrils were already starting to escape around her face and neck. But just as she was starting to fret about her hair, she saw Carlos coming down the street, the windows of his car down and his arm nudging out the side. He lifted his hand in a wave and she waved back.

'I hope you're hungry,' he said with a grin as she opened the door.

'My stomach is growling, I haven't eaten since the plane,' she said.

'Mateo is unofficially the best cook in Havana. Once you've

tried his food, you won't want to eat in a restaurant the entire time you're here.'

She laughed as he pulled away from the kerb, enjoying the breeze blowing through the open window. 'I thought you said your grandmother was the best cook in Havana?'

Carlos just shook his head, still grinning. 'She's the best *aside* from Mateo. Just don't tell her I said that.'

They both laughed, and Claudia shut her eyes, tipping her head slightly towards the wind. The air felt different in Cuba; there was a different smell, a different sensation compared to what she was used to in London, and it made her realise how long it had been since she'd had a holiday and been somewhere different. As a teenager she'd vowed to travel and had a burning desire to discover new places, but then she'd ended up on the hamster wheel that was life; university, internship, first job.

I did the right thing leaving it all behind. This is what life is supposed to feel like. This is what I'm supposed to be doing. This is me truly living.

'Carlos,' she said, opening her eyes and turning to him, 'I just realised I haven't paid you for your driving yet. I'm so sorry.'

'Just buy me dinner, it's worth more than my driving skills.'

Claudia didn't have time to answer, because he was pulling over then and she could see exactly where they were going. There was a line on the street outside a small truck that was like nothing she'd ever seen before, it was so old; in fact, it appeared it had been towed there like a trailer. It was an off-white colour and had a tent beside it, presumably for people to stand inside and eat, and there was a sandwich board positioned on the pavement with a menu written in chalk.

She followed Carlos, seeing that 'Mateo's Food Truck' had been painted on the side as they walked closer. She found it curious that the words were in English, but then she imagined he catered largely to tourists.

'It's busy for so early,' she said.

'He's always busy. Sometimes the line stretches all the way down the street.'

Claudia looked at the board and noticed that a few items had NO written beside them.

'I'm surprised to see locals here, I thought it would be mainly foreigners.'

'Sometimes,' Carlos said, 'it's why I told you to buy me dinner. One meal here for a family is five hundred and fifty pesos, just to eat burgers and have a soda. That's a third of the monthly minimum wage.'

Claudia looked at the faces in the line, imagined how tight their budgets must be just to survive. She was certainly going to buy Carlos dinner, *and* pay him as well for his driving time.

'It's one of the reasons we love tourists here and have them to stay in our homes,' he said as they inched forward in the line. 'It gives us a way to make some extra money, to be able to buy better food.'

She nodded, feeling a prick of tears in her eyes as she thought about how different her life in London was compared to someone in Cuba. But Carlos was back to smiling again, calling and waving our Claudia followed his gaze and caught a glimpse of the man in the food truck, leaning out with his shirt sleeves pushed up to his elbows. As they moved closer, she saw that he wore a black apron tied around his middle, and he had thick dark hair that was pushed back off his face. She didn't know what she'd been expecting, but it certainly wasn't someone as young and handsome as the man she was looking at.

'The croquettes are incredible,' Carlos said beside her, and she pulled her eyes from the man she guessed was Mateo to listen to him and look at the board. 'He also does juicy, delicious chicken, that's what some of the locals are here for, although they'll buy it whole, and his empanadas are,' he smacked his lips together, 'so good you'll be back for them again tomorrow. Or you could try his ropa vieja. It's a traditional dinner here, made with shredded beef, tomatoes, onions, peppers and wine. Heaven on a plate.'

Carlos's enthusiasm was contagious and had her mouth watering within seconds.

As the people in front of them parted ways, she eventually found herself at the front of the line, watching Mateo as he wiped his hands on his apron, apologised and came through the little door on the truck. He had a piece of chalk in his hand and wiped out the ropa vieja, which caused a groan from the people still in line behind her.

'Sorry,' he said when he reappeared, leaning over and resting his arms on the edge of the open window. 'What would you like?'

'Mateo!' Carlos greeted him like a long-lost friend, which perhaps he was. 'You're working alone tonight?'

He frowned. 'It's why the queue is taking so long. Who's your friend?'

Claudia smiled, realising that she was the friend when Carlos said her name. Mateo turned his gaze back to her, and she found herself lost in his cocoa brown gaze. There was handsome, and then there was Mateo; his features were strong and dark, his skin a deep shade of golden brown, and he had a smile that was as easy and warm as Carlos's.

'Mateo,' he said, reaching out a hand.

She lifted hers and he shook it, before giving her a wink. 'Empanadas?' he asked, turning his back and stirring one of the large pots.

'Give her a little of everything you have, and the same for me,' Carlos replied. 'This girl needs to try real Cuban food, it's her first time here.'

Mateo turned back a minute later with the first plate piled high, which he passed to Claudia with a grin, and then another for Carlos.

'Enjoy,' he said.

'Hey Mateo,' Carlos said as they stepped away, before the next person could order. 'What time do you finish?'

'Maybe an hour?' he called back. 'Everything is selling out fast tonight.'

'We'll wait. I want you to meet Claudia properly.'

Claudia knew he was only asking because of the questions she had about the Diaz family, but her cheeks still burned, especially when Mateo raised his eyebrows and gave her a smile that almost melted her on the spot.

It had been a long time since a man had been able to make her stomach flutter.

She smiled to herself. *A very long time.*

She sat near the water as the sun began to set, casting a web of pink across the sky and even the water. She'd read about the Malecón on the plane, and how popular it was for both tourists and locals, and there was something about watching people pass by that made her feel content. Carlos had seen someone he knew and had disappeared, wandering off and sharing a cigarette with a woman who'd seemed very pleased to see him, and so Claudia had the chance to simply sit. Her mouth was still alive with flavour after the incredible plate of food she'd consumed, and she could see exactly why Mateo had such a line outside his truck. Every bite had been delicious, although now she was full to bursting.

'You know what they say about the Malecón?'

Claudia turned at the deep voice, immediately recognising it as Mateo's as he stood nearby on the pavement, dressed in a fresh T-shirt and the same worn jeans, and without his apron tied around his waist.

'What's that?' she asked, as her pulse started to race.

His smile was mischievous as he stepped closer and lowered

his voice. 'It's where women come to lie in the arms of their lovers.'

She was thankful for the pink sky, which was hopefully disguising her equally pink cheeks. 'I've only been in Havana a few hours, so no time for any lovers yet,' she quipped, despite her embarrassment.

'Carlos said he wanted me to meet you,' he said, his hands in his pockets as he came to stand beside her and stared out at the ocean. 'You and he are—'

'Oh, no! We're not,' she said quickly. 'I mean, he's my driver and I'm staying with his grandmother. I've never been to Cuba before, but somehow he found me when I was on my way to a hotel.'

Mateo smiled, likely amused by how quickly she'd rebutted him. 'And yet he wanted us to meet?'

She nodded. 'I've come to Cuba with questions about my grandmother.' Claudia reached into her bag and took out the box, passing him the paper. 'His family recognised this immediately when I showed it to them, and they thought you would, too.'

'Many people in Havana would recognise this,' Mateo said, barely looking at it before passing it back to her. 'The question is, why do you have it?'

'Somehow it's connected to my grandmother, it was one of the only things left for her by her birth mother,' she said, before explaining to him how she'd come to be in possession of it.

'And Carlos told you about my grandfather? That's why he wanted us to meet?'

'He did.'

Mateo started to walk then, very slowly, and she fell into step beside him. 'From the stories I've been told, Julio Diaz treated my grandfather as if he was a member of the family. They were the wealthiest family in all of Havana, but also one of the humblest, or at least Julio was.'

'He was the patriarch of the family?'

'Sí.'

'But they all left Cuba for America, after the revolution? There are no family members left here?'

'They all left, yes, but the ghosts of the past are still here. There are still people who knew them, people who grew up with the Diaz girls or at least knew of them. They're not the kind of family that anyone forgets.'

She imagined what the Malecón must have been like then, when the Diaz family lived in Havana; young women walking arm in arm with handsome men, as a chaperone trailed behind, their dresses far too lavish for a seaside stroll yet somehow completely appropriate. Mateo was right, it was as if even a tourist could sense the past, as if somehow when Cuba had been frozen in time, it had also captured the memories of the past, which still whispered on the breeze.

'How do you think your grandmother is connected to the Diaz family?' he asked.

Claudia didn't tell him that she wondered if she herself were a descendant. Perhaps the connection wasn't one of blood, but for it to be only one of two clues left behind, wasn't that the most obvious link?

'I'd only be speculating if I tried to explain,' she replied. 'To be honest, I'd hoped to find a relative of the family, or someone who could trace the connection. Perhaps someone who knew about a child being adopted?'

Carlos joined them then, his happy, carefree demeanour infectious. 'You've told him?'

She nodded. 'I have.'

'And?'

This time it was Mateo who answered. 'And I think your little friend needs to learn more about the Diaz family while she's here.'

'Are you going to the be one to teach me?' Claudia asked.

'Tomorrow,' Mateo said. 'Be ready at nine.'

With that he waved and walked backwards a few steps, before shoving his hands in his pockets and walking quickly down the promenade. Claudia found herself looking after him, surprised at how quickly she'd been drawn to him and how quickly he'd left.

'Claudia?'

She turned and saw that Carlos's face had drained of all colour, and when she looked over her shoulder to see what he was looking at, she saw a very angry, very beautiful, woman marching towards them.

'Who is—'

'My wife,' he whispered. 'And she's going to kill me. You need to go.'

Claudia laughed, before seeing that Carlos wasn't joking. 'Why didn't you tell me you had a wife! I would never have let you drive me so late! She could have joined us for dinner.'

It turned out that Carlos's wife didn't care to even look at Claudia, she was more interested in her husband, whom she grabbed by the ear and marched all the way back to his car, while he spoke rapidly in Spanish as she yelled.

Claudia shook her head, pleased she'd avoided being drawn into the conflict, and looked both ways to get her bearings. Walking back would take her a while, but she didn't feel unsafe and it wasn't overly late yet. The sea splashed gently to her left as she walked, past groups of young men and old, past lovers intertwined in each other's arms, and past people like her who chose to wander or sit alone. Maybe she was naïve, but she certainly didn't feel unsafe.

When a car pulled up beside her, the engine rumbling, she didn't look sideways straight away, until the driver spoke.

'Would you like a ride?'

Claudia turned, seeing Mateo leaning out of an old pickup truck, not so much beaten up in appearance as starting to fade.

'Please,' she replied. Even if she had known the way home better, she'd have still said yes.

'Let me guess, his wife saw him with you?' Mateo leaned across and opened the door for her.

'How did you know?' She climbed in.

'Carlos is harmless, but he's very friendly with the ladies.' Mateo laughed. 'Let's just say that his wife would prefer he came home for dinner, or at least before bedtime.'

She hoped he wasn't in too much trouble, he'd been helping her after all and hadn't done anything inappropriate where she was concerned. Claudia let her head tip back and stared out the window into the almost dark as the Malecón made way for buildings, and before she knew it they were parked outside Rosa's house.

'Thank you,' she said, turning slightly towards him.

Mateo held her gaze, and even though she felt her cheeks flush, she didn't look away. He was the exact opposite of her ex fiancé; Mateo was dark where Max had been fair, his car worthless and his clothes casual and well-worn, whereas Max had worn designer suits that wouldn't have been complete without his Rolex glinting on his wrist. But the difference was that Mateo was authentic; he was himself. There was nothing to hide who he was, and she liked it.

'I'll see you tomorrow,' he said.

'Tomorrow,' she repeated.

And as she stood on the pavement and watched him drive away, red tail lights disappearing into the distance, she realised that she couldn't wait until morning.

Claudia smiled to herself as she walked up the stairs to her room, and stepped inside. The windows were thrown open and her bed had been turned down, and as she flopped down onto the bed, she reached into her bag to feel for the little wooden box.

You sent me here, Grandma, and somehow coming to Cuba was exactly what I needed.

I only wish you were still here so I could tell you all about it.

11

THE RITZ HOTEL, LONDON, 1950

Being the centre of attention wasn't something Esmeralda was usually uncomfortable with, but without her sisters by her side, she was finding it a far more daunting experience. Despite wishing she could fit in rather than stand out, her father had presented her with an extravagant diamond necklace that twinkled brightly, and he asked her to wear the powder blue dress he'd given her before they'd left Havana. Although she'd loved it at the time, she was now acutely aware of how different it was to the fashion in London, and she wished she could wear one of her new dresses that she'd purchased the day before.

But she forgot it all when Christopher reappeared by her side. She looked up at him and into eyes that were the most brilliant shade of blue, and from the way he was looking at her, he liked the way she looked very much.

'Your father has given me permission to ask you to dance,' he said.

She looked up at him, eyes widening in disbelief. 'He has?'

'Admittedly only within this fine establishment,' he confessed. 'I wouldn't like to be presumptuous though. Esmeralda,' he said, holding out his hand. '*Would* you like to dance?'

'Yes.' The word came out on an exhale and she smiled at how breathy she sounded. Is this how other girls had felt when they'd been asked to dance back home? She was finally starting to understand their behaviour and why her sisters were always so giddy when they arrived home after a night out.

The music changed then to something entirely unfamiliar to Esmeralda, and she gratefully caught Christopher's hand when someone bumped into her, with couples flocking to the dance floor around them. She laughed as she spun around, still holding his hand, as she watched the other couples all begin dancing in a way she'd never seen before.

'What is this?' she asked, her eyes wide as Christopher smiled down at her.

'This is the jitterbug,' he said. 'You've never heard of it?'

'Never!'

'Come on then,' he said with a laugh. 'I'm not sure I'll be the best teacher, but follow my lead. I'll try not to stand on your toes.'

Esmeralda couldn't remember a time she'd smiled so much or laughed so freely. There was something liberating about being away from home, about doing different things and not being surrounded by the same people she'd been in the company of her entire life. She knew how lucky she was to live in Havana, that it was the kind of paradise that so many people yearned for, but going to London had truly opened her eyes to the world.

If only she wasn't leaving in just a few days' time.

She looked up at Christopher and imagined what it would be like if he lived in her world, if they weren't separated by a country and their cultures. Her father liked that she was impressing him, and all the other business acquaintances that she'd met, but if he knew for a second how she truly felt, he'd have her on a plane back to Havana before she had time to pack her bags.

The song ended then, but Christopher reached for her hand, gently grasping her fingers with his. 'Would you like to get some fresh air?'

She swallowed, looking first at their hands and then over her shoulder to where her father was. She couldn't see him, although that didn't mean he wasn't watching her.

'He's retired to the smoking room for a cigar,' Christopher whispered in her ear.

His words hung between them for a moment before she nodded. She'd noticed women in London moving about with freedom, not seeming to need chaperones, which made her think they would hardly be noticed if she did step outside with Christopher. The last thing she wanted was to anger her papá. *But what he doesn't know won't hurt him.*

Christopher let go of her fingers and covered her palm with his instead, and she ducked her head, finding it hard not to imagine everyone staring at them. Until he leaned close and whispered in her ear.

'They're not looking at you because you're holding my hand,' he murmured. 'They're looking at you because they've never seen anyone like you before.'

She flushed at his words, at the way his eyes met hers when he leaned in close, the warmth of his breath against her skin. Their shoulders bumped, her bare skin against the fabric of his jacket.

When they stepped outside, onto a terrace that overlooked London, there was a chill in the air, which almost took her breath away. Christopher had already noticed her gasp and quickly took his jacket off, draping it over her shoulders. She snuggled into it, loving the smell of his aftershave so close to her body.

'Thank you. I'm not used to the cold,' she said.

'Tell me what Havana is like?' he asked, stepping around her and gesturing for her to follow. 'Is it truly such a paradise?'

They were tucked away from the doors now, in an almost dark part of the terrace that concealed them from view. Esmeralda should have been nervous, alone with a man she barely knew, but all she could think about was his coat around her shoulders, about how chivalrous he'd been with her.

'It's so different from here,' she said. 'I feel as if it's a world away. It's hard to explain, but in answer to your question, yes, it truly is paradise on earth.'

She saw the way he put his hands in his pockets, watched as he stepped away and then immediately turned back around to her. Her eyes had adjusted to the dark and she could see the way he was looking at her, searching her face.

'I wasn't lying before, when I said the people in there had never seen anyone like you.' Christopher stepped closer, their bodies so close to touching as he lifted his hand and ever so gently cupped his palm against her cheek. 'Because *I've* never seen anyone like you, Esmeralda. Every time I see you, you steal my breath away.'

Esmeralda's breath quickened as she looked up at him. *I shouldn't be here. I could step around him and go back inside. Papá will never even know I was out here.*

But she didn't move.

'May I kiss you?'

'Yes,' she whispered, without hesitation.

His lips were so soft as they brushed gently against hers, and Esmeralda found herself leaning towards him, looping her arms around his neck as he kissed her again. His mouth moved against hers and she finally understood the excitement of being touched by a man.

Only this was forbidden. Christopher wasn't a man from a good Cuban family, he wasn't a man she should even have been allowed to be alone with, he wasn't a man she would ever have permission to marry.

When his lips left hers, Christopher pulled her closer and

she went willingly into his arms, hidden by his jacket as she tucked against his chest. His mouth touched her hair and she inhaled the scent of him as tears filled her eyes.

Neither of them had to say anything. They both knew that there was no way they could be together. And yet still she didn't move.

Because there was nowhere else she wanted to be than in Christopher's arms.

'It's been a pleasure doing business with you,' Esmeralda's father said, shaking Christopher's hand in earnest on the final day of their trip as she watched on, trying to keep her face impassive even though her heart was breaking.

'It's been a most enjoyable week, Julio. Thank you for travelling all this way.'

When Christopher turned to her she smiled sedately, conscious of her father watching her, knowing what was expected. But in truth she was ready to burst, desperate to have a moment alone with him, knowing this was likely the last time she'd ever see him again.

Her memories were going to have to last her a lifetime, because no man would ever compare to Christopher Dutton, of that she was certain.

'Thank you for entertaining my daughter, too,' her father said. 'Without my wife by my side, I have to say it's comforting to have Esmeralda with me, although perhaps selfish to drag her all this way.'

'Selfish?' she repeated, before Christopher had the chance to reply. 'Papá, don't say such a thing! This has been the most wonderful experience of my life coming to London! I will be forever grateful that you asked me to join you.'

She looked at Christopher as she said that last part. London had been special because of him.

'Sir, I thought it would be nice to take Esmeralda for what we call high tea here in London, before your departure,' Christopher said. 'It's something my mother and sisters adore, and in fact they scolded me for not taking her earlier.'

Esmeralda held her breath, maintaining her composure as she turned expectantly towards her father. *Time alone with Christopher?* She admired his boldness in asking.

'Of course you may join us, Julio, if you'd like? Although I'm certain you have business to attend to before...'

'You will be with her the entire time?' Julio asked. 'At her side?'

'Of course,' Christopher replied. 'We shall be on the fourth floor at Harrods, one of the finest establishments in all of London.'

Her father looked at her and she nodded, holding her breath until he eventually waved his hand. 'My daughter has become very well acquainted with the womenswear department at Harrods, so please avoid that floor at all costs.'

They all laughed and, ever the dutiful daughter, she stepped forward to kiss her father's cheek.

'Thank you, Papá.'

'Stay close to Mr Dutton at all times,' he cautioned, before holding his hand out to shake Christopher's. 'I trust this man with your life.'

Esmeralda swallowed and smiled, careful not to react.

If only Papá knew that it was Christopher Dutton he should have been keeping her away from.

The tea rooms at Harrods were exquisite, with a stained-glass ceiling and tables set with military precision, but Esmeralda barely noticed her surroundings. All she could think about was the fact that she had her hand slipped through the crook of Christopher's arm, his shoulder close enough for her to drop her head to as they stood and waited to be shown to their table. When he lowered his arm, she let her hand drop away, already missing his touch.

'This way, please.'

They followed the waitress and then sat across from each other as an assortment of delicate finger sandwiches and patisseries was placed in front of them, with Christopher ordering them tea. Once they were alone, she placed her hand on the table, thrilled when he covered it with his own. She resisted the urge to look over her shoulder; no one here knew her, she didn't have to worry about them being seen.

'Es—'

'Chris—'

She laughed nervously as he graciously indicated that she should speak first.

'Thank you for bringing me here. I know how intimidating my father can be.'

Christopher's fingers moved gently against hers. 'You're right. I didn't think twice about negotiating deals worth millions of pounds with him, but asking to take his daughter to afternoon tea, with me as her chaperone?' He laughed. 'I was certain he was going to notice the sweat on my brow.'

She didn't want to talk about leaving, or ask him whether they might ever see each other again. She was returning to Havana, and his life was in London; what future could they possibly have? All she knew was that she wanted to enjoy every moment she had with him. If this was their last hour together, then so be it, she was going to soak up every second.

'What are these?' she asked, gesturing to the fluffy looking pieces of bread covered in jam, with a dollop of cream on top.

'That, my love, is an English scone,' Christopher said, putting one on a dainty plate for her. 'It's tastes heavenly.'

Esmeralda carefully picked it up with her fingers and took a bite, and then another. 'Oh, it is amazing! I think I need another.'

They both laughed as he filled her plate with another scone, as well as a tiny cucumber sandwich and some sort of pastry. The waitress returned with their tea, and although she was more used to strong Cuban coffee, she happily sipped the English Breakfast tea that was placed before her. She'd become used to it since they'd arrived in England.

'You're even exquisite when you eat,' Christopher said with a sigh. 'I've never met anyone like you, Miss Diaz.'

She dabbed at the corners of her mouth with a starched white napkin. 'And I've never met anyone like you either, Mr Dutton.'

They stared at each other across the table, neither of them needing to say a thing. She'd wondered if he felt the same way about her as she did him, whether he was merely indulging in spending time with an inexperienced woman he saw as exotic, but something about the way he looked at her, the way he smiled at her so thoughtfully, made her think otherwise. It made her believe his feelings ran deeper than that; after all, he'd been nothing other than a gentleman.

'Esmeralda, may I write to you?' he suddenly asked.

'Yes!' she replied, before lowering her voice. 'Only you'll have to write to my maid and she'll pass me the letters. If my papá found out you were writing me, he'd kill you.'

Christopher visibly paled. *If only it weren't the truth.*

'This can't be the end,' he said, his fingers intertwining with hers again.

Esmeralda nodded, although she had no idea how it *wouldn't* be the end. Finding a way to see Christopher again felt as good as impossible.

12

HAVANA, CUBA, PRESENT DAY

'Where are you off to this morning?'

Claudia looked up as Rosa sat down at the table with her and poured herself a coffee. 'I met Mateo last night,' she said. 'He kindly offered to show me around.'

The older woman smiled. 'Mateo is a good boy, I know his mother.'

Claudia laughed. 'Well, that makes me feel better.'

'If anyone can help you discover more about the Diaz family, it will be him. Who knows? You might find all the answers to your questions.'

She nodded and finished the piece of fruit she was eating. Her breakfast had been delicious, with fresh fruit, coffee and fresh Cuban bread, and she was even more grateful to Carlos today than she'd been the day before, for insisting that she stay in a home rather than a hotel. The hotel breakfast would likely have been nice, but eating Cuban food, sitting at a little outdoor table in the sunshine, had been the best way to spend the morning. Somehow it felt fitting, being in a family home when family was what had drawn her to Cuba.

'Leave all this, I'll clean up once you've gone.'

'You're sure?' Claudia glanced down at her plate and coffee cup. 'I don't mind helping.'

'Your pesos are helping me more than you realise,' Rosa said, patting her hand. 'Now go, enjoy your day. Mateo is nothing if not great company, and I want you to fall in love with Cuba.'

Claudia was already seeing how easily she could fall in love with Cuba, there was certainly something special about it, if not simply because it was so different to what she was used to. But spending the day with a man she barely knew felt more like a date, and she hadn't been on one of those in a very long time, which was making her nervous.

'Will you be having dinner here tonight?' Rosa called after her.

'Yes please! I've heard all about your famous cooking.'

'Oh querido,' she heard her mutter, before shaking her head as if to realise she hadn't spoken English. 'Oh dear. I have a lot to live up to.'

Claudia laughed to herself as she ran up the stairs, getting herself ready before picking up her bag and heading back out into the sunshine again, just in time to see Mateo pull up outside. His car was as old as everything else around, although his looked every bit its age. The paintwork certainly wasn't polished to a shine like Carlos's, and when he stepped out and walked around to greet her, she noticed that he wore the same scuffed boots from the night before, faded jeans and a T-shirt. She cleared her throat and lifted her gaze. He was almost impossible not to stare at.

'Buenos días, Claudia,' he said, opening the passenger door for her.

'Good morning,' she replied, unable to hide her smile as she slid into the car. She'd hoped for a slightly cooler temperature once she was in, but it was just as hot as outside with no air conditioning. She wound her window down as far as it would go.

'So tell me,' Mateo said once he was behind the wheel again, 'what do you know of the Diaz house?'

'Absolutely nothing,' she replied. 'Honestly, this is all so new to me, I know very little about the family or their home. I'm at your mercy.'

Mateo looked sideways at her and she tried to pretend her face wasn't on fire, her cheeks no doubt a dark shade of pink. Perhaps saying she was at his mercy hadn't been her best turn of phrase.

'So let me get this straight,' he said, one arm out the window, the other loosely holding the wheel. 'You received this clue of yours, you know nothing about the family, and you just booked a ticket and decided to come to Cuba?' He clicked his fingers. 'Just like that?'

Claudia sighed. 'Exactly. Although hearing you say it makes it sound crazy.'

'Not crazy,' he said with a grin. 'Impulsive perhaps, but not crazy. Not many people can make a fast decision like that.'

She toyed with how much to tell him. He was still a stranger, after all, but she wanted him to understand. The person she'd once been would never have done anything so spontaneously. 'A year ago, I was living a very different life, with a stressful job and little time for myself. I suppose I was trying to make everyone else happy, or live up to the expectations they had of me. But now I'm trying to live in the moment more, to just enjoy my life.' What she didn't say was how fortunate she'd been; she'd made enough money in finance to give her independence, and she knew not everyone was so lucky.

'I like it,' Mateo replied. 'It's brave stepping away from what everyone else expects of you. We only have one life.'

She nodded, pleased she'd told him, although not wanting to talk too much about herself.

'We're not so different, you and I,' he said, with a quick glance in her direction. 'It's why I do what I love. I mean, I could be a chef in one of the hotels, or I could have left Cuba altogether, but if I'm going to slave away for hours over a stove, I want to meet the people eating my food, I want to *see* them eat it, and in the country I love, too. Nothing beats watching someone's face when they eat my empanadas for the very first time.'

'That's what I had last night.' She would never forget that burst of flavour.

He grinned again. 'I know. And your face told me exactly how good they were.'

Claudia was convinced the car had become a hundred degrees hotter, and she was grateful when he sped up, which made the wind feel cooler against her skin. But just as she was enjoying the breeze, he pulled the car over and stopped.

'What are we doing?' she asked.

'Getting coffee,' he said, gesturing for her to get out and follow him.

They walked a short distance before Mateo stopped, and she noticed there were a few people standing with little ceramic cups, gathered on the street and narrowly avoiding the passing cars.

He went up to a window that she wouldn't have even noticed if she wasn't with him, and turned back to her with two cups.

She took one, still puzzled. 'Unexpected, but thanks.' Claudia took a sip, surprised at how sweet it was. 'Is this someone's house?'

Mateo nodded. 'The owner makes coffee every morning, it's a popular spot for locals.'

She sipped again, starting to get used to how strong Cuban coffee was, although not the sweetness of this particular brew.

'Finished?' Mateo asked.

She took a final sip and passed him the cup, which he in turn passed back through the hole in the wall.

'Gracias,' she called out, as more people stepped forward to get their morning fix.

They started to walk back to the car again, Claudia following in Mateo's footsteps and wondering if there were any more surprises in store. 'Are there any other hidden places reserved for locals?'

Mateo's eyes lit up. 'Maybe later I'll take you for pizza,' he said. 'We eat it differently here, you'll like it.'

'Pizza?' Her stomach growled loudly enough to make them both laugh.

'It's very simple pizza, made with Cuban tomato sauce and cheese,' he said. 'The base is doughy, but it's good, and you just fold it in half and eat it. It's one of the few things that can always be made, because the ingredients are so simple.'

They were almost at the car when he grabbed her hand. 'Here, follow me. All this talking about food has made me hungry.'

She glanced at her hand in his but went with it. 'You can get pizza in the morning? I've only just had breakfast!'

'Of course, it's a great breakfast food!'

Within minutes they were at another window, this one slightly more obvious than the coffee one. Mateo lined up and a few minutes later he passed her a whole small pizza in a napkin.

'Like this,' he said as he demonstrated with his own, folding it in half and eating it more like a burrito. 'Now you can eat pizza like a Cuban.'

Claudia laughed but followed his direction, folding it over and taking a bite. He was right, it was doughy, but it also packed a punch of cheese and homemade tomato sauce.

'This is good,' she said, as they slowly walked and ate at the same time. 'Not as good as the food I had last night, but still good.'

They were back at the car now, and they stood on the pavement as they finished, before wiping their hands on the napkins.

'Let's go,' he said.

'You know, I'm curious about your grandfather,' Claudia said once they were driving again. 'Did you become a chef to follow in his footsteps?'

'My grandfather worked for the Diaz family for almost two decades, when the house was run by Julio's mother, and he stayed on there when Julio married and had his own family. He always spoke very fondly of that time.'

'He must have been close to them after all those years?'

Mateo nodded. 'He was. He thought of them as his own family. When my mother was young, she was often invited over to swim in the pool and spend the day with the Diaz girls, and she's always quick to recount how kind they were to her. They were a good family, and my grandfather always said the girls were brought up to respect everyone, whether they were maids or businessmen.'

Claudia couldn't help but think how strange it was. Families like the Diazes seemed to be such a huge part of Havana's identity, so to know they'd all fled, that only memories of them remained, almost felt as though part of Cuba's history had been erased. She wondered if some had chosen to stay, and if so, whether they were still grieving the Havana of their youth all these decades later.

'I grew up hearing so many stories. Even though I never met the old families of Havana, I almost feel like I know them. My grandfather told tales in a way that brought them to life, although I always wondered if he'd embellished them over the years.'

'When did he pass away?' she asked.

'When I was about fourteen, although he lived on through my father and we went on to open the food truck together and cooked side by side for years, often talking about him and how much he would have loved it.'

She noticed the change in Mateo's voice, the way his hand tightened for a moment over the steering wheel. She could suddenly see the whites of his knuckles.

'He's not alive now, either?'

'No, he's not, but I can still feel him here sometimes, especially when I'm cooking.'

'Are they his recipes? Did you cook the same food with him?'

'They're actually my grandfather's recipes,' Mateo said. 'Although the rumour is that my grandmother was the true chef, and my grandfather simply copied her. Either way, they've passed down through my family, almost identical even after all these years.'

Claudia smiled to herself as she imagined the generations of Mateo's family, and how special it was that they all shared such a deep love of food. It was so different to her own family. Her father was almost guaranteed to burn whatever he tried to cook on the barbeque, and her mother had perhaps four recipes in her repertoire that she'd cooked on rotation when Claudia had been a child. But her grandmother, she'd been something else; her food had brought them all together every week, all of them looking forward to whatever dish they'd requested. They'd all missed it terribly since she'd been gone, and wished they'd taken the time to learn from her instead of taking it for granted that she'd always be there. Claudia wondered if her grandma might have left behind a cookbook full of her famous recipes, and made a mental note to ask her mother the next time they spoke.

After a comfortable silence that involved Claudia gazing with interest at everything passing them by, Mateo suddenly cleared his throat.

'This is it.'

She looked up from her thoughts as the car slowed and

glanced to where Mateo was pointing. The house was enormous, a true mansion by anyone's standards, set close to the road and impossible not to notice. The bricks had turned grey and were covered in moss, with plaster peeling off in other parts, and she wondered if perhaps the house would have once been a more vibrant colour, or even simply a rich, flawless cream. It was as if she was seeing it in black and white, instead of colour, as if the years had stripped everything away that had once made it unique, other than its sheer size. Because as huge and imposing as it was, there was something so sad about the state of repair it was in. *It needs someone like me to breathe life back into it again, to make it sparkle and return it to its former glory.* There were missing roof tiles and the windowsills were overrun with peeling paintwork, and she could only imagine what the garden could have been like, because it appeared even more unloved than the house now.

'Wow,' she said on a breath. There was nothing else to say; it was incredible and sad all at the same time, but it was still *wow*, simply due to the sheer size of it.

'It's still quite something, isn't it?' he said, pulling the car over farther up the road. 'It's quite a change from its days as the home to one of Havana's high-society families, although at least it hasn't fallen into complete disrepair. It might look bad to you, but some of the homes around here are much worse.'

Claudia craned her neck to look back at the house, but there was no need as Mateo got out and opened her door, beckoning for her to join him.

'It is still beautiful,' Claudia said as they strolled slowly past together, giving her time to appreciate it. 'It's actually as I imagined, if I'd had to try to visualise it.' Perhaps she'd romanticised the Cuba of old, but the house certainly lived up to her expectations, despite the state of repair. There was truly something magical about it.

She loved architecture and design, and she would have

done anything to spend more time looking at the house, perhaps even going inside. Since she'd started renovating real estate for a job, architecture and interiors had become her obsession. All of the places she worked on were older, they all had history regardless of their architecture, and she always saw it as her job to preserve something of the past, to not completely strip away history.

'Come on, let's take a look,' Mateo said, reaching for her hand.

'Inside? Do you know the people who live here?'

'Not exactly.'

She swallowed, shaking her head, not convinced. 'Mateo, I'm not sure.'

'Come with me, there's a gate around the corner,' he said. 'Let's just look through the front door if it's open.'

She dragged her feet, convinced they were being watched and that she would end up being arrested, but Mateo appeared as relaxed as could be, as if they were about to visit a friend. The last thing she needed was to be thrown into a Cuban jail.

'This is the gate the Diaz girls used to go through, when they were sneaking home late at night,' Mateo whispered, leaning closer.

'Really?'

He laughed. 'I'm only guessing. But after all the stories I've heard over my lifetime about how stunning they were, their beauty striking enough to stop a man on the street, I can imagine they might have snuck out at night. Wouldn't they have stayed out late at parties or met young men in secret under the cloak of darkness?'

She'd created an image of them in her mind herself now, these raven-haired beauties who could seduce every man in a room. In reality, she imagined their personalities might have been quite the opposite, but Cuba had her imagination running wild. She wished she could see a photo of them to see what they actually did look like.

'There's a large garden and courtyard around the back, and there was once the most incredible swimming pool. I still remember my grandfather saying that everyone wanted an invitation to the Diaz family pool. It was the largest in town, with a fountain at one end that splashed water all day long.'

'When would this have been?'

'The late forties I suppose,' he said. 'Perhaps early fifties?'

She tried to remember what year her grandmother was born, wondered if she could somehow have been part of this, could have been connected to the people who'd once called this home. It seemed so unlikely, a world away from the life her grandparents had had in London, and she still couldn't see a clear connection from the Diaz family to her own.

At the gate, Claudia hesitated. 'I feel like we're trespassing.'

'We're only taking a look,' he said. 'Besides, people return to Cuba all the time these days, and they all go to their former homes to see how they've fared. It's no different to what we're doing.'

Her feet were still rooted to the spot. 'I just—'

'Come on,' he said, his eyes lighting up as he tugged at her hand, reminding her of being a schoolgirl and trying to decide whether to smoke behind the gym building with the others or return to class. 'The people who left here, they walked away without anything, thinking they would return and step back into the lives they'd left. It was as if they were leaving for the season, their paintings still on the walls and their clothes still hanging in the wardrobes.'

She swallowed. Flying to Cuba on a whim was one thing, but being arrested for trespassing? That wasn't just being impulsive, that was being outright reckless.

'Claudia?'

She fought against her better judgement.

'Fine, but just a peek through the door. I don't want to get caught.'

'I'll be the one to get in trouble, not you. I promise.'

Claudia kept a tight hold on Mateo's hand as they walked quickly to the front door, and she couldn't believe his audacity when he simply turned the handle to see if was unlocked. It was, and he immediately pushed it open and then stepped back to let her in.

'Go in,' he whispered. 'You'll be fine.'

She took one furtive step, about to turn and tell Mateo that she couldn't do it, but the moment she looked inside she was captivated. There was no way she couldn't take just a little look.

She tipped back her head to look up at the high ceiling, absorbing the chandelier and then the sweeping staircase at the other end of the hall. The carpet had seen better days and was almost threadbare, but as she stood there she could imagine what it must have been like, could almost see the Díaz family sweeping past her, the girls running for the stairs, their dresses swishing as they held them above their ankles. She could see maids scurrying, everything polished and gleaming, living up to its name as the most extravagant home in Cuba.

'It's quite something, isn't it?' Mateo said quietly as he stood so close they were almost touching. 'And look here, these are some of the paintings they left behind. Apparently Julio Diaz's art collection was worth millions, and of course much of it was sold by the regime, but some remain.'

Claudia heard voices then, and Mateo grabbed hold of her hand again and they hurried the few steps back for the door. He closed it quietly behind them and they ran across the front of the property and back through the gate.

Breathless, they stood outside, shoulder to shoulder, pressed to the wall, and when Claudia looked over at Mateo she burst out laughing. 'I can't believe we did that!'

He shrugged. 'Was it worth it?'

She closed her eyes a moment, still catching her breath. 'Yes. Yes, Mateo, it was worth it.' *I just wish I could figure out what my connection to it all is. What my grandmother's connection was.* It wasn't any clearer to her now than it was when she'd first seen the clues.

'Come on,' he said, pushing off from the wall and gesturing for her to follow him again. 'We can walk around here and see the back of the property, and take a look at the other homes in the neighbourhood.'

'But no going inside,' she said. 'That's the one and only time I'm doing that. I've never done anything criminal in my life before!'

His smile was easy and she followed him, surprised by how carefree she felt. At home she'd never have dared to be so bold as to spend the day with a man she barely knew, not to mention going into a house without being invited.

'Look, there's a large crack in the fence here.'

He stood back and she edged forward, placing her hands on the cool concrete wall and slowly bringing her eye towards the large hole. She half expected someone to be looking back at her from the other side, but there was nothing other than an enormous backyard. Claudia pressed forward, staring at the large palm trees of the former Diaz property, the huge expanse of lawn, and most impressive of all, the paved area that led down to an extravagant swimming pool. There were statues of lions beside it, as if they were the pool's guardians, and an ornate feature at the end that she guessed would have once been the water fountain that Mateo mentioned, only now the entire thing was dry.

'It's amazing,' she said, finally drawing her gaze away. 'I can't imagine how those families could walk away from all this, from a home like this.'

'I don't think anyone imagined that those families wouldn't return,' Mateo said, and they fell into an easy step beside each other as they continued walking. 'Havana without its most affluent families, families who'd employed so many people in their sugar factories and fields, and in their homes, would have seemed impossible to believe. But these weren't to be their homes anymore, they were all to be taken from them.' Mateo sighed. 'Julio Diaz wasn't a bad man, he treated his workers much better than most of the other businessmen did, but of course many of the wealthy were not known for their generosity, and that was fuelled by years of government corruption. Some were pleased to see them lose their mansions.'

She knew enough history to understand roughly what had happened in Cuba, but to hear it from the mouth of a Cuban was something else entirely.

'So many families that lost a brother or son to the revolution, they all believed so fervently in our country needing change, but sadly the change was a step too far.'

'Was it better though?' she asked. 'For the people? After the revolution, with Castro in power?'

'No, Claudia, it wasn't. Cuba needed change, but Castro didn't live up to his promises,' Mateo replied. 'Or perhaps the people were so desperate to overthrow the government, they didn't see the truth of the man they had put all their faith in. At least that's how my father told it, and he lost his own brother to the fighting.'

They strolled in silence for a while, and Claudia looked around, at all the large houses around them. The Diaz home was in a slightly better state of repair than many, but all she could think was how heartbreaking it would be for any of those families to return and see what remained of their former residences.

'There were many affluent families living down this street and the blocks surrounding them,' Mateo said. 'Some say that the families who fled buried their cash and jewels, that the ground is full of wealth, but I'm sure Castro searched for it and found anything that was left.'

They kept walking, and Claudia kept thinking, pondering on what Mateo had told her, and what she already knew. *If the Diaz family had fled Cuba for Florida, how did her grandmother end up being born in London if she was indeed related to one of them? Or had Julio Diaz himself been having an affair, and the connection wasn't one of the Diaz daughters, as she'd originally wondered?*

'Mateo, did you ever hear anything about an illegitimate Diaz child? Could Julio have had a secret love child, perhaps? Or could his wife have had a secret child?'

He shrugged. 'With a family like theirs, who would know? It wouldn't be unheard of for a man like him to have a mistress.'

Claudia stopped and looked back at the Diaz home, wishing she could spend more time there exploring the house and searching for clues, looking at family portraits to see if there was a resemblance to her grandmother in any of them. *If only those walls could talk.*

It had been a long morning that had stretched until long past lunchtime as they'd explored the once-affluent streets of Havana, but Claudia still wasn't ready for it to end. She sat with Mateo on the steps of his food truck, their legs nudging together as they leaned forward. He'd told her to sit and enjoy the sunshine while he prepared lunch, and she hadn't really known what to expect, although when he'd returned with two paper plates and joined her on the step, she'd known immediately it was going to be delicious.

'This is a famous Cuban sandwich,' he said, as he took a bite, gesturing for her to do the same.

She did, and she couldn't hide the little groan of pleasure

that escaped her lips as she chewed it. 'Oh my gosh, this is incredible,' she said. 'What's in it?'

'Leftover pork from last night, with pickles, a tangy mustard and Swiss cheese,' he said. 'I came in early to make the bread, before I picked you up.'

'Wait, you'd already been in the kitchen this morning?'

He shrugged and took another bite. 'I make everything from scratch. It's all part of the job.'

She kept eating, loving the saltiness of the sandwich and knowing she was going to have to try to replicate it when she was home. It was heavenly. Perhaps she could collect recipes and take her grandmother's place as the family cook after spending more time with Mateo.

'Thank you for today,' she said, setting down what was left of her sandwich and dabbing at the corners of her mouth. 'It was a lot of fun.'

Mateo finished his sandwich and leaned back a little. 'How about tomorrow I take you out to see the sugar mill?'

She felt her eyes widen. 'Really?'

'You can't learn about the Diaz family without seeing where they made their fortune,' he said. 'Who knows? It might help you with your search.'

A flutter of excitement touched Claudia's stomach. 'I'd like that, thank you, but only if you're certain? I mean, I'm sure you have better things to do than be my personal tour guide.'

Mateo stood, dusting himself off and looking down at her. 'Taking a beautiful tourist around Havana isn't exactly unenjoyable, Claudia. It would be my pleasure.'

She didn't know what to say to that, so Claudia just smiled and diverted her gaze back to her sandwich; it seemed a much safer bet than looking at Mateo.

'Are you okay to walk back?' he asked. 'I have to start preparing for this evening.'

Claudia passed him the paper plate and napkin, nodding. 'Of course.'

Mateo watched her for a long moment, slightly higher than her as he stood in the truck and looked down at her where she stood on the step, and for a second she thought he was about to move closer. But instead he just grinned and turned away, firing up his stove and sending delicious aromas into the air from whatever he'd already prepared in the pot.

'Hasta luego,' Mateo called out.

She had no idea what he'd said, but she guessed it was some sort of goodbye, and as she walked away from the truck, she couldn't help but smile. It had been a great day; one of those days that would make her happy just from the memory of it for hours to come. But she was quickly pulled from her thoughts about Mateo when she saw a sign for an internet café across the road. Her internet on her phone had been patchy at best since she'd arrived, and she wanted to check her emails.

A few minutes later, she was sitting at a computer, with archaic internet speed that made her wonder if it was worth it. Although when she saw that the first email was from her dad when she was finally in her inbox, she was pleased she'd persisted.

Claudia clicked.

Hi darling,

I hope you're having a wonderful time in Havana. How's the search into the Diaz family going? I've had some minor success with the business card, after drawing on all my old finance contacts. Christopher Dutton appears to have been a very successful young businessman back in the very late forties. Very little is known about him, other than that he left the firm in Capel Court in 1951, and that when he died in 2001, he left the entirety of his estate to the maternal research centre at St Thomas' Hospital here in London. He appears to have no descendants, and other than what I've outlined above, my research has largely come to a dead end.

Your mother is peering over my shoulder and wants to know all about what you're up to, although I've told her you may not have mobile reception.

Let us know how you're getting on when you can, and good luck with your search.

Dad xx

She sat back and reread her father's email. Why would a man, with no family of his own, leave his entire estate to *maternity* research? Was this man's connection to Hope's House, the place Mia had spoken of, rather than to her own grandmother? Was that why he'd wanted to give money to maternity care?

More confused about her clues than before she'd read the email, Claudia sent a quick reply to her dad before logging out, with this Christopher on her mind as she tried to unravel what it all meant, and how her family was connected to any of it. *If we even are at all.*

What if Grandmu's mother was simply a maid to this family? What if she wasn't related by blood to the Diaz family at all?

But in her heart, Claudia knew the connection was deeper. The pull she felt towards the house, the inescapable connection she had felt at just glimpsing the interior, all told her that there had to be something more, something that linked her own blood to the Diaz family.

Or perhaps I've just fallen in love with the history of the family and can't stand the thought that I'm not directly connected to them in some way.

She logged out and picked up her bag, deciding to walk back to the house so she had time to gather her thoughts.

13

THE DIAZ RESIDENCE, HAVANA, CUBA, 1950

'Tell me all about him!' María whispered, as they all sat on Esmeralda's bed. 'Was he truly so gorgeous?'

Esmeralda sighed, flopping back onto the row of plumped-up pillows behind her. Her sisters were both sitting on her bed with her, which was covered in clothes and trinkets that she'd brought home for them, but her mind was still consumed with Christopher. She'd been desperate to arrive home and tell her sisters all about him—in the end she'd not dared write home in case her letters were somehow seen by Papá—and as her maid finally left the room, she was able to lift her voice above a whisper. Her sisters were waiting to lap up every detail she was prepared to share, and she couldn't wait to tell them.

'He was a true gentleman,' she said, staring up at the ornately carved ceiling rose above her. 'From the moment I met him, the moment my eyes caught in his, I knew I was in trouble. There was something different about him, and he was so handsome!'

'So it was love at first sight?' María asked.

Esmeralda pushed up onto her elbows. 'It sounds silly, but it was the first time I'd understood why you two get so excited about parties and dancing. If I'd met Christopher here, I'd have danced in his arms all night and dreamed of him for days afterwards. You never would have heard the end of it.'

'Who would have thought, our Es in love with an Englishman,' Gisele teased. 'I thought you were going to come back with your head full of business, not romance.'

'Business?' Esmeralda laughed. It wasn't the silliest comment, she'd always loved learning about their father's sugar business and liked nothing more than walking the sugar mill with him, but she'd forgotten all about that during her travels. Christopher had consumed her.

'Tell us what he looked like?' María asked. 'I need to imagine him in my mind.'

She dropped back onto the pillows again, seeing him as if he were there, smiling at her, his hand reaching for hers as they'd sat across from each other at Harrods. 'He was so handsome, with eyes as blue as the ocean. But it was the way he smiled at me, the way his face changed the moment I walked into the room, that's what made me notice him. He looked at me in a way that no other man has.'

María laughed. 'That's how *all* the boys look at you, Es! Every party we go to, their eyes follow you around the room while we clamber to turn one head. I just think you haven't noticed it before.'

'Nonsense!' Her eyes flew open and she swatted at her sister as she sat up. 'Don't say that! I see plenty of young men drooling over you, it's not me that they're looking at.'

They all giggled, heads bent together now.

'She's right, Es,' Gisele said. 'You light up the eyes of every man in every room you walk into, so what was it about this man? What was so different about him?'

Esmeralda sighed. 'I don't know. I just knew from the moment I met him, the moment Papá and I arrived for dinner on our very first night, that he was different. He made me *feel* different.' She remembered back to the first moment she'd set eyes upon him. 'We had a connection, as if we were destined to be together.'

Both of her sisters sighed, too, as if their hearts were full alongside hers, but it didn't take long before Gisele and María started to look at all the things she'd brought for them from Harrods, their attention diverted, leaping up and trying on dresses and laughing to one another as she watched on, trying to show interest. But it was Gisele who returned to sit beside her on the bed, reaching for her hand; her sister instinctively knowing she was hurting.

'You miss him already, don't you?'

Esmeralda nodded as tears clung to her lashes. 'I'm afraid I won't ever see him again.'

Gisele didn't reply for a long while. 'You don't know that, Es. Perhaps your paths will cross again, perhaps something will happen to bring you together?'

'I can't imagine a life without him,' Esmeralda whispered, blinking furiously as tears filled her eyes. 'One day soon, Papá will need to make a decision about my future, he won't let me become a spinster, and I want to marry a man who makes me feel like Christopher did. I fear that no one will ever live up to him, that I'll never fall in love with another man like I fell for him.'

María came to sit on her other side and Esmeralda threw her arms around her, as Gisele nestled into her back on the other side, tucking her body tightly alongside hers. And they sat like that, her sisters stroking her hair and soothing her cries until her maid knocked on the door and told them it was time for dinner.

Gisele rose to get a tissue, gently dabbing Esmeralda's eyes and cheeks, before pressing a warm kiss to her hair. 'Time heals all hurt. This will get easier, I promise.'

Esmeralda rose and nodded, staring at her reflection in the

full-length mirror and wishing her eyes weren't so red. It was obvious she'd been crying, although she hoped that with some artfully applied makeup, she could disguise it and explain it away as tiredness. The last thing she wanted was to answer questions from her maid or her father about her appearance, and she knew they'd both notice if something was wrong.

'Gisele's right, it will get easier,' María said as she rose to leave, also kissing her. 'It's like when we lost Mamá. At the time, I thought I'd never be able to rise from my bed ever again, but look at us now? We've flourished despite our loss, because we've had one another. We're always here for you, no matter what, just like you've always been for us.'

Esmeralda nodded and smiled at her sister, knowing how true her words were, but the moment she shut the door, leaving her alone, she crumpled to the floor; a fallen ballerina, her dress a puddle around her.

I'm never going to forget how Christopher made me feel. I'm never going to forget the way his skin felt against mine. I'm never going to stop wishing I was in his arms.

She closed her eyes and saw his face, remembered the feel of her hand tucked in his arm, her head dipped to his shoulder; the moment they'd shared alone on the balcony in the almost dark.

I have to find a way to be with him again. I cannot live the rest of my life, married off to a man I don't even love. I cannot live a life that doesn't have him in it.

'Esmeralda?' Her name was followed by a gentle tap on the door. 'It's time for dinner, may I dress you?'

'Just a moment!' she called back, quickly regaining her composure and standing, taking a moment to still her breath, before finally letting her maid in.

'Is everything all right?'

She nodded, fixing her smile. 'Of course, I'm simply tired and wishing for bed. The trip to London has sapped all my energy.' She sighed and turned around. 'Please select a dress for me while I attend to my complexion. Whatever you choose will be fine.'

And just like that, Esmeralda stepped back into the life that was expected of her, donning a beautiful dress and gliding downstairs to join her family, the woman of the house once more. Her father must never know how she felt, and as she walked around the table to kiss his cheek before taking her seat beside him, she tried to ignore her broken heart. It would do her no good to mope, but at least she had her memories from London, at least she'd had that magical week.

Those memories might have to last me a lifetime.

'María, how are the final plans coming along for your party?' she forced herself to ask. 'I'm so looking forward to the celebrations, you must be terribly excited?'

María's smile warmed the table, and also Esmeralda's heart. Her sister deserved the world; it was the biggest day of her life so far, and Esmeralda was going to do everything she could to make it a day her sister would never forget. That was one thing she *could* do, as their mother had once done for her.

'I have my final dress fitting in the morning,' María said. 'I tried it on when you were away and I felt like a princess.'

'As you should,' Esmeralda said. 'Papá, do you need me tomorrow, or may we all go for the dress fitting and out for lunch? I'd like to spend time with María and make sure everything is perfect for her special day.'

Her father sat back, smiling at his daughters as he so often did at dinner, with a look on his face as if he were the luckiest man in the world. She knew he'd do anything for them; his generosity was unrivalled, as was his kindness. But if he found out that she'd kissed Christopher, that the man he'd trusted to chaperone his eldest daughter had done anything other than protect her, his temper would know no bounds. She'd never pushed him before, never disobeyed him, never stepped outside of what was expected of her. Until one person had made her question everything about her life.

She pushed Christopher from her mind, fearful that her father might be able to read it if she wasn't careful.

'Enjoy telling your sisters about your travels. I'm sure they've missed you greatly and want to hear all about London,' he said. 'But bring me home the chocolate your mamá used to get, would you?'

Esmeralda nodded, grateful for the excuse to be out of the house come morning. The last thing she wanted was for him to ask her to join him at his office. 'Si, Papá, of course.'

María and Gisele began talking about the party again, and her father seemed to have missed Cuban food while they were away, for he ate heartily and didn't seem to notice when she placed her fork back down, barely able to stomach a mouthful.

14

HAVANA, CUBA, PRESENT DAY

Claudia would have been lying to herself if she'd said she wasn't looking forward to seeing Mateo again. She'd tossed and turned in the night, wondering what she was even doing spending time with him, but then the other voice in her head had said, *Why not?* She was single and she was on holiday. What did it matter whom she was spending time with? Not to mention he had a connection to precisely what she'd come to Cuba to investigate.

Just relax and stop overthinking everything.

And just like that, Mateo's car appeared. She smiled at his easy grin and the way his arm was hanging out the window, his hand tapping a beat on the door. When he pulled up at the kerb she found her feet moving of their own accord, her mouth drawing into a smile as Mateo turned down his music and raised his eyebrows.

'Morning.'

'Morning,' she replied, sliding onto the passenger seat.

'I have something for you.'

'You do?' she watched as he leaned over into the back seat, his T-shirt riding up and giving her a glimpse of his golden body. She stifled a sigh. *When did a man last make me sigh?* Max had been... perfect. He'd had a perfectly slender body, just like he'd had a perfectly pleasant personality and a perfect job. But some time in their final months together, she'd begun to wonder just how much she wanted *perfect.*

'This,' he said, passing her a thick book of some kind, 'is something my mother found.'

'Your mother?'

He laughed. 'Yes, my mother. She was most intrigued by the Englishwoman looking for details on the Diaz family. Gossip spreads fast here, and it seems that Rosa had told her all about you.'

Claudia looked at the book in her lap and realised it was an old album. She carefully turned the first page as Mateo began to drive, her eyes moving slowly over the young people in the black-and-white photographs.

'Whom am I looking at?'

'My mother and the Diaz sisters,' he said. 'Do you recognise the swimming pool?'

She nodded. It was the one she'd glimpsed through the fence the day before, only this photo was from its heyday. Claudia squinted and brought the album closer to her face, staring at the stunningly beautiful women in the photo. There were more photos, some elsewhere, at a party with everyone all dressed up, but try as she might she didn't see her grandmother in any of the girls pictured. The dark hair, certainly, but there was nothing in particular that made her believe she was related to anyone she was looking at.

Claudia closed the album and looked out, her arm on the open door to catch the breeze as she watched Havana pass them by. The trees were tropical, waving ever so in the wind, but it was the Malecón she was drawn to again as they passed, the sun painting everything a pretty golden colour. She watched the water lapping and suddenly wished to dip her toes into the ocean, to find their way to a beach somewhere so she could just lie and think everything through.

She found herself glancing over at Mateo, who had one hand on the wheel.

'You mentioned the mystery of the eldest sister the other day,' she said. 'I can't stop thinking about what might have happened to her.'

'Esmeralda?' he asked. 'I think everyone is intrigued by what happened to her.'

'So she just vanished into thin air?' Claudia asked. 'Would her family not have turned over every stone, no expense spared, to find her? She can't have just gone missing?'

Mateo shrugged. 'It was such a long time ago, but the rumour has always been that she ran away.'

'And you think that's true?'

'I think that a family like hers would have had the power and influence to find out what had happened to her,' he said. 'If they'd wanted to.'

She mulled that over in her mind for a moment, opening the album again and studying the very first photo, her eyes searching for the oldest girl. Esmeralda. *What happened to you?*

'So you think that she ran away, and that her family stayed quiet to avoid a scandal?'

'From what I've heard, they say that one day she just vanished, and from then no one in her family ever spoke of her again. And there was no search party, no police involvement, nothing.'

The mystery of it all intrigued Claudia—even if it hadn't been connected to her own family, she'd have still wanted to find out what had happened. A family with so much wealth and in such a position of privilege, why hadn't they gone to the ends of the earth to find their beloved daughter? Or had they, and just not told everyone what they'd found?

'Was she known for being rebellious?' Claudia asked.

He shook his head. 'From what I understand, the girls all loved their father and their father adored his daughters. The stories I've heard paint a picture of an eldest who was the apple of her father's eye though, who was often at his side after his wife had passed. It's why so many Cubans gossiped about it at the time, because they were always looked upon to be the perfect family. Even after their mother died, the girls continued on, raising their baby sister, devoted to their father.'

'So perhaps it wasn't so perfect after all?'

He nodded. 'Exactly. Although who knows what really happened? Perhaps the story is like a legend, becoming more of a mystery with each retelling. There must be someone who knows the truth.'

But who could that someone be?

She sighed, looking out the window once more and seeing how much the landscape had changed. She'd been so busy looking at the album and lost in her own thoughts, that she hadn't taken the time to notice the changing scenery. Claudia soaked up the lushness of the fields, the grass such a vivid green that it looked to be painted by an artist's brush, the rolling hills in the distance like sleeping giants ready to stretch and rise. The sky was so blue that she marvelled at how perfect it was, with barely a cloud passing by.

The car began to slow and Mateo stretched out his arm. 'This is what I wanted to show you.'

'This is the sugar mill?'

'The one and only,' he said. 'It wasn't the only mill Julio owned, but this one was his largest and most successful. Apparently it was the last mill to be owned privately after the revolution, and when this was taken from him, that's when he finally left Cuba.'

She wondered if he'd stayed for his sugar, or because he was waiting for his lost daughter, or perhaps a combination of the two. Or perhaps he'd already long ago given up on his daughter ever coming home, if what Mateo was hinting at was true. If he knew she'd run away, then presumably he'd have known where to find her if he'd wanted to, given the resources at his disposal. So perhaps the Diaz family had allowed everyone to believe she was missing, to cover up the truth about what she'd done? Surely there would be police files on the case, if she were ever listed as a missing person though.

They sat in the car a long moment, before Mateo got out and she followed, less worried about being seen looking at the sugar mill than she had been the house. Here, they were simply pulled over on the side of the road, gazing at fields filled with tall green stalks that she wouldn't have even known were sugar if she hadn't been told. She wasn't exactly used to looking at crops, and the production of sugar wasn't something she'd ever thought about before, especially not when she was tipping it out of a little paper sachet at her local café to pour into her coffee.

There was a tall building in the distance that she imagined was the mill, and she held up her hand and squinted, wondering if anyone was in there.

Mateo came and stood beside her, his shoulder brushing hers as he lifted his hand and looked in the same direction. 'The fortune the Diaz family made from this sugar,' he said with a whistle.

She shut her eyes and imagined the field full of men, of the sugar canes being cut. And then she imagined further back in time, wondering if the field would have been full of slaves, worked to the bone as their master became rich beyond anyone's wildest dreams. Mateo had said that Julio was a respected boss, kind to his employees, but she still couldn't help but wonder how the family's fortunes must have begun.

They stood awhile longer, and as Claudia's mind drifted from thoughts of the past, she became acutely aware of just how close he was standing to her, especially when he moved away.

'Let's take a walk.'

She followed, ignoring how hot and sticky her skin felt or the way the grass scratched her feet. She wished she'd worn trainers instead of her sandals, although it was slightly better when they walked along the dusty road. Her feet would be filthy afterwards, but at least it was soft.

'I haven't asked how long you're in Cuba?'

'One week,' she replied. 'Although if I need to stay longer, I will.'

'So I have only one week to show you my country.'

She looked around her, at a lush green landscape she couldn't have even imagined a week ago. 'You've been so kind, driving me around. I don't expect you to take me anywhere else.'

'But I want to show you the Cuba I know,' Mateo said, turning and starting to walk backwards, his gaze dancing against hers. 'Old Havana gives you a glimpse of the old Cuba, and the Malecón is like nowhere else in the world, but I want to show you where I live, what it's like where the tourists don't go.'

Claudia smiled shyly at him. 'That all sounds amazing.'

'May I ask you a question?'

She nodded, for some reason at a loss for words after his impassioned speech about showing her his world. *He wants to show me his Cuba?* Her heart was beating too fast and she hoped he couldn't sense how nervous she was.

'Do you have someone waiting at home for you? A boyfriend? Lover?'

He'd almost stopped walking now, and so had she. 'Ah, no, not anymore I don't.' *There, I've said it. There's no one waiting for me.*

'Good,' he said with a grin, before turning back around, slinging his arm around her shoulder as he fell into step beside her. 'Although maybe not so good for the other guy.'

Claudia laughed; she couldn't help it. Meeting Mateo had certainly been an unexpected upside of her impromptu trip.

'Let's just say that he was the one who ended things.' *Why did I say that? I ended things when he refused to let me grow, to let me be whom I needed to be. When he walked out the door and turned his back on me.*

Mateo shook his head. 'All the better for me. He must be loco.'

She laughed. 'Loco?'

He grinned in reply. 'Crazy in the head.'

That made her laugh even more, loving the way his fingers brushed her shoulder as they walked.

'Thank you,' she said.

He gave her a quizzical kind of look. 'For what?'

She dropped her gaze for a second and he stopped walking again. 'Just for this, for all of it.'

Mateo raised a brow, but it was the way his eyes dropped to her lips that made her breath catch in her throat. He stepped into her, unexpectedly touching his fingers to her chin as he leaned in, brushing his lips to hers. The kiss was soft and warm and ever so sweet, but it made every part of her body tingle, goose pimples rippling across her skin despite the sticky heat.

'Shall we go look at the sugar mill?' he asked, his voice husky.

Claudia just nodded, but when he turned and caught her hand in his, she lifted her fingers to her lips, touching where his mouth had been, surprised by how her afternoon was turning out.

It's not only the mystery of the Diaz family that's taking me by surprise on this trip.

Claudia was numb. She stared at the screen again, not sure why it hurt so much, or perhaps it wasn't hurt so much as shock.

He was getting married.

She reread the email from her friend. She'd come straight from Mateo dropping her off to the internet café to see if her father had been in touch; she certainly hadn't been expecting this.

I thought this was better coming from me rather than you seeing it on Facebook, but Max just announced his engagement in *The Times*. I can't believe he's moved on so quickly, I'm so sorry. Anyway, how's Havana? Call me! I'm dying to hear all about it!

Claudia took a deep breath and clicked on the attachment. This shouldn't hurt, it shouldn't have any effect on her, but she'd have been lying if she said her heart wasn't just a little broken that he'd moved on so fast. It had been almost a year since she'd left him, but since then he'd told her he was giving her space to reconsider, telling her she'd made a big mistake that she'd regret, telling her repeatedly that he wanted her back.

Clearly he'd been doing less waiting and more searching for a new Mrs Right.

The engagement is announced between Maxwell, son of Mr & Mrs Henry Lawford of London, and Priscilla, daughter of Lord Stewart Henderson and Lady Helen White

She closed the screen, not wanting to look at it again. Good for him. She'd sent him back the ring, after all; she'd made up her mind that there was no looking back. She just hadn't expected him to have someone else waiting in the wings to propose to, to have meant so little to him after their years together that he'd not only met someone else, but also had time to propose! Perhaps he'd had a backup wife waiting in the wings in case she failed all along. *I should have kept the damn ring.*

Claudia stretched her fingers before placing them on the keyboard. All she wanted was to pick up the phone and call Charlotte, to hear her voice and listen to her friend tell her what a bastard Max was. But the truth was, perhaps him moving on so publicly was exactly what she needed. At least it closed their chapter for good.

> Well, it seems he found someone to move on to quicker than expected. Thanks for letting me know, I'm happy for him, or at least I think I am, I just can't figure out why it stings so much when I don't even want to be with him. Phone reception is terrible here. I'm sitting in one of those old school internet cafés that don't even exist back home anymore, because there's no Wi-Fi! Although if I'd stayed in the fancy hotel I was supposed to be in (long story) I might have been able to at least send emails. Anyway, will call soon, so much to fill you in on, including a gorgeous Cuban man who may just break my man drought. Don't go getting too excited though, it was just one kiss...
>
> C xx

Claudia smiled to herself as she scanned through the rest of her emails. Charlotte was going to have a fit when she read that last line, especially when she couldn't just pick up the phone and demand a debrief of exactly what was happening.

So Max is getting married. She sighed. It only hurt because it felt so fast, but perhaps it should be a relief. He deserved to find the woman he wanted—that woman just hadn't been her. *We would have been miserable together.*

Now Mateo, he was a different story. Mateo was young, single and carefree. Mateo's kiss had made her feel like a giddy teenager; he didn't seem to care who she was or what she had.

He's just a fun holiday romance, but maybe he's the one to make me feel like me again.

She liked the way she was around him. With Max it had been like performing a role; she'd had to host dinner parties on a Saturday night after an eighty-hour work week, charm his parents despite the fact they'd made it clear she wasn't as successful as their own daughter, not to mention their constant insistence that she sign a prenuptial agreement despite the fact she earnt the same amount of money as their son. It had been a life that had sent her into a spin and left her breathless, like there had been a weight on her chest that she'd barely been able to breathe past. So if this Priscilla wanted that life, then she could have it.

Claudia left the café and started to walk, and within minutes she found herself in front of Mateo's food truck, the smell of his cooking filling her nostrils. She stood a moment, indulging in watching him, music playing softly inside the truck as he prepared for the customers who would soon be queuing to order dinner.

She took a breath before clearing her throat, and when he turned and looked at her, she felt it; a flutter inside of her that told her everything she needed to know. Max had twisted her stomach into a knot when his eyes had met hers, as she'd anxiously hoped she was good enough at every turn, whereas Mateo ignited something different inside of her. *Anticipation. Mateo makes me want to step closer instead of run away.*

'Could you do with an extra pair of hands tonight?' she asked shyly.

Mateo's grin was all she needed, and as she stepped into the truck he held up an apron, stepping close to her to slip it over her head in the small space. But it was when his fingers brushed her middle, tying the apron around her waist, that her breath caught in her throat. He placed his hands gently on her hips for a moment, his breath against her ear.

'It's going to get hot in the kitchen tonight,' he said as his hands fell away.

Claudia had no idea whether he was talking about the heat between them or the actual cooking, all she knew was that her skin was on fire and she doubted her temperature was going to drop anytime soon.

15

HAVANA, CUBA, 1950

Esmeralda had her arm linked through her sister María's as they walked into their sitting room to join her father. Their maid had come dashing up in a hurry to tell them there was a visitor, and that they were expected to come downstairs immediately, but it wasn't an unusual request. Her father liked to show his daughters off; they were his pride and joy. Before, when her mother was alive, her parents would have likely entertained guests without need for their daughters to do more than whisk in and out of the room, but now her father preferred his girls by his side. He liked nothing more than to see them smile and entertain his business associates and friends, his eyes always lighting up when they entered a room, as if he was never more content than with his daughters.

But today was different. Today, for the very first time, Esmeralda lost her perfectly practised composure, her feet stopping of their own accord even though María kept walking and tried to tug her along, even as Gisele glided into the room behind them and bumped her shoulder on the way past, eager to see who the unexpected guest was.

Because there, sitting on their opulent gold-edged sofa,

rising slightly as she and her sisters entered the room, was Christopher.

My Christopher is here. Her heart skipped a beat and her mouth went dry. *It can't be. How is Christopher here in Cuba?*

'Esmeralda, you remember Mr Christopher Dutton, from London?' Her father beamed at her, a cigar in hand as he waved her into the room. 'And these are my daughters, María and Gisele.'

Esmeralda forced her feet to move, not wanting her father to know how affected she was by Christopher's presence, and she was grateful for the way his eyes only fleetingly met hers, his composure impeccable. Had she imagined what had happened between them? The looks he'd given her when she'd been in London, the way their hands had brushed, their little fingers just touching as she'd walked away from him that very last time?

'It's so lovely to see you again, Esmeralda,' Christopher said, standing and nodding, before gently taking first María's hand and then Gisele's. Her cheeks heated as she watched him, as Gisele glanced over her shoulder at her, eyebrows raised when he pressed a kiss to the back of her hand. Of course Esmeralda had told her sister all about the handsome Englishman, her thoughts had been consumed by him since she'd returned from London, but never in a million years had she imagined he'd come to Cuba to visit. When it came to her turn, Christopher kept hold of her hand just a second too long, his lips lingering against her skin, his eyes locked on hers.

'What, ah, what,' Esmeralda quickly corrected herself, clearing her throat as he dropped her hand. 'What brings you all the way to Havana, Mr Dutton?'

'Your father was most insistent that someone from the company come here to see the production first-hand,' Christopher said, sitting back down as her father gestured for them to sit, although his eyes barely left hers. 'I have to say, he's a very hard man to say no to, and I couldn't resist the opportunity to come to Cuba myself, especially after all the stories you regaled me with of Havana. You certainly painted a beautiful picture of your exotic country.'

One of their maids rushed into the room then, and with her father's attention diverted, she indulged in truly looking at Christopher, the knot in her stomach dispersing when he smiled, his expression somehow telling her that he was as relieved to see her as she was him.

Perhaps I didn't imagine his feelings towards me.

The last time she'd seen him had replayed in her mind ever since; sitting at Harrods, wishing she didn't have to say goodbye, wondering what could have been. *And now he's here.*

'A bottle of our finest champagne in honour of our guest,' her father announced as he lit his cigar, puffing the pungent smoke into the room as their maid scurried off to fulfil his request.

Christopher didn't look quite so comfortable when her father leaned forward to light his cigar, coughing a little as they all looked on, but he quickly righted himself, his eyes somehow always making their way back to her.

When Esmeralda moved past Christopher, her breath stilled in her throat as she brushed so closely to him that the fabric of her dress must have touched his knee, and he caught her finger in his. It was only a split second, their fingers intertwined in a hold so brief that no one could have possibly noticed, but it told her everything she needed to know.

He didn't just come to see Cuba.

He travelled all this way to see me.

A little thrill ran through her body as she sat down and took the glass of champagne that her maid passed her, taking a little sip and avoiding Christopher's gaze at all costs. But she couldn't avoid her sisters; they both looked ready to burst with excitement, their eyes darting constantly in her direction. She studiously avoided them, hoping that if her father noticed, he simply thought his two youngest daughters giddy with excitement at meeting a man all the way from London.

'Christopher, my daughters would love to show you Havana while you're here, wouldn't you, girls?'

Esmeralda nodded along with her sisters.

'Yes, Papá,' she said. 'It would be my honour to show Christopher the sights.'

This time she couldn't *not* look at Christopher, and the look he gave her sent a ripple of anticipation through her like she'd never felt before.

Dinner that night was almost painfully slow, most especially because Esmeralda had to force herself to swallow each mouthful when all she wanted was to steal Christopher away and have him to herself. Her sisters seemed to be taking great pleasure in speaking with him and sharing stories about Cuba, while she sat at the farthest point from him, indulging in watching him without having to say a thing. But it was also the closest seat to her father, which meant she had to watch her every movement, every word she said, more carefully than ever.

She glanced up and caught her father's eye, smiling at him sweetly as a maid stepped forward to pour him more wine. She took little sips of air, her smile composed, even though her heart was racing so fast she was almost certain everyone else at the table could hear it hammering away in her chest. She still couldn't believe he was there.

'Christopher, tell my daughters about London,' Julio said as he filled his plate with more food. 'They haven't seen beyond Cuba, other than Esmeralda here of course.'

Christopher smiled. 'It was such a delight to have Esmeralda in London, I most enjoyed taking her to Harrods on your last day.'

She held her smile, refusing to meet Christopher's gaze. She knew that if she did her cheeks would blush an even deeper pink than they already were, and then her father would be certain to notice that something was amiss.

'Your sister has no doubt regaled you with stories about her travels, but London is so different to your beautiful country, ladies,' he continued. 'It's all concrete pavements and gloomy days when I compare it to the lushness and sunshine of Cuba.'

'Listen! He says it like he's been here before!' Julio laughed. 'Esmeralda, can you arrange for Christopher to be shown all over the island? I want him to be the envy of all his colleagues when he returns home full of tales of what it's like here.' He frowned. 'You'll have time in between the party preparations? If not—'

'Sí, Papá, of course,' she said quickly. 'It would be my pleasure and all the preparations are now complete.'

One of her sisters kicked her beneath the table and she swiftly kicked back. They both knew exactly how much she'd like to show Christopher around, because it would mean time with him away from her father's prying gaze.

'You're planning a party?' Christopher asked. 'Is there a special occasion?'

'It's my quince party,' María said, her smile showing her shyness as she ducked her head down slightly.

'It's the biggest moment of girlhood in our culture,' Esmeralda explained. 'The celebration is second only to a wedding, as we celebrate a girl becoming a woman when she turns fifteen. It's often something families spend months, if not years, planning for, so it's causing quite the excitement.'

'Esmeralda has taken over the role of organising it all,' Julio said. 'Since my wife is no longer with us.'

Christopher nodded. 'Well, I'm certain she's doing an excellent job,' he said. 'I wouldn't want to take her away from that if—'

'Nonsense!' Esmeralda checked herself as she realised how enthusiastically she'd spoken. 'I mean, it's not every day we have a visitor all the way from *London*, and everything is already well ahead of schedule for the party.'

'You will be our guest of honour on the night!' Julio said enthusiastically. 'We can celebrate our joint success, and what this means for both our firms now that we've come to an agreement in regards to our business dealings.'

Esmeralda held her smile. 'The deal with the Dutton's firm is complete?'

Her father beamed, and she took the chance to quickly glance at Christopher, who was doing an excellent job of not giving her too much attention. But when their eyes met, it was almost impossible to look away.

'We will sign the papers while he's here. The biggest sugar deal ever brokered!' Her father reached for his wine and took a large gulp.

'Congratulations,' Esmeralda managed. 'I'm so happy our trip to London was such a success.'

'Christopher is an honorary member of our family now,' Julio said as he stood and went to stand behind him, clapping Christopher on the back.

She nodded and lifted her glass of champagne. 'To the most successful sugar deal ever made then,' she said. *And to Christopher becoming part of the family.* If only her father knew how desperately she wanted Christopher to be a legitimate family member.

She took a sip and then another, enjoying the bubbles as they rippled down her throat.

'Ladies, I think it's time you retired for the evening,' Julio said, gesturing for the maids to clear the table. 'Christopher, join me for another cigar.'

'Of course, Papá.' Esmeralda nodded and indicated for her sisters to rise with her. It took all her strength not to look back

over her shoulder at Christopher, hoping instead that he might
come and find her after dark.

She smiled to herself as she walked, as María grabbed her
hand on one side and Gisele on the other, both squeezing hard
as they walked out of the room, before breaking into a run for
the stairs.

16

HAVANA, CUBA, PRESENT DAY

Claudia lay in bed and stared up at the ceiling. She had five days left in Cuba, which seemed on the one hand long enough, and the other far too short to actually achieve anything. She'd discovered plenty about the Diaz family—she knew their names, she knew where they lived and what their house looked like, and she'd discovered a mystery that involved the eldest daughter. But it wasn't getting her any closer to figuring out what it all meant and how her grandmother was connected to it.

If she could call Charlotte, she knew what her friend would say; they'd been close friends long enough that she could hear her voice in her mind. *Go and explore Cuba! You've wanted to travel for as long as I've known you, so just go and enjoy yourself. Splash in the water, get sand beneath your toes, soak up the old architecture and find a gorgeous man to drink beer with and steal kisses from.*

She smiled to herself. So far she'd succeeded in the kissing-a-boy part, of which Charlotte would wholeheartedly approve, but she hadn't yet done any of the others. *And don't think about your ex.* That's the other thing Charlotte would say, because she'd be able to read her mind. The lack of internet in Havana had at least meant she couldn't spend hours googling and Facebook stalking the happy new couple.

Claudia sat up and changed, brushing her hair into a high ponytail and putting on some minimal makeup. If she didn't go down soon she'd miss breakfast, and her stomach was starting to rumble. *I'm getting used to the gorgeous spread Rosa puts on each morning.*

Sure enough, the moment she went downstairs it was to the now-familiar smell of coffee and freshly baked bread that filled the small kitchen, and all thoughts of her ex and the old life that she'd had with him disappeared from her mind.

'Good morning, Rosa,' she called out.

'Buenos días, Claudia,' Rosa replied, greeting her with a big smile. 'Take a seat outside.'

A couple were sitting there already, and Claudia didn't feel like sitting with them. Most of the time she'd managed to avoid seeing anyone else who was staying there; she was more interested in talking to Rosa than other tourists.

'May I help you in here?' she asked, instead. 'I don't feel like sitting.'

Rosa gave her a quizzical look. 'You're my guest, you can't help!'

Claudia just laughed. 'Fine, then I'll just stand here and drink my coffee, but if I get under your feet please tell me.'

The older woman murmured something, but she was still smiling and Claudia had a feeling she was more amused by her behaviour than annoyed. She didn't like to sit idle, and she would have happily helped tidy up or prepare the food for something to do. And besides, she liked talking to Rosa; in a way it was like being back with her own grandmother, watching her in the kitchen and telling her all about what was happening at school or with her friends. Her grandma had loved to hear all about whatever was going on in her life.

'I helped Mateo in his food truck last night,' Claudia said as she poured herself coffee, stirring in some sugar before taking a sip.

'It must have been nice for him, having the company.'

Rosa disappeared out to the courtyard for a moment and Claudia watched her, following her with her eyes and wondering about the life she'd led, about whether she'd been married and how hard it had been for her to keep her house. Life must be hard with so little money to go around, even with tourists staying.

'Next time try to get his ropa vieja recipe though,' Rosa said when she walked back inside. 'I've been trying to convince his mother to give it to me for years.'

Claudia reached for some fruit, eating some papaya and savouring the sweet taste as Rosa moved around her, making more coffee to take outside and then starting to wash some dishes. She moved closer to her and took the tea towel from Rosa's shoulder where she had it slung, starting to dry the plates before her host could protest.

'Rosa, what do you know of Esmeralda Diaz?'

Rosa went still a moment, her hands still in the soapy water but no longer scrubbing.

'Both you and Mateo mentioned her disappearance, and it's made me curious about her,' she said. 'Were you a similar age to her?'

'I was only twelve when she disappeared, but everyone knew who Esmeralda Diaz was.' The washing resumed again.

'Mateo mentioned there were rumours she may have run away? That maybe the circumstances around her disappearance weren't as suspicious as first thought?'

She reached for another plate to dry as Rosa spoke. 'Some secrets are supposed to stay that way. Why ask questions about something that happened so long ago? The girl disappeared and no one ever spoke of her again, that's all. If she ran away, then it's not something I know about.'

Claudia moved back to her seat once she'd finished drying and took a bread roll. 'I suppose I want to know what happened to her, in case it has something to do with my grandmother,' she said. 'I just can't stop thinking about why a family like Esmeralda's would just let her go like that?'

Rosa sighed and gave her a look that told her she didn't want to keep talking about it. 'If other girls had gone missing, then everyone would have been searching for Esmeralda, but the police refused to comment at the time, and the family asked for privacy. We don't ask questions, especially not of a family like that, not back then.'

'So they *did* know what happened to her? The family, I mean?'

Rosa muttered something under her breath before replying. 'If they knew what happened, they certainly kept it to themselves. People did talk about it for months, behind closed doors, the scandal of it all, but there was so much else going on in Cuba at the time. The revolution was all anyone spoke about for years, so no one cared about a wealthy society girl who'd decided to run away with a man.'

Claudia almost dropped her coffee. 'A man? Everyone thought she'd run away with *a man*?' That was certainly something Mateo had left out. And it seemed that Rosa knew a lot more than she was letting on!

Rosa shook her head. 'You ask too many questions. Sometimes it's better for the past to stay in the past.'

'But—'

Rosa waved her hand. 'Go and enjoy the day. Explore Havana! Do you want Carlos to drive you somewhere? I can call him for you.'

Claudia held her tongue even though it pained her. How could Rosa say something like that and then not tell her more! But she knew better than to ask when the subject had so clearly been closed, and she also knew better than to upset her host.

'Thank you, Rosa,' she said with a smile. 'I'd love you to call Carlos for me. I'm sure he knows exactly where to take a tourist like me for the day.'

Rosa waved her away out of the kitchen and Claudia took her coffee with her, her mind full of questions. *That's the trouble with this place, I keep having more questions than answers!* But perhaps a few hours out with Carlos was exactly what she needed; time to take in the sights and forget about everything.

She'd wanted a beach holiday for longer than she could remember, and suddenly here she was in paradise and she still hadn't even curled her toes in sand. Even if she never found out what she'd come searching for, at least she'd have had a lovely holiday in a country that she might otherwise never have visited.

Later that night, after a lovely day out seeing the sights with an enthusiastic Carlos, and a simple yet delicious meal that Rosa had prepared, Claudia lay on her bed, staring up at the ceiling. There was no television to watch and she hadn't brought any books with her, and she was lying there too relaxed to move yet not tired enough to sleep. She couldn't stop thinking about what Carlos had told her either, shining some light on Mateo and how devastating it had been for the family when his father had passed. It sounded as if the entire town had been in mourning for the larger-than-life man, a man whom Mateo was apparently the spitting image of. It only reinforced her feelings that he was kind and genuine, and now she knew that he would also understand what she'd been through. He'd hinted that there had been another tragedy in the family, but he hadn't elaborated, and Claudia hadn't wanted to pry.

It had been a tough past year, losing both her friend and her grandmother, and she knew that only someone who understood loss would ever be able to comprehend her pain.

A soft knock at the door startled her, and she stretched before half rising. 'Come in!' she called, expecting Rosa to be bringing her something. She'd mentioned making her a drink before bed, although she hadn't expected her to bring it up to the room.

She smiled as the door opened, but her smile turned to surprise when she saw Mateo standing there. 'Mateo!'

'You said to come in,' he said, clearly registering her surprise.

'Of course, I was only expecting Rosa, that's all.'

Mateo pushed his hands into his jeans pockets, looking as awkward as she felt standing in the room. It was a distinctly feminine space, with a floral bed cover and a small flower arrangement on the little bedside table, and he looked so out of place she almost laughed.

'You've finished for the night?'

He nodded. 'I have. I missed you tonight.'

'I wasn't sure if I was a help or a hindrance last night, so I thought it best if I stayed away.'

His grin made her smile in reply. 'Hindrance? I'm guessing that means not helpful?'

'I think your grasp of English is better than you think.'

'It was nice having you there. I always used to have company in the truck, so the last year has been difficult.'

She tried to recall when his father had died, but she was certain he'd said it was more than a year ago since he'd passed. She opened her mouth to ask but Mateo spoke before she had the chance.

'I thought you might like to go for a walk?' he asked. 'There is nothing quite like the Malecón at night.'

'I thought you said it was for women and their lovers,' she teased.

He met her gaze and she bravely held it, even as her skin heated.

'Will I need my jacket?'

He shook his head. 'No.'

Claudia wished she had time to freshen up, but Mateo hadn't looked away from her and she didn't want to ask him to wait. She didn't bother taking anything with her—she had no use for her phone or her bag—and followed him out the door after she'd slipped on her sandals, shutting it gently behind her. Mateo stood back and let her go down the stairs first, and she felt his eyes on her and wished she was the one following behind.

She saw Rosa sitting in the courtyard when she got to the bottom, a candle burning and some lights on that only just illuminated the table.

'We're going for a walk,' she called out.

'Look after our girl, Mateo,' Rosa said.

He disappeared for a moment and Claudia watched on as he went to see Rosa, pressing a kiss to her cheek and holding her hand a moment. She wasn't sure what he said, but she saw Rosa's face light up as he backed away.

'What did you say to make an old woman grin like that?' Claudia asked when he was beside her again.

'I told her not to worry if you didn't come home.'

'Mateo!'

He just laughed and caught her hand in his, as they walked past his car, which he'd parked outside. This time when he spoke, he leaned in closer to her.

'I'm only teasing. She's been asking me for a recipe for years, and I told her I'd show her how to make it.'

She wasn't sure if she believed him or not, the glint in his eyes made her think he enjoyed teasing her, but she didn't care. It was nice to be around someone like him, someone who made her feel relaxed and excited at the same time. And Rosa had mentioned a recipe, so it was plausible.

'Last night,' he said, 'when you came to help me.'

She nodded. 'I *was* a hindrance, wasn't I?'

He laughed. 'No, Claudia, you were not this *hindrance* that you keep speaking of. It was nice to have company. After so many years working with another, it's hard to be alone sometimes.'

'You hide it well,' she said, squeezing his hand, remembering her palm was against his. 'That first night I met you, you looked so happy.'

'I am happy,' he said. 'Happy to share my cooking and to have a job, but—'

His mouth smiled, but it didn't reach his eyes. 'Your father?' she asked.

Mateo shook his head, pulling her in a little closer to him and letting go of her hand to slip his arm around her shoulder instead. 'What I wanted to say was that something was different about you last night.'

She wondered whether she should tell him or not, whether she preferred to be anonymous in a way with him, not letting him know that she was damaged goods. But on the other hand, what did it matter? Anything that happened with Mateo would be over within days; she was leaving Cuba for London and she would never see him again.

'I found out my ex-fiancé is engaged again, just before I came to see you,' she admitted.

'You still love him?'

She laughed. 'No. That's the thing, I don't love him at all. Sometimes I feel sad for the future I thought I was going to have, but I chose not to be with him, and it was the right decision.'

His fingers moved against her shoulder and she tentatively slid her arm around his waist.

'You're hurt that he didn't love you like you thought he did,' Mateo said. 'If he truly loved you, why would he move on so fast?'

She blinked away unexpected tears. Mateo's words hurt because they were true; that was exactly how she felt. But what didn't hurt was the way he took her hand and pulled her close, her hips brushing against his as his other hand gently cupped her cheek.

'But you know what else?'

She stared up into his eyes, wondering how she'd managed to cross paths with a man who made her feel like Mateo did in a country full of strangers.

'What?' she whispered.

'You're in Havana, walking the Malecón, with a man who very much wants to be with you.' His mouth moved closer to hers, his words turning to whispers. 'I only have you for a few days, and I want to enjoy every second.'

Her lips parted but she didn't speak, couldn't with his mouth hovering above hers, his eyes never leaving hers. So instead of speaking she inched upwards and kissed him, looping her arms around his neck as he tenderly kissed her back, his hands moving to her waist, fingers splayed out across her lower back.

Don't overthink this. Just enjoy the moment. Enjoy the gorgeous man who wants you.

Mateo took his time when he kissed her, like he had all the time in the world, his touch soft. And when he finally pulled away, he kept his head bent and pressed his forehead to hers.

'We both have things we want to forget,' he murmured.

She wasn't sure what thing he needed to forget, but she was more than happy to be the distraction he needed. Claudia tucked herself to his side as they started to walk again, as she inhaled the salty, damp sea air and watched the other couples dotted along the stretch of pavement ahead of them.

'How many foreign girls have you walked the Malecón with?' she asked.

He made a grunting kind of sound and dropped a kiss to the top of her head. 'None.'

'None?'

Mateo went silent then, and she didn't ask more, content with the feel of his body against hers and the sound of the waves lapping beside them. And it was then she wondered what demons he might have, whether being with her was distracting him from something else. She thought of the way he'd mentioned being alone, and glanced up as they walked, seeing the way his eyes were almost lost in the distance, as if he were a million miles away.

'Mateo,' she murmured.

He looked down at her, back in their world again as she reached for his face, stroking his cheek as they stopped walking again. His eyes told her that she was right, that something was troubling him.

It was the first time his smile had been sad, as he stroked his thumb down her cheek. Neither of them said anything; they didn't need to. He understood her pain because he knew it himself, because something inside of him was broken, too. She could see that now.

They started to walk again, and she tucked herself tighter to him, this beautiful man whom she already couldn't imagine never seeing again once she left Cuba.

'Someone broke your heart, too?' she finally asked. Was there more to his pain than losing his father? Is that what Carlos had been hinting at?

His breath was more of a shudder that she felt run through his body. 'Our hearts are amazing things,' he said. 'Somehow they always manage to heal, eventually.'

They walked in silence for so long that she lost all track of time, until Mateo finally stopped and took her hand, sitting down on the stone wall and drawing her to him. She sat on his knee, more brazen than she ever would have been at home. But with the still-warm sea breeze against her skin, and Mateo's hands cupped around her, the only thing she cared about was drinking in his kisses and losing herself to his touch.

'You didn't believe me that this was a place for lovers,' he murmured.

'Oh, I believed you,' she said, thinking back to that first night she'd met him. Never in a million years had she expected to end up in his arms, though. Or in any man's arms for that matter.

They sat together a long while, turning to stare out at the moonlight glinting off the water, listening to the gentleness of it. If there were a more romantic place in the world, she couldn't imagine it. And it was then that Claudia said something that sounded foreign to her own ears.

'Would you like to stay the night with me?'

Mateo's eyes met hers, and something unspoken passed between them as he wrapped her in his arms and kissed her again.

'Sí, hermosa chica,' he whispered against her skin. 'Sí.'

She had no idea what he'd even said to her other than *yes*, but whatever it was sounded beautiful in his language. And when he rose, taking her hand and cupping his palm to hers, she imagined he'd be whispering in Spanish against her skin all night long.

17

HAVANA, CUBA, 1950

Esmeralda couldn't help but steal glances at Christopher as they walked. Her sisters were trailing behind, giving them time alone, but she was careful to keep her distance, to stay far enough away that her elbow couldn't absently bump into his. In London they'd enjoyed an anonymity that she'd taken for granted; in Havana, everyone knew whom she was, and that meant it would take only a whisper of scandal for her reputation to be in tatters. Not to mention for word to get back to her father.

But whenever he spoke, whenever his eyes graced hers or she had to move around him, her breath caught in her throat, her fingers aching to reach out to him.

'You weren't exaggerating about how beautiful your country was,' Christopher said as they strolled.

'When it's all you've ever seen, it's hard to understand that the rest of the world isn't like this,' she replied.

'Trust me, it's one of the most stunning places on earth.' He stopped walking then and his eyes caught hers, and for that moment in time neither of them moved. Esmeralda was certain she barely breathed.

'Shall we sit?' he asked.

She nodded, sitting on the low stone wall and watching as he did the same, positioning himself so that he was facing her. Esmeralda gave her sisters a sharp look and they kept walking, clearly understanding that she didn't want them hovering.

'Christopher,' she said, finally able to speak freely with no one nearby to overhear them. 'When we were last together, the day before I left London, I never thought I was going to see you again.'

His smile was as warm as the sun above them, and she loved how much more relaxed he looked in Cuba, the way he'd undone the top button of his shirt and done away with his tie.

He went to reach for her hand but she quickly folded it in her lap and gave a small shake of her head. 'Not here,' she murmured. 'There will be someone watching us.'

Christopher nodded, his voice low when he spoke. 'I know I promised to write, but after what you said, about the possibility of your father intercepting our letters, I decided it wasn't worth the risk.'

'I thought it was a sign that our time together hadn't meant anything to you.'

His smile fell then. 'I've thought of little other than you since you left.' Christopher placed his hand on the low wall and edged his fingers closer to her. She took a shaky breath and placed her hand down, too, glancing around before carefully moving her fingers forward until they were touching his. Her pulse ignited, knowing what would happen if they were caught by her father.

'How many days are you here?' she asked.

'I'm here for a week. I couldn't take any longer away from work.' He chuckled. 'My father was furious that I was taking so long, but I convinced him that I had to see Julio again in person to sign the final papers. That he expected me to come here.'

She breathed in his words, studied every inch of his face as they sat. 'You came for me?'

He smiled. 'I came for you. Esmeralda, of course I came for you.'

Esmeralda closed her eyes, listening to his words, letting them wash over her. *He came for me.* All the hours she'd spent wondering if he'd felt the same, imagining that perhaps what had meant the world to her had perhaps meant nothing to him, and her thoughts couldn't have been further from the truth.

'So I have six more days with you?' she said when she finally opened her eyes.

'Six more days,' he repeated.

Before they could say anything else, Esmeralda noticed her sisters returning.

'Meet me outside our gate tonight, once the house is asleep,' she said, leaning in closer to him as she started to rise. 'I want to come here with you when it's dark.'

Christopher's eyes widened. 'Tonight?'

She smiled sweetly and stood back for him to stand. 'This is where everyone strolls with their lover after dark,' she whispered.

Christopher's cheeks turned a deep shade of pink then, and she laughed as she fell into step with her sisters and linked arms with Gisele, still smiling over at the man who'd stolen her heart. It was nice, for once, to see that it was him blushing instead of her.

'He's everything you said he'd be,' Gisele whispered.

'I still can't believe he's here.' She sighed. 'I have a week of seeing him. A week before we have to say goodbye again.'

'Perhaps you should talk to Papá,' Gisele murmured. 'There's a chance he would understand?'

'That I fell in love with a business associate of his who isn't Cuban? Of course he wouldn't understand! Papá would be furious with me, it could ruin everything.'

Gisele's head fell to her shoulder. 'You're his favourite, Es. If he'd forgive anyone for anything, it would be you.'

She didn't reply, because she knew her sister was right; she *had* always been his favourite, even though she didn't like to acknowledge it. But her falling for Christopher wasn't just a little mistake, an indiscretion that could be forgiven and forgotten. Her father expected more from her, she was the one her sisters looked to for guidance, who set an example for their entire family.

No, Papá would never forgive her if he found out, just like he'd never accept Christopher into their family as a son-in-law, no matter how proud he was of the business deal they'd agreed to. Which meant that she was going to have to decide what was more important to her—her family, or the man she'd fallen in love with.

She blinked away tears, quickly wiping her cheeks as Gisele lifted her head from her shoulder.

'What's wrong?' her sister asked, her face etched with such concern it broke Esmeralda's heart all over again.

'Nothing,' she said. 'Nothing's the matter. I'm just happy, that's all.'

Gisele tucked close to her again and Esmeralda squared her shoulders, not wanting anyone to see the turmoil inside of her. *No matter how much I love him, no matter how much I yearn to be with him, nothing will ever take me from my family.*

Our love simply cannot be.

Esmeralda lay beneath her covers that night, her heart hammering ferociously in her chest as she waited. The house had been quiet for some time, darkness long since blanketing the sky, but she had to wait until there wasn't a chance of being discovered by her father making his way to bed or maids scurrying about as they finished their final tasks for the evening.

Christopher and her father had retired after dinner once more, as they'd done the previous night, for cigars and a drink, but she'd kept her door open a crack and listened, waiting for all the usual sounds of the house winding down for the night. She'd put her little sister to bed hours earlier, said goodnight to everyone else, and told her maid that she wouldn't need any assistance preparing for bed. Then she'd changed into a simple dress and found a scarf to tie around her hair, which she'd braided to help with her disguise. She hoped no one would recognise her beneath the cover of night, but if they were noticed then she wanted to do everything she could to look a little less Diaz and a little more everyday Cuban girl.

After what felt like an eternity, Esmeralda rose, avoiding the floorboard that always made a noise when she stepped on it and placing the scarf in her pocket, not wanting to use it until she was out of the house. If she was seen with it tied around her hair, it would only make it obvious that she was sneaking out.

Esmeralda paused at the top of the staircase, her eyes adjusted to the dark after so long waiting, and she could see all the bedroom doors were shut, with not a blade of light shining beneath any of them. She took a deep breath and slowly stepped down the stairs, as light-footed as could be as she finally made it downstairs and crept silently across the hall, choosing to go through the kitchen and out the side door rather than the heavy front door. She should have cautioned Christopher, but then if he were caught he could simply say he was going for a walk to clear his head or some other such excuse—men were never questioned no matter what the hour.

When she was outside, the side door shut behind her, Esmeralda reached for her silk scarf and carefully positioned it over her hair, tying it and smoothing her fingers over it to hold it in place. But then her heart started to hammer all the more, for she was within a few steps of finding out whether Christopher was indeed waiting for her on the other side of the wall. She hurried on, glancing over her shoulder before she stepped through the gate, but finding the house still dark behind her. No one had heard her.

She left the gate open slightly to avoid the creak it might make, and found herself standing alone on the street, her back pressed to the wall. And just as she started to fret that he'd changed his mind, just as her heart began to race, a figure stepped from the shadows.

'Christopher?' she whispered.

'It's me,' he said, and she ran into his open arms without thinking, her hands sliding around the back of his neck as he tucked her tight against his body, his fingers around her waist.

They should have waited until they were farther away from the house, but Esmeralda had been waiting since the night before, consumed by thoughts of him, imagining him lying in one of their sumptuous guest bedrooms so close to her own yet so far away. Christopher's lips touched softly against hers and she willingly kissed him back, transported to the night they'd spent together in London, dancing and then kissing on the balcony.

'We need to go,' she whispered against his skin, knowing how easily they could be caught. Her headscarf wasn't going to fool anyone who knew her well, especially one of their staff from the house should they happen upon them.

She slid an arm around Christopher's waist and they began to walk, his arm around her shoulders, and for a long while they didn't say a thing, somehow content to simply be together. But the farther they walked, the farther away from her family residence they became, the bolder she felt about being with him, and eventually she pulled the scarf from her head and let her hair fall over her shoulders. If this was to be one of their only evenings together, then she wanted to feel like herself.

'Where are you taking me?' Christopher asked, squeezing her shoulders gently as he spoke.

'Back to the Malecón,' she said. 'Or anywhere else you'd like to go.'

'Would it sound too much to say that I'm happy to be anywhere with you?'

She leaned into him. 'Not at all.'

They continued on in a comfortable silence again, until eventually they were exactly where she wanted to be. She'd seen couples walk the Malecón together most of her life and wondered what the fuss was about; the slow walk hand-in-hand, the even slower kisses at night when they thought no one could see them, or the tears as they parted. But she understood now.

'Shall we sit?' she asked.

Christopher let go of her and sat, and she positioned herself so close to him she was almost in his lap. His arms encircled her and she dropped her head to his chest, her hair lifting and billowing around them in the light sea breeze.

'Esmeralda, I know we've only been acquainted a short time, but if I were to talk to your father—'

'No!' she lifted her head and stared into Christopher's eyes. 'No, you mustn't. He would never approve.'

Christopher stroked her hair as he looked down at her. 'Even though he respects the business we've done together? You don't think that's enough? If he understood that I had honourable intentions, if—'

She shook her head. 'My papá would never allow it,' she told him. 'If he had so much as an inkling that there was something between us, that you'd acted in any way other than my trusted chaperone in London, he'd be more likely to quickly marry me off to a Cuban man than allow me to be with you.'

Christopher dropped his hand to her cheek, his thumb gentle as he brushed it over her skin. 'I cannot leave Havana without you, Esmeralda. Or at least without a promise of what's to come.'

She refused to cry, blinking away the tears that clung to her lashes. 'Sometimes we can't have what we want.'

Christopher's thumb dipped lower and smoothed across her chin, before he leaned in to her as if to kiss her again.

'Esmeralda?'

She jumped back, arms wrapped protectively around herself as she turned. 'Alejandro?'

Her cousin stood with his arms folded over his chest, a beautiful young woman tucked to his elbow. She couldn't decide if he looked angry, or amused.

'What are you doing here so late at night?' he asked. 'Who is this?'

'This,' she said, gesturing towards Christopher, who was already on his feet. 'This is Christopher Dutton. He's visiting from London.'

Alejandro took a step forward and she noticed that his female friend stayed where she was, her hand falling from her cousin's arm.

'Does your papá know you're out so late? And with a man?'

'What do you think, Ale?' she said, shaking her head and moving to stand in front of Christopher. 'And don't you even think about telling him.'

'I'm sorry, this is your—'

'Cousin,' she said quickly, before taking hold of Alejandro's hand. 'My beloved *favourite* cousin who wouldn't dare let our secret be known.'

Alejandro laughed, his face softening into the expression she was used to seeing. 'Your favourite cousin, hmm?'

'You've always been my favourite, you know that,' she said, smiling up at him. When she let go, she stepped back and took her place beside Christopher again. 'Christopher and I became acquainted when I was in London.'

'And you thought it a good idea to sneak out of the house

after dark for a stroll on the Malecón?' Alejandro said, before letting out a whistle. '*Prima*, you're braver than I thought.'

She stepped forward. 'You won't breathe a word of this, will you?'

'How many times have you snuck out at night?' he asked.

Esmeralda glared at him, one hand on her hip. 'Never.'

The woman he was with stepped forward and he shrugged, laughing as he shook his head. 'You know your secret is safe with me. But if Julio finds out...'

'He won't.'

She stood back as Alejandro extended a hand and shook Christopher's. 'You must be something special for her to risk her neck like this.'

Christopher said something she didn't hear, before Alejandro stepped back, pulling his companion closer to him. It wasn't until they'd started to walk away, her heart pounding at being caught, that she realised she hadn't asked the name of his friend, although she guessed it was the young woman he'd mentioned to her before.

'That was close,' Christopher said when they were alone, as she stood staring after Alejandro.

She turned. 'If it had been anyone else, if someone else had recognised me '

Christopher's arms closed around her and she lay her cheek on his chest as he held her. 'But it wasn't. Our secret is safe.'

She knew he was right, but she also knew that he couldn't possibly understand the repercussions if she were caught.

'Shall we walk?' he asked. 'Or would you rather sit?'

'Let's walk,' she said, her mind already racing, trying to figure out something safer, wondering where they could meet next time, somewhere they couldn't be caught.

And as Christopher kept her tucked against his body, she wished there was some way she could spend an entire evening with Christopher without anyone even noticing she was gone.

'I know you don't think your family would approve of me, but my mother would love you,' Christopher said. 'She'd be showing you off to all her friends, dragging you to lunches every week.'

She tried to imagine it. After so long without her own mother, it was almost impossible to imagine a life that would involve an older woman taking her under her wing. She'd always been the eldest, always been the one to take care of everyone else, even her papá.

'You truly think so? That she'd approve of me.'

'Yes, Esmeralda, I know so,' he said. 'One day she'll think of you as the daughter she never had. Not to mention you'll be her favourite person in the world if you give her the grandchildren she's been yearning for all these years.' He smiled down at her, his fingers tracing gently down her arm until he caught her hands in his.

As Christopher's lips met hers, as she lost herself to the touch of his mouth against hers, she truly believed that anything was possible. That somehow, no matter what the obstacles, they were going to find a way to be together again.

18

HAVANA, CUBA, PRESENT DAY

Claudia had decided not to second-guess herself when it came to Mateo. She felt like her skin was still glowing from the night before; still flushed from his touch and the way he'd made her feel. She smiled as she thought back to earlier that day, to waking up with him beside her that morning.

Her stomach had rumbled and Mateo pushed the sheet away and pressed a kiss to her bare skin.

'You're hungry.'

She groaned and reached for his face, pulling him up closer to her and indulging in another kiss. It turned out that she couldn't get enough of him, and even as sunlight filtered through the blinds, she found she wasn't even self-conscious of him seeing her body. There was something about being away from home, with a man she knew she'd never see again, that had given her a newfound confidence. Or perhaps it was just this particular man.

Mateo eventually lay back against the pillows and she curled against his chest, listening to the rise and fall of his breath, tracing circles against his skin. He had a sprinkle of dark hair there, his skin the most beautiful golden shade of brown beneath her paler skin.

'How many days do you have left here? I'm losing count.'

'Three,' she whispered, already wishing it were longer if it meant more nights like the one they'd just had.

'Three days of you in my arms,' he whispered against her hair. 'That's not nearly long enough with this body of yours.'

She knew she was blushing as he ran his fingers across her hip and down the top of her thigh. They'd barely slept and she knew she would find it impossible to keep her eyes open later, but being with Mateo had shown her that she most definitely didn't have feelings for her ex any longer. He'd been the last thing on her mind as she'd walked hand in hand with Mateo back to her room, and she expected it would be Mateo who would be the only man on her mind for many, many months to come. In fact she doubted she'd ever forget their rendezvous for as long as she lived.

'I'm going to have to go soon,' he said. 'Although I'd stay here all day with you if I could.'

She curled even tighter to him, wishing they could stay in their little bubble for longer, just the two of them, but within minutes Mateo was extracting himself from her, dropping a slow kiss to her mouth before rising.

Claudia indulged in watching him, admiring his lean, muscled body as he dressed, eyes dancing across his chest when he turned, standing only in his jeans. But he wasn't looking at her, he was looking past her to the little box she'd left on the bedside table.

She stretched back and reached for it. 'These are the clues left behind for my grandmother,' she said, drawing the sheet around her as she sat up in the bed. 'This little box is what brought me here.' Without it, Cuba was not a country she'd ever likely have visited.

Mateo sat back down beside her, reaching for the box and

running his thumb across the smooth surface. 'The crest was folded inside this?'

She nodded and reached to take off the lid. 'It's still in there. It had been hand-drawn, which was the strangest part.'

'Someone must have known it intimately to draw it by hand, especially so well. It's not something that would be easy to remember.'

'We overlayed it with colour, just to see how it would look,' she said. 'Well, my father did. He was most excited about the history of it all.'

'And it was just folded in this box?'

'Yes. The box was tied together with string, and a little handwritten note bearing my grandmother's name was attached to it.'

Mateo turned the box over in his hands, studying it carefully, before looking inside it again and taking out the business card. She watched him read it before placing it all back again.

'This was the only other thing inside?' he asked.

She nodded. 'Yes. Just the crest and the card.'

'I can see why you're so intrigued by it all.'

She took the box from him and placed it back beside the bed. Claudia almost felt as if she were moving further away from the reason she'd come to Cuba in the first place, and looking at the box again only made her frustrated that she hadn't succeeded in her search. Being with Mateo was amazing; in a way it was exactly what she'd needed.

'Are you free tomorrow?' Mateo asked, reaching out and stroking her hair as it fell over her shoulder.

She smiled. 'You forget, I'm on holiday. I'm free every day.'

'Then come to lunch with my family,' he said. 'Perhaps my mother can help.'

She tried to hide her excitement over meeting his family. His mother had already been so kind as to share her photo album, which made her curious to meet her, and Claudia was interested to glimpse his world and see what his life was really like. Where he lived, the neighbourhood he'd grown up in and what his family were like.

'Te veo pronto, mi amor,' he said, bending to kiss her one last time.

'I still have no idea what you're saying to me,' she sighed. 'But I could listen to it all day.'

Mateo chuckled, turning when he was at the door. 'I said see you soon, my love.'

She waited until he'd closed the door before flopping back onto the pillows, eyes shut as she wondered if she were perhaps the luckiest girl in the world.

Claudia smiled as she walked, remembering the way she'd stayed lying there, satiated in a way she'd never been before. And when she came within sight of Mateo's food truck, her skin had tingled just seeing him. There was something about the man; the way he looked, the way he made her feel. She couldn't get enough of him.

'Claudia!'

It was Carlos. She saw Mateo look up and smile as she turned. Sure enough, Carlos was walking towards her, his white hat sitting jauntily on his head, his shirt unbuttoned just a little too low. But it was the woman on his arm that made her smile— this time she didn't look like she was in danger of killing anyone.

'Claudia, I want you to meet my wife,' Carlos said.

Mateo had stepped out of the truck now, a small towel thrown over his shoulder, his black apron contrasting against his white T-shirt, as he came to stand beside her.

'Pleased to meet you—'

'Amber,' the other woman said.

Carlos was grinning ear to ear, his arm slung around his

wife's shoulders, even though his wife was openly studying her in a way that wasn't overly friendly.

'What have you been doing? I thought you'd be needing me to drive you?' Carlos asked. 'Has Mateo here been keeping you busy?'

Claudia laughed, glancing at Mateo, but he only shrugged. 'I have to get back to work. Come back and have dinner later. I'll save you something,' he said to Carlos.

Claudia turned slightly and Mateo unexpectedly kissed her, long and slow, as if they didn't have company. But when he pulled away and gave her a wink, she saw that Amber suddenly appeared a lot more friendly towards her, no longer scowling.

Carlos let out a low whistle. 'I see Mateo is doing more than just helping to solve your mystery?'

She chose not to be embarrassed—she was a grown, single woman enjoying the company of a man. 'I'm not going to lie, I'm so pleased you introduced us.'

'Well, I'm happy for you both,' Amber said. 'Mateo deserves something good to happen to him, even if it is only for a few days.'

Claudia couldn't help but notice the sharp look Carlos gave his wife.

'What?' Amber said with a shrug. 'It's true. After what he's been through, it's nice to see him happy.'

Claudia hesitated, looking between them. 'After what happened?' It was the second time someone had referred to Mateo's past. 'Do you mean his father passing?'

Carlos looked past her, and she knew he was looking at the food truck. 'He's a good man, our Mateo. Keep making him smile, it's nice to see him happy again.'

She watched them go, Carlos tugging his wife away, although not before his wife mouthed *sorry* to her. Claudia stood a few moments, before turning to look at Mateo, who was whistling in the truck as he cooked, as if he didn't have a care in the world. *What was all that about?*

Suddenly she felt like it wasn't just her grandmother's mystery she had to solve. Whatever had happened to Mateo, it seemed that no one liked to talk about it, or at least they didn't want to talk about it with her.

'Come on, chica,' Mateo called out. 'Are you just standing there to look pretty or are you coming to help?'

She smiled, entering the truck and moving to stand beside him. *He'd said something about being happy to have company in the truck again. Had someone else, other than his father, worked with him before? Had he lost someone else?*

But she didn't have time to ask, because Mateo was moving expertly around her, the compact kitchen full of the most delicious aromas, and even if she'd wanted to, she couldn't have brought herself to ask him anything that would ruin the lightness between them.

'So all I do is stir?' she asked, glancing over her shoulder at Mateo who was busy slicing something to add to the stew she was cooking. 'What did you call this again?'

'This is ropa vieja, the dish Rosa wanted the recipe for,' Mateo said, coming to stand beside her, his chin over her shoulder as he leaned forward, his pelvis nudging against her. 'It's our national dish, but I make it a little different.'

'Ropa vieja,' she said, trying out the words.

'Vieja,' he corrected, and she tried not to laugh as she repeated after him.

'Better,' he said. 'Now, try this.'

He took out a small piece of meat and shredded it with his fork, before indicating that she should open her mouth. Mateo fed it to her, watching her face for her reaction.

'It's amazing,' she said. 'It just dissolved in my mouth, it's so tender.'

'The key is cooking it slowly, and then you shred the meat into long pieces over the top of rice to serve it. The sauce is so full of flavour with the bell peppers, onions, garlic and wine, but you have to cook it with love, and that means hours of tending to it.'

He leaned over her again and dipped a spoon into the sauce, lifting it to her mouth again. She obliged.

'Mmmm, it's so good!'

He nudged his pelvis into her, whispering directly into her ear again this time. 'It's all in the time I take with it.'

She wasn't sure if they were talking about the sauce or something else entirely now, but Mateo had already moved past her and was back to slicing something for another recipe he was working on.

'What can I do to be helpful?' she asked.

'You can dish the food out,' he said. 'Listen to me carefully and I'll guide you through every step.'

She gulped. Just because she wasn't doing any of the cooking didn't mean she still couldn't make a mistake, and she didn't want to let him down, not when his food was so renowned.

'What are you doing now?' she asked, sidling a little closer to him.

'Finishing off the yuca con mojo,' he told her, as he chopped garlic. 'Here, you can squeeze the limes for me.'

She moved closer and reached for the limes. 'Do you have a squeezer?'

Mateo laughed. 'Use your hands, tonta.'

'Tonta?'

That made him laugh all the more, although he didn't look up as he used a very sharp knife to slice the garlic.

'Silly,' he said. 'It means silly.'

She picked up a much smaller-looking knife and cut the first lime in half, squeezing it by hand and realising it actually felt much more satisfying by hand than if she'd used a utensil. She moved on to the next one, eventually filling up the bowl he'd nudged in her direction.

'What else do you put in?'

'This dish is made with the root of the cassava plant, and you cook it in a vibrant sauce made of garlic, lime juice and olive oil. It's one of the most delicious vegetarian dishes you'll find here.'

She nodded, using her arm to wipe her forehead, her fingers dripping with lime juice.

'Cooking suits you,' he said, nudging her with his shoulder.

Claudia nudged him back, grinning as she did so. Perhaps cooking wasn't such a chore, after all.

'That was quite the evening,' she said, exhaling and trying to blow the hair from her face. Her skin was sticky from the heat of the kitchen, her T-shirt tacky against her skin, and after smelling such delicious food for so many hours, she was starving hungry. But despite all that, it had been one of the best, most enjoyable nights of her life.

'Here, come and sit with me and eat this,' Mateo said.

She greedily eyed the plate, groaning with delight as she saw what was on it. It was the ropa vieja she'd been stirring at the very beginning of the evening. 'I thought you said we'd sold out of this?'

'I put that aside for you hours ago,' he told her. 'I can't pay you, but the least I can do is feed you.'

She went to sit on the step as they'd done the last time they'd eaten together, her mouth watering, but Mateo indicated for her to keep moving. As if she'd ever let him pay her for the meagre amount of work she'd done—for all she knew, she'd been a hindrance!

'Why don't we stroll and eat? I need to stretch my legs.'

Claudia was happy to walk, and as they slowly meandered, mostly in silence as they ate, she realised just how relaxed she was around him. There weren't many people in her life she felt that way around, other than her parents or her friend Charlotte, and she couldn't help but think how nice it was.

'I have to say I'm envious of the work you do,' she confessed. 'You've found something you're so good at, you get to have fun every night and you seem so happy. It's a beautiful thing to watch you cook.'

Mateo swallowed and slowly nodded. 'You're right, but I'm envious of you being able to travel,' he said. 'And it sounds like your job makes you happy, too.'

She looked up at him and knew she had to tell him. It was something that she kept inside, hating to go there in her mind even though she knew it wasn't something she could lock away forever, but for some reason she wanted Mateo to understand why she'd made the choices she had. Why she was able to travel, the ways in which her life had changed.

'I thought I loved my old job,' she said, as they started to walk even more slowly. 'I got my dream job out of university, and the money I was earning was incredible. It's the only reason I can travel now or choose to do the work I do.'

Mateo was watching her as he ate, and she took a deep breath, moving her meat around on her plate with her fork.

'I had two best friends, we met at university and we all went out into the world with big dreams,' she said, seeing it in her mind, remembering what they'd been like. *The three musketeers, ready to conquer the world.* 'None of us truly realised the hours we'd be expected to work or the pressures we'd face, although my friend Charlotte had a different culture in her law firm compared to what we did in finance.'

'That's why you left? Because of the hours?' Mateo asked, appearing genuinely interested. 'I can imagine they make the young ones work the hardest.'

Her breath came out as a shudder, her appetite gone. 'Lisa and I had desks side by side, in an area they called the bullpen because they just crammed us all in there. Only the best would graduate to get their own desk, and we both thought we'd made it when we were shoulder tapped to move. Life seemed amazing.'

'What happened?'

'After months of hundred-hour weeks and constant pressure to perform, we were both struggling. It was a lot to cope with, but everyone kept telling us we were doing so well, that we should be grateful for the opportunities given to us.' She blinked away tears. 'Until one day Lisa didn't come in to work, and she wasn't answering her phone. I left work because I knew something was wrong, and because I had a key to her flat. My boss was furious with me for leaving during the middle of the day, but I didn't listen.'

Mateo lowered his plate, his eyes on hers.

'It turned out she'd been taking pills to stay awake, to cope with the hours we had to work. The coroner ruled it was an accidental overdose, and I didn't even know she'd been taking anything.'

Mateo shook his head. 'I'm so sorry. I can see why it made you want to leave.'

'Add to that a fiancé who couldn't understand why I no longer wanted to work in an industry that was so broken, that took one of the people I was closest to in the world, and my life kind of imploded.'

'Death makes us evaluate our lives,' he said, indicating that they should sit. She followed his lead, toying with her meat and rice before making herself take a mouthful—it was delicious and she wasn't going to let her memories stop her from enjoying what he'd made for her. 'Some people take a few days, others make major changes, they see death as a way to approach their own life in a different way.'

She looked up at him, saw the lump in his throat and the way he was staring off into the distance.

'You sound like a man who has first-hand experience,' she said.

'One day I'll tell you my story,' Mateo said. 'But that day isn't today.'

Claudia was curious, she couldn't not be. After what had been said earlier, the way Carlos had glared so sharply at his wife, and even Rosa had alluded to a sadness or loss that she'd never explained. But she simply nodded, nudging her knee against his. When he was ready, he'd tell her.

'Come closer to me.' His voice was huskier than she'd heard it before, his eyes searching hers.

She did what he asked, moving closer, surprised when he took her plate and put both of them behind him. Perhaps the reason they'd been drawn to each other was because they both wanted a fresh start, because when his mouth covered hers, she understood that he was trying to lose himself, too. Running from memories, living in the moment, not letting his past define him.

'You can go home and remember being kissed on the Malecón,' he whispered. 'You can remember Havana, and how it brought you to life, how it let you live without thinking about the past.'

She didn't bother asking him how he knew, because she could already tell that she was a different woman now to the one she'd been when she'd arrived.

And maybe to avoid his memories, and definitely to avoid hers, she kissed him again, her palm against his soft, warm cheek as she indulged in the holiday romance she'd never even dreamed she'd be having.

Carpe diem. She'd made that promise the day of Lisa's funeral, both she and Charlotte had, and while her friend had gotten married and had a baby on the way, Claudia had quit her job and changed her lifestyle.

Although if I'd known about Cuba, I might have started my journey of self-discovery here, instead.

She looked up at Mateo through hooded lashes, drinking in the sight of him and committing the feel of him to memory. *This is going to be a holiday I'll never, ever forget.*

19

HAVANA, CUBA, 1950

'I can't believe it's tonight.'

Esmeralda placed her hands on her sister's shoulders, smiling at her in the mirror as she stood behind her. 'You look beautiful, María. No one will be able to take their eyes off you.'

'Except Christopher,' Gisele called out from where her maid was helping to dress her. 'He only seems to have eyes for you.'

Esmeralda gave her a sharp stare, but it was her own maid Sofia assisting them, and she knew she could trust her with her secrets. She wouldn't have trusted anyone else in the house, but Sofia was almost like a sister to her.

'Mamá would have been so proud of you,' she said, whispering in María's ear as she placed a diamond chain around her neck. 'I can't believe you're fifteen already.'

'Esmeralda! It's beautiful.'

She smiled, watching as her sister turned and admiring the glint of the diamonds under the light. 'Papá asked me to find something special for you. I'm pleased you like it.'

'I love it. It's perfect.'

'Mamá would have loved to see you tonight, to see you

become a woman before her eyes,' Esmeralda said as she stared at her own reflection in the mirror for a moment, hoping she'd chosen the right dress for the occasion. It was a burgundy colour with a low-cut neckline, her small waist accentuated, with fuller fabric around her hips. 'It's hard to believe we're all women now.'

They all looked at one another, and Esmeralda recognised the sorrow in both of her sisters' eyes. Becoming young women and yearning for love and a husband was one thing, but to think of a time when they wouldn't all be living beneath the same roof was enough to break each of their hearts, and that day was beginning to feel closer and closer.

'I'm nervous about my dance, what if—'

'Your dance will be perfect,' Esmeralda assured her. 'You've rehearsed it so many times, it will be fine.'

María sighed, staring at herself in the mirror again. Esmeralda remembered all too well how nervous she'd been when it was her turn, how she'd lain awake worrying for hours the night before, terrified she might make a misstep in her waltz.

'I'm going to say goodnight to Marisol before everyone begins to arrive,' Esmeralda said. 'I'll see you both downstairs soon.'

She gave María a quick hug and left them to finish getting ready in her room, walking down the hall to find a pouting Marisol sitting on her bed.

'What are you doing, little one?' she asked, trying not to smile when Marisol's nanny muttered something beneath her breath. 'You should be all tucked up in bed.'

'But I want to go to the party,' she said. 'Why can't I go? Papá says I'm too young but I'm not!'

'Marisol,' she said, sitting down and putting an arm around her, drawing her little sister close. 'One day you will go to parties all year round, and you'll become like me.' She laughed.

'Tired of parties and wishing you didn't have to dance all night in uncomfortable shoes.'

Marisol made a face. 'I would dance all night.'

'Maybe, my love,' she said. 'Maybe you'll be more like Gisele and María and love every party and all the dancing in the world, but there's plenty of time for that. One day you'll be the quinceañera, wearing the most beautiful dress you've ever seen, and with a gift of diamonds from Papá.'

Marisol's little arm went around her and Esmeralda hugged her, pressing a soft kiss to the top of her head.

'Please let Marisol watch from upstairs for a few moments so she can see some of our guests arrive,' she instructed the nanny—news that was received with a squeal of delight from her sister. 'But after that, she's to go straight to bed.'

Marisol wrapped her arms tightly around her and kissed her cheek. 'To bed when you're told?'

Her sister nodded. 'Yes, Esmeralda. Straight to bed after.'

She left her then, knowing it was almost time to position herself at the door with her sisters to greet each guest as they arrived, greeting them by name, kissing cheeks and welcoming them into her home. Her papá would expect nothing less, and it wasn't in her nature to disappoint him.

It wasn't until the traditional dance had begun that Esmeralda saw Christopher. There were more than 300 guests filling every inch of their home, and she'd barely made it two steps without someone stopping her to talk or introduce themselves, so it had made it impossible to seek him out. But as María and thirteen of her friends did a well-rehearsed waltz, carrying candles around fourteen boys holding roses, as her eyes should have been on her sister, Esmeralda found herself instead meeting Christopher's gaze. They stared at each other across the room, and she found she couldn't look away, no matter how hard she tried.

Her time with Christopher was coming to an end, and although she'd imagined many stolen moments with him, they had been few and far between.

'You look like a woman in love.'

She jumped at the words whispered close to her ear, swatting at Alejandro when she turned and saw him standing behind her, leaning close.

Esmeralda didn't reply, instead giving him a sharp look, not wanting anyone to hear their exchange, but Alejandro didn't back away, instead stepping closer to her and taking her arm. He was her beloved cousin and everyone knew it, so when the official dance was over and everyone began clapping to celebrate the quinceañera before finding their own dance partners, no one noticed them as they began to waltz together. Esmeralda could dance in her sleep and Alejandro made dancing appear effortless, which meant they were well versed at dancing together and talking, without worrying about standing on each other's toes.

'He's the one, isn't he?' Alejandro murmured.

'I'm not going to deny it,' Esmeralda said. 'You're the only one who's seen us together though, so please keep your thoughts to yourself.'

'What are you going to do?' he asked as they continued to dance. 'Will he propose?'

'He wants to ask my father after his return to London. We both think it's best if he waits until their business deal is completed, and I think it would be best if he wrote to him, to give Papá time to think about it.'

Alejandro went silent and she found herself searching his face, wanting to know what he was thinking.

'You don't agree?' she asked.

He gave her a long look as they spun around the dance floor. 'I think that he should want to move heaven and earth for your hand, Es. So many men would give anything to have you as their wife.'

She swallowed, close to tears. 'You don't think he's prepared to fight for me? Is that it?'

'I never said that,' he replied, as the song changed and couples moved away from them, making way for new dancers.

Her breath caught in her throat as she stared back at him.

'Then what are you trying to say, Ale? What is it?'

He lifted her hand and pressed a kiss to it. 'I'm saying that you're the most wonderful girl I know, Esmeralda, and you deserve the world. I only want to make certain he's prepared to give you it.'

As if on cue, Christopher appeared behind Alejandro. Now her breath wasn't caught, it was instead causing her chest to rapidly rise and fall.

'May I cut in?'

'You may,' Alejandro said, stepping aside and giving her a warm smile.

But she forgot all about her cousin the moment she was standing in front of Christopher. The touch of his hand against hers, the other at her waist as he stared down at her, sent ripples of excitement down her spine.

'Do you know how to waltz?' she asked, her voice whisper soft and not sounding at all like it belonged to her.

'Thankfully I do,' he replied, and she noticed how careful he was to keep his body distanced from hers. With Alejandro she danced close to him and didn't think about the way she moved, remembering her steps as if they were second nature, but with Christopher she felt every bump of his body against hers, so acutely aware of the air between them, of the way her feet moved, of the way his fingers felt against hers. It was almost impossible to remember the dance steps with him holding her, without fretting that someone would observe them and somehow see the ripple of chemistry that ran between them.

'I feel eyes upon us,' he murmured as they danced. 'Does everyone always watch you like this?'

She daren't look around, smiling up at him instead. 'I'm one of the sugar king's unmarried, eligible daughters,' she told him. 'The only reason they watch me is because they want me to marry their sons.'

He dared to speak in a low voice directly into her ear. 'Have you ever considered it's because you're the most beautiful woman in the room?'

His compliment washed over her like a ray of sunshine on a gloomy day, but it was tipping her head back for a moment and looking up that made her smile. Standing upstairs, in her nightgown and peering down at all the dancers spilling from the ballroom into the hall, was Marisol, and she was staring right at her.

Esmeralda lifted her hand from Christopher's arm and gave her a little wave, to which Marisol replied with a wiggle of her fingers and a naughty smile as she leaned over the banister. Clearly she'd snuck out of her room long after bedtime, her nanny none the wiser, and Esmeralda certainly wasn't going to scold her. If she wanted to watch the dancing, then so be it.

'Would you ever leave them?' Christopher asked as he followed her gaze. 'London is a long way from Cuba, after all.'

She turned her attention back to him and gazed into his eyes. 'Yes, Christopher, I would.' *I would follow you all around the world if you asked me.*

The song ended then and they stopped dancing for a moment, and much to her dismay another young man was waiting to ask her to dance and Christopher, ever the gentleman, stepped aside.

All she wanted was to snap at her new dance partner to find someone else to waltz with, but of course she would never be so rude, and even when he stepped on her toe she kept her smile fixed and followed his lead. When the song finally ended, she made her excuses before anyone else could come along and headed for the door, in desperate need of a breath of fresh air, but it wasn't to be. A hand caught her arm and she turned to see her father standing there, his smile stretching his face wide.

'Dance with your papá?'

'Of course!' She glanced longingly at the door, but quickly turned her attention to her father.

'You were going somewhere?'

She took his arm and they walked back to the dance floor. 'Only a breath of fresh air. I've been dancing so much I felt lightheaded is all.'

Esmeralda had always enjoyed dancing with her papá; her mother had been a graceful, enthusiastic dancer and had insisted her husband join her at all times. But tonight she was nervous, wondering if somehow he'd seen the way she looked at Christopher or sensed something had developed between them.

'I wanted to thank you for being such a gracious host to Christopher,' he said, smiling down at her. 'You've had a lot to contend with, organising this party, travelling with me. Your mother would have been so proud.'

'Thank you,' she said. 'But it hasn't been a hardship at all. I enjoy being busy.'

He leaned in a little closer. 'Esmeralda, look around you. This is the most spectacular quince party, you have truly outdone yourself. Everything you do reflects on our family, and you've done nothing but make me proud.'

She swallowed, hoping he didn't feel the dampness of her hands or the sweat forming on her brow.

'You're welcome, Papá,' she said, forcing a smile.

'Are you all right, Esmeralda? You seem flushed?'

'It's simply the excitement of the night and all this dancing,' she said quickly. 'It's why I was disappearing for air before.'

Her father nodded and they didn't speak for the rest of the song, but to her relief an acquaintance waved out to him and he kissed her cheek before dismissing her before the next song began. Esmeralda kept her head down as she hurried towards the door, needing the air more than ever now and not wanting anyone to stop her. She held her dress a little higher as it swished, rushing through the open doors and gulping air as if she'd been deprived.

'Esmeralda?'

She turned and found Alejandro standing behind her on the balcony, with an expression on his face that she couldn't read. But she saw him glance sideways and followed it, seeing Christopher standing alone, away from the crowds, near their swimming pool. It looked magnificent, with water flowing through a statue to create a constant splash, but it wasn't the water she was captivated by.

'Take this,' Alejandro said, pressing something into her palm.

She opened her hand, no longer looking at Christopher, and found herself in possession of a key. 'What's this for?'

'It's the key to my family's beach house in Santa María,' he said. 'No one is there, we haven't been there in weeks, and it's yours for the night. My driver will be waiting for you, he's at your disposal for the evening and I can assure you of his absolute discretion.'

Esmeralda stared back at him, blinking, not entirely certain what he was trying to say. 'Why would I...'

Her words faded as she followed Alejandro's stare again. He was looking at Christopher. And then it dawned on her the gift he was giving her.

'Take it,' he said, gently closing her palm and leaning in to whisper a kiss to her cheek. 'This way you have a choice. If you want to be alone with him, you can be.'

'Why?' she murmured. 'Why would you do this for me?'

'Because I've known you my entire life, and you've never looked at anyone the way I've seen you look at your Englishman.'

Esmeralda stood, stunned by what he'd done for her, as she watched Alejandro walk away and disappear into the crowd. Esmeralda clutched the key so tightly in her hand the sharp metal edges dug into her skin, before slipping it into her pocket, grateful her dress even had one.

'Es, what are you doing out here? I've been looking everywhere for you!' María's face was pink, her eyes bright as she caught her arm and leaned in close. 'Come and see who I've been dancing with, he's so handsome!' Her sister kept talking but Esmeralda didn't hear a word; her head was pounding as she imagined the weight of the key in her pocket, what it would mean, the gift that Alejandro had given her. Despite her thoughts she obediently followed her sister, nodding and smiling as if she had her full attention, all the while searching desperately for Christopher, who seemed to have disappeared into the crowd when she wasn't looking.

She only hoped he'd be as excited as she was.

'There you are.'

Christopher's deep, warm voice washed over her as she stood near the door with a glass of champagne. The bubbles tickled her throat but she'd needed to have one for courage, although so far it was only making her stomach dance as she thought of the key in her pocket. It was almost like a heavy weight, impossible not to feel with every step she took.

'Are you enjoying the party?' she asked, demurely glancing up at him. She didn't want to give him her full attention, not when so many eyes could be on them, but she did afford him a small smile.

'Very much so. The hostess did an extraordinary job.'

She turned her body to face him, finding it impossible to maintain such a distance when all she wanted was to be close. He was dressed impeccably in a shirt and suit, but unlike when she'd seen him in London he wasn't wearing a tie, and she found she liked it. Although she would have been the first to admit that she would have liked him no matter what his choice of attire.

'Chris—'

'Esmer—'

They both laughed, and he gestured that she should speak first.

'Alejandro gave me a key,' she said, her voice barely louder than a whisper. 'For us. To his beach house.'

Christopher's face appeared to drain of colour as he stared at her. 'You mean, for us to...'

She smiled sweetly, as if they were talking about the weather. 'Yes. For us to use, tonight, if we so wish. For us to be alone.'

'And this beach house is where?' he asked, clearing his throat.

'Santa María,' she told him. 'It will take about twenty-five minutes by car. It so happens his driver is at our disposal.'

A waiter went past holding champagne flutes high on a silver tray, and Christopher reached for one, draining half of it as she watched. It took him only a moment to regain his composure, his eyes searching hers as if trying to be certain that she was saying what he thought she was.

'This is what you want?' he asked. 'To go together to this house?'

Esmeralda nodded, breathing heavily as she met his gaze. She wanted it more than anything, but it didn't mean she wasn't terrified. 'Yes,' she said boldly. 'It's what I want.' *I've never wanted anything so badly in all my life.*

Christopher took a step closer, far too close to be appropriate, but she found she didn't want to step away. 'Then we should go when no one will notice us,' he said. 'In a few hours' time, when everyone has had too much to drink to realise our absence.'

She nodded. 'I have no further obligations,' she said. 'Everyone will assume I've retired to my room. I'll tell my sisters I have a headache.'

Esmeralda stepped back then to maintain a proper distance, clearing her throat. 'I shall see you later. I'll pass you and touch your arm when it's time to leave, and you can wait fifteen minutes before joining me.'

'It was lovely to have a moment talking with you, Miss Diaz,' Christopher said, his voice louder now. 'Perhaps we could dance again before the night is over?'

'Perhaps,' she replied, her voice equally loud in case anyone was trying to listen to their exchange, smiling sweetly before turning on her heel, champagne glass still in hand as she tried not to skip across the room in excitement. All she'd ever wanted was to be alone with Christopher, and aside from their afternoon in Harrods and then their one night walking the Malecón she'd barely had the chance. *Until tonight.* And all thanks to Alejandro.

She looked up and saw that Marisol was still watching the crowds below, so she lifted her skirts and hurried up the stairs, determined to get her to bed so she didn't see her big sister slip from the crowd later, lest she disclose her secret to Papá.

The last thing she needed was for her plans to be foiled by an almost four-year old.

20

A butterfly soft shiver ran down Esmeralda's spine the closer they got to Alejandro's beach house in Santa María. She knew the place intimately, having been there so many times with both of their families, but arriving in the dark, and with her hand tucked into Christopher's as they sat together in the back seat of the car, was something else entirely. Their plan had worked perfectly, with her sneaking from the house first, the touch of her fingertips to Christopher's arm as she'd silently passed him sending ripples of anticipation through her, the wait in the car until he joined her almost impossible to stand. She'd half wondered if he wouldn't come, but right on cue he'd appeared on the street, his eyes alight when he'd joined her in the back seat.

It didn't matter that it was dark, she could still see where they were going in her mind—could see the hill of Santa María Loma in the near distance, the palm trees gently waving in the breeze and the grassland that stretched beyond the sand. It had always been one of her favourite places to visit, and now it was going to hold an even more special place in her heart.

'We're almost there,' she whispered to him, tucking closer as her stomach did a little leap. What she was doing went beyond forbidden, but no amount of reminding herself of that fact had made her hesitate.

Christopher's fingers tightened around hers for a moment as the car began to slow, and she wondered if he was as nervous as she was.

'Shall I ask the driver to wait for us?' Christopher asked, his voice barely a whisper. 'I'll need to have you home before daybreak.'

She nodded against him, curling her hand around his arm. She didn't want to think about daybreak, because that would mean saying goodbye and she wanted to soak up every moment with him rather than fret about what couldn't be. But Alejandro had made it clear that his car and driver were theirs for the night.

When the car finally rolled to a stop, she listened as Christopher spoke to the driver, before opening the door and reaching back in for her. She held his hand as she stepped out, her eyes adjusting to the dark as she led Christopher to the front door. The residence was silent, set alone away from other beach houses, and her hand shook as she fumbled with the key.

Christopher seemed to sense her nerves and took it from her, placing it in the lock and then opening it, waiting for her to step through before securing it again behind them. Her heels sounded hollow on the tiled floor, her stomach twisting even more violently with every moment that passed. But when Christopher's hand claimed hers again she found her breath and they quietly walked through the house, his touch calming her.

'This is a beautiful home,' Christopher said as they walked to the doors, which opened out to the beach. 'I wish we could have spent the entire weekend here.'

She sighed. 'So do I.' Esmeralda would have done anything

to have more than a handful of stolen moments with him; what a luxury an entire weekend would be.

'Imagine us living somewhere like this,' he marvelled. 'Children running from room to room, waking up to the ocean view.' He turned to her. 'It would be magical, wouldn't it?'

She found herself lost in his fantasy, imagining their life together, imagining what it would be like if he could somehow move his business and life to Havana. But she knew how dangerous dreams were, how painful it would be to believe it would happen one day only to be let down.

'Shall we find something to drink?' he asked.

Esmeralda smiled, forcing herself to be in the present instead of lost in her thoughts. 'Yes, and I know just where to find the champagne.'

She turned a light on and disappeared, going into the kitchen and finding not one but numerous bottles of Dom Perignon. She took one out and rummaged around until she found two glasses, taking everything out to Christopher. He'd opened the doors and was standing outside on the patio, and she set everything down on the table nearby, pausing to listen to the soothing sound of the ocean. He was right—this place was magical, and not just because they were there together.

'You weren't lying when you told me that Cuba was paradise,' Christopher said, turning to her. 'I don't think I could have imagined how beautiful it was.' His voice was husky as his eyes searched her face, and she suddenly wondered if they were still talking about Cuba or whether his words were for her.

He wasn't wrong, it was paradise, but somehow it wouldn't feel like paradise if she was going to be left behind while he returned to London. It would seem more like a prison, she the bird in the gilded cage. But before she could say anything, Christopher had turned away from the ocean and was opening the champagne. He poured them both a glass, the moonlight and the light from inside that she'd turned on earlier casting just enough light for them to see by.

'To being together,' he said, touching his glass gently to hers. 'This has turned into a very special evening.'

'To my cousin Alejandro,' she replied with a nervous laugh, before taking a sip. 'He's always been my favourite, now I know why.'

'He may just be my favourite person now, too,' Christopher said, his brows arched. 'Other than you, of course.'

Her face heated and she took another sip of champagne. *This is not my time to be a wallflower. I need to be bold.* Christopher was a gentleman, she knew that he wouldn't press her to do anything she didn't want to do, which was why she needed to make her intentions clear.

She took a large gulp of champagne to settle her nerves before setting her glass down and taking a step towards him. Her hands were shaking but she reached for his jacket, her fingers clutching his lapel as she tilted her face back up, looking into his eyes before lowering her gaze to his mouth. Christopher didn't need further encouragement, not now that she'd made the first move, his lips immediately finding hers and kissing her so tenderly that she couldn't help but sigh. Esmeralda pulled back only to take his glass and set it beside hers, their drinks forgotten as she turned back to him and slid his jacket from his shoulders, before exploring his arms and back now that he was only in a shirt.

This time it was Christopher kissing her, his arms around her waist, his hands dipping lower than he'd ever dared before. She knew she should have stopped him, that the way he was touching her was beyond forbidden, but she wanted it as much as he did, wanted one night in his arms to remember him by when he was gone. She didn't know how long it might be until she saw him again.

Christopher scooped her up into his arms then, his mouth

never leaving hers, his kisses insistent as he started to walk farther into the house.

'Where are the bedrooms?' he asked, his voice husky.

'Upstairs,' she whispered, pressing her cheek to his chest as he carried her, as she listened to the ragged in and out of his breath.

Within moments he was nudging a door open with his shoulder, before placing her gently on the bed. He stood above her, looking down, as if trying to decide what to do. Esmeralda kicked off her shoes and sat up a little, staring at Christopher's silhouette.

'Come to me,' she murmured.

He hesitated, as if he was doubting their decision to come to the house, as worry started to knot in her chest, but then he took off his own shoes and lowered himself gently over her body, his arms framing her head.

'Esmeralda,' he whispered, 'my beautiful, enchanting Esmeralda.'

She lifted one hand and gently touched his cheek, his skin soft beneath her fingertips. She wanted to commit every part of him to memory—the smell, the feel, the taste of the man she loved.

'One day you will be my wife, Esmeralda. This is just the beginning for us, the start of our life together. I won't take no for an answer from your father, but we have to be patient.' He paused, tenderly stroking her face and then her hair. 'I promise you we'll be married. Once the papers are signed, after I've returned to London, I will ask his permission.'

She smiled up at him, surprised to feel tears in her eyes as his words washed over her. She had no reason not to believe him, *wanted* to believe him, but she also didn't want to talk and whisper promises. Not now. 'Kiss me,' she whispered back.

'Are you certain you want to do this?' he asked, his voice a murmur. 'I can take you home, we don't have to—'

Esmeralda reached for him, cupping the back of his head and drawing his mouth to hers. She was lost for words, but she knew what she wanted, and there was no way she was going home, not now, not now that she had him all to herself.

She loved Christopher with all her heart, and she'd never wanted anything so badly in all her life.

It was still dark when Esmeralda rose. She pushed the sheets back and looked down at Christopher, his breathing telling her he was still asleep as she leaned down to press a barely there kiss to his lips, not wanting to disturb him. She also couldn't stand to have to say goodbye; they'd just shared a night of passion together, and that's how she wanted to remember him. She'd send the driver back for him, but she wanted to travel separately.

Esmeralda silently stood and gathered her clothes, the moonlight filtering through the open drapes meaning it wasn't completely dark as she slipped back into her dress. She reached for her shoes, leaving them to dangle from her fingers as she tiptoed across the room and down the hall, silently making her way down the stairs and letting herself out the front door and shutting it quietly behind her. She stood a moment, catching her breath, wrestling in her mind with the idea of running straight back to bed and into his arms, but she knew that she had to be stronger than that. There was no future for them if they were caught like this; she needed to get home before her absence was discovered.

Alejandro's driver had waited for them all night as Christopher had requested, and as she approached the car she could see that he was slumped down, asleep behind the wheel. She softly tapped on the window before opening the door and getting into the back seat, wanting as little contact with him as possible as she curled into the corner.

'Sorry, I—'

'No need to apologise,' she said, her cheeks flushed when he looked at her in the rearview mirror at her. It was no doubt obvious what she'd been doing, and it was embarrassing leaving without Christopher, especially when she was used to having a chaperone with her at all times. At least he would have been the one to give directions and fend off any questions if he were there, and she could have tucked silently to his side, not caring what they'd been doing. 'Please take me back to where you collected me from.'

'We're not waiting on your gentleman friend?'

She lifted her head and looked out the window. 'No, we are not. You are to return for him after taking me home.'

Tears burned her eyes and clung to her lashes as she imagined Christopher lying in bed as she'd left him, his body warm from slumber, the sheets crumpled, her perfume on his skin. As she imagined him waking and reaching for her, wondering where she'd gone. Despite the promises he'd made, she knew nothing would be easy when it came to him asking for her hand. Her papá wanted his girls to live close by, to have husbands chosen by him, from families he wanted them to align with. Even a highly successful businessman from London wasn't going to find it easy to get her father's consent, no matter how much she wished to imagine otherwise.

Christopher was returning to London before the end of the day, which meant this might very well have been her last moment with him, save for when they all lined up to bid him farewell as he departed. She would be forced to stand with her sisters, reaching for his hand and shaking it, formally, as if those very hands hadn't explored every inch of her body, as if he were nothing more than a business associate to her. She would have to tell him what a pleasure it had been to make his acquaintance again, as her father watched on, as she did her best to be demure under his watchful eye, always the one to set an example for her sisters.

Esmeralda let her tears fall freely then, as she pressed back into her seat, wishing she could curl into a ball as the beach finally gave way to the city, her home only minutes away as she continued to stare out the window, daybreak almost upon them. She wished the drive was longer so she could have had more time to compose herself, but at the same time she wanted to run for her bedroom and hide beneath the covers for as long as she possibly could.

When the car stopped, she whispered her thanks to the driver and got out, not waiting for him to open the door for her, running barefoot across the concrete to the little gate around the side of her house, shoes still hanging from her fingertips as she let herself silently into the house and tiptoed to her bedroom.

She could still smell Christopher on her skin, could still feel the brush of his body against hers, the way he'd held her, so tenderly, in his arms. She fell on her bed, still fully dressed as she sobbed into her pillow, clutching it as she cried and wished things could have been different, that they weren't destined to live worlds apart.

Only a fool would give her body to a man before she were married. They were words she'd learnt as a young woman and constantly reminded her sisters of, and despite knowing better, it was precisely what she'd done.

21

HAVANA, CUBA, PRESENT DAY

Claudia stood outside Mateo's home and took a deep breath before lifting her hand to knock. Carlos had driven her, raising his eyebrows when she'd told him where she needed to go, and although she'd been excited earlier, now she was a ball of nerves. *What am I even doing here?* She had zero experience with holiday flings, but she was fairly certain they didn't usually involve meeting the family.

Regardless, she tapped her knuckles against the door. It was a different home to Rosa's, much less Dr Seuss looking and more of what she guessed was a regular home in Havana, away from the tourist areas. It had an adobe, nondescript off-white plaster finish, but it was the brightly coloured flowers in planter boxes along the window frames that made it stand out. It looked like a happy home, the kind of house that would put a smile on her face just from walking past each day.

The door opened.

'Hola!'

'Hola.' Claudia laughed. She'd expected Mateo, and instead she'd ended up with a pint-sized version. The little boy grinned at her and grabbed her hand, and she barely had time to shut the door behind her before he tugged her down the hall to the kitchen. It was only small, but the aromas were like nothing she'd ever smelt before, even at the food truck, and it took a few moments before either of the cooks looked up.

'Claudia!' Mateo was the first to see her, stopping to wipe his hands before taking off his apron and coming towards her. 'I'm so happy you came.'

He greeted her with a kiss to the cheek and ruffled the hair of the boy who was still standing near her. She looked between them, not sure whether she was looking at his son, whether he'd kept something rather important from her, or...

'This is my nephew, José,' he said. 'He's been looking forward to meeting you.'

'Hola, José,' she said, taking an immediate liking to the little guy as she breathed a sigh of relief. His smile was impossible not to return, and when she looked up at Mateo she realised it was the same smile as his uncle's.

She didn't have time to tell Mateo though, because within seconds they were joined by two other women. One was obviously his mother; her eyes were almost the same as Mateo's, cocoa dark and warm as could be, and her embrace was no different.

'Claudia, it's so good to meet you,' she said, her English heavily accented. 'The girl who put a smile back on my Mateo's face.'

She blushed as she hugged her back. *I put the smile back on his face?* She was fairly certain he'd had a big smile the night she'd met him, and she was fairly certain that had had nothing to do with her, either.

'I'm not sure his smile has anything to do with me,' she replied. 'But thank you for inviting me into your home.'

She passed his mother the chocolates she'd purchased on the way, as well as a bottle of rum. She'd taken her time trying to figure out what to bring, and Rosa had told her she couldn't go wrong with taking alcohol and chocolate.

'Thank you. You didn't need to bring anything though.'

José was quick to eye up the chocolates, and she grinned at him, hoping he was allowed to eat them after their meal.

'I'm Ana,' the other woman said. 'Mateo's sister.' She too stepped forward, kissing her cheek, although her embrace wasn't as warm as her mother's, perhaps not as certain about having her in their home.

'It's so lovely to meet you, Ana.'

'Come, sit,' Mateo said, taking her hand and brushing a quick kiss to her cheek, before leading her to a table in the courtyard. It was similar to Rosa's, only theirs had a pergola with a vine growing across it, and Claudia could only imagine how wonderful it would look strung with fairy lights. They had a simple candle in the middle of the table in a glass jar, and she wondered if she'd be staying late enough to see it lit when the light started to fade.

'Do you have a family lunch every Sunday?' she asked.

Mateo sat beside her, pushing his chair back a little so his nephew could climb into his lap. She guessed he was perhaps four or five years old and clearly very attached to his uncle as he tucked his little legs up.

'Since I was this one's size,' he said. 'We all love cooking and eating, so it's not a chore for any of us.'

'And who does most of the cooking?' she asked. 'You must be so tired of food after all those hours making food for other people.'

'Mamá does the cooking on Sunday,' he said. 'She's the one who brings us together, I couldn't say no to her food even if I wanted to.'

'So perhaps you were right, when you told me it was the women in your family who had the real skills?'

'My mother runs a paladar from our home on Friday and

Saturday nights,' Mateo said as he sat back, stretching his arm across the seat beside him. 'Trust me when I say the woman can cook.'

Claudia grinned. 'I don't doubt it.'

They sat for a moment as she looked around, thinking how lucky she was to be having such an authentic experience while she was in Havana. Everything had been incredible, but she had a feeling that the food she was going to eat tonight would be her best yet.

'Your sister's husband isn't here?' she asked, suddenly realising that she hadn't met the young boy's father.

Mateo cleared his throat then. 'José, go see if Abuela needs any help.'

'She doesn't!' he exclaimed.

'But how about you see if she does?' Mateo asked softly. 'For me.'

She smiled at José as he reluctantly left, wondering why Mateo didn't want to speak in front of him, but she could sense he had something to tell her.

'Ana isn't my sister by blood,' he said. 'She's my sister-in-law.'

'Oh,' she said. 'I'm so sorry, I—'

'I think of her as a true sister, she's as much a part of this family as I am,' Mateo said. 'And José is as much my son as he was my brother's. I'd do anything for him.'

'Was?'

Mateo sat back in his chair, toying with the edge of the placemat. 'My brother was killed by a drunk driver,' he said. 'It's been a rough past year.'

Claudia's eyes filled with tears, her skin covered in goose pimples as she reached for him. 'I'm so sorry, Mateo. I wish I'd known sooner.'

He squeezed her fingers back. 'I liked that you didn't know. Sometimes it's easier talking to a stranger than someone who's seen my pain. I could be the old me when I was with you.'

'It's why you understood how I felt losing my friend,' she said.

'Sí,' he said. 'I lost my brother, and then my father died soon after. The doctors told us it was his heart, and my mother believes it was broken after losing his child. Life was too hard without his youngest son, he simply couldn't go on.'

'Did he work in the food truck too?' she asked.

'It was the three of us. We used to take turns, but we always made sure there were two of us on each shift.' His eyes lit up with the memory. 'We used to play music and talk and laugh. It was the best of times.'

No wonder he'd liked having the company when she'd joined him; the silence since losing two family members must have been deafening sometimes.

'Ana works with me as often as she can now, and sometimes my mother, but this past week they were both sick and I wanted them to rest. I'm lucky though, my customers are vibrant and full of life, they make me smile every day and it keeps my mind from going, how do you say, too dark?'

'I understand,' she said. 'It's one of the reasons I was worried about leaving my job, knowing I'd have so much time alone to my own thoughts, without anyone to distract me.'

She selfishly wondered if she wouldn't have met Mateo the way she had if his sister-in-law or mother had been by his side—perhaps fate had had a hand there, too.

As if on cue his family came out onto the terrace and the mood changed with the arrival of food. Mateo went to stand but his mother put her hand on his shoulder, saying something to him that Claudia guessed would translate to him staying put, and then he gently touched his mother's hand, looking up at her. The moment was tender, and Claudia hoped that one day if she ever had a son, he'd look at her and treat her the way Mateo did his mother. It was something else.

He caught her eye when his mother walked away, and Claudia had the most overwhelming feeling of how lucky she was to be there.

'Lunch is served,' his mother said when she returned, setting one enormous ceramic dish in the middle of the table and then taking her seat.

'It looks incredible,' she said. And it wasn't an exaggeration —it was a banquet of food on one plate.

'This is Mamá's famous Cuban paella. She loves seafood, so this is a special one filled with locally caught fish and shellfish. You're going to love it.'

'Please tell me she didn't buy seafood because I was coming? I didn't want any fuss.'

He shrugged. 'She didn't, I did.' She was going to scold him for spending extra money on her when all she cared about was being with him and his family, but she was quickly distracted.

She watched as they all held their hands out, and she did the same, taking Mateo's on one side and Ana's on the other. And it was Ana who said grace for them, her head slightly bowed and her eyes shut.

'Gracias, Señor, por esto alimentos y bendice las manos que los prepararon,' she said. 'Thank you, Lord, for this food, bless the hands that made it,' Mateo whispered, leaning in towards her to translate.

'Amen,' Ana finished.

'Amen,' they all said in unison.

They all sat silent a moment, looking at one another before dropping their hands, and Claudia instinctively knew that they were silently remembering those who weren't there. Her own family weren't religious, but being part of their blessing and seeing the food in front of her, knowing now how hard it was for many families in Cuba to simply put that food on the table, it made her appreciate being part of their tradition all the more. There was also so much love around the table, a quiet, unspoken feeling that warmed her just to be a part of.

'Claudia, Mateo tells us that you came to Cuba searching for answers,' his mother said. 'You have family you're trying to find?'

She nodded as Mateo served her, piling the rice and seafood on her plate.

'That's right, although I've all but abandoned hopes of discovering anything. I haven't had much luck yet.'

'So soon?' Ana asked. 'But you must keep searching if that's why you came here, no?'

'Mateo has been kind enough to show me around, but to be honest I don't know where else to search.' She didn't add that Mateo had been such a distraction that she'd probably not looked as widely as she should have. 'I think I was a little too ambitious, believing I could just come here and figure everything out, but it's been the most incredible trip anyway, so I'm very grateful all the same.'

'Your grandmother left you these clues that you have?' Ana asked. 'Mateo has told us a little about your journey.'

'It was actually her birth mother who left the clues, my grandmother passed before they were even found,' she explained. 'Which is how I ended up here trying to find out what her link to Cuba might be, if there even is one.'

They all started to eat then, and she watched the way José tucked into his food with gusto, eating so much more widely than she was used to seeing children eat. She tried not to groan with pleasure as she tasted the paella, smiling at Mateo when he caught her eye again. She doubted it would matter how many days or weeks passed by, he managed to make her stomach dance every time he looked at her.

It was only because Mateo's mother spoke that she looked away from him.

'Claudia, am I correct that you're trying to find out more about Esmeralda Diaz? Do you truly think she could be the connection?'

Claudia swallowed and set her fork down, reaching for her napkin and dabbing at the corners of her mouth. 'Yes, I think she could be. I thought perhaps the mystery surrounding her might have something to do with my grandmother, but that could just be my imagination getting carried away.'

'Esmeralda's maid is still alive, if you'd like to meet her,' his mother said. 'She's ninety-two years old and sometimes she's more lucid than other times, but if anyone knows the truth about what happened all those years ago, it's her.'

Claudia's heart skipped a beat. 'You could arrange that for me? I could actually meet her?'

'Did you not hear how grateful I am for my son's smile?'

She looked across at Mateo and saw him shaking his head at his mother, which only made her smile all the more, and José had started to giggle, clearly sensing his uncle's embarrassment.

'How much longer do you have in Cuba?' his mother asked.

'Only two days.' The words caught in Claudia's throat as she said them. *Two days.* She looked at Mateo, and then her eyes travelled around the table before landing on him again. *How can I fly back to London in two days, knowing I'll never see him again?* It wasn't so long ago she'd sworn off men for good to focus on herself. *I just didn't happen upon falling for someone in the place I least expected it.*

'Well, we'd best visit her tomorrow, then. I can't promise she'll give you the answers you need, but perhaps it's time the secret of the Diaz family is finally revealed? It's been a mystery far too long.'

'Thank you, it really does mean a lot to me.'

'Family is the most important thing in the world to us, Claudia,' his mother said, tears shining in her eyes. 'If me taking you to meet someone helps you to better understand your own family and your heritage, then of course I will do everything in my power to help you. It's important to under-stand the past, to feel the connection to those who've walked before us.'

Mateo's hand found hers beneath the table—he caught her fingers and let them rest over her knee. If there was one thing she'd learnt about Cuba, or *Cubans*, it was that nothing seemed more important to them than family and food. Not to mention how generous they all seemed to be.

Grandma, is it a coincidence that those were the two most important things in your life, too?

She'd missed her terribly since she passed, but right now as she sat surrounded by Mateo and his family, she felt an even deeper pain. A sadness that there was so much about her past that her grandmother hadn't known, that she could have been on this journey with her if the clues had been discovered a couple of years earlier.

But if they had been, she might never have met Mateo, or seen Havana with her own eyes.

She'd been married to her job then, so it was highly likely she would have said no, even if it meant the trip of a lifetime with her grandmother. By the time she'd left her job and changed her lifestyle, her grandmother had already passed.

'I'm going to miss you when you're gone,' Mateo whispered, his fingers warm against her leg. 'Does that seem strange, after only knowing you for a few days?'

She smiled at him, even though there was sadness in her heart just at the thought of saying goodbye. For some reason, it wasn't strange at all, because it was exactly how she was feeling. How had they only known each other a handful of days?

'I'm going to miss you, too.'

José jumped up then, declaring it time for chocolate, and they all laughed as they watched the little boy run back inside to the kitchen. This family had lost so much, Mateo had lost so

much, and yet they were still able to find joy in a child's enthusiasm, or in sharing a long lunch.

If anything, being in Havana had shown her that the decision she'd made to change her life had been the right one, that
living more simply was the right life for her. She just hadn't
banked on wishing she could do that somewhere that wasn't
London.

'Claudia, the last I heard of the Diaz family, they were
living in Florida,' Ana said, interrupting her thoughts. 'I'm not
sure if that's helpful or not? A friend of mine had read something about them in a newspaper a tourist left behind. She was
cleaning their room and glanced at the page they'd left it
open on.'

'It's unbelievably helpful, thank you,' she said, surprised at
how interested Ana seemed, or that she'd spoken at all after
being so quiet for the rest of lunch. 'Did it say anything about
them? What they're doing, perhaps?'

'Only that there was only one sister left, the youngest I
think, and some of the grandchildren had gone on to run the
company.'

'The company?' Claudia asked. 'The *sugar* company?'
She'd presumed the sugar empire had collapsed when the
family left Havana.

Ana shrugged, and when she glanced at Mateo he shook his
head, clearly not having any knowledge of what the company
was. She hadn't thought that it would still be operational,
because when she'd googled their name and tried to find out
more about Julio, everything had related to his prosperous years
in Cuba. But perhaps they'd changed the company name? She
knew he'd had business dealings in London and New York, he
was the largest seller of sugar in the world back then, after all, so
it made sense that he would have moved to America and started
over. Or maybe he'd simply closed one arm of the company and
continued on?

Mateo's mother reached for her hand over the table and gave it a pat. 'Leave it all with me, and I'll try to find out if anyone local has stayed in touch with the family. It's unlikely, but I can ask around at my church group and perhaps someone knows more about where the descendants are now?'

Claudia smiled her thanks as José reappeared, having already started eating the chocolate, evidenced by the smear of brown across his mouth and cheek.

'José!' his mother scolded.

But he ran straight past her to his uncle, who happily scooped him up onto his lap again without telling him off. It was clear the little boy knew exactly whom to run to when he was in trouble, for Mateo just shrugged and held out his hand for some chocolate, which José happily gave him.

'Chocolate?' José asked Claudia with a cheeky smile.

She grinned back at him. 'How could I resist?'

The next day, Claudia went back to the internet café—other than Mateo's food truck, it was the place she'd visited most during her time in Havana. But this time she didn't log in to her emails straight away, instead going to the British Airways website and cursing how long it took to open. Her fingers were restless on the mouse as she waited, her legs jittery as she finally clicked through to see if she could change her flight. She'd barely been able to sleep the night before, her stomach painfully full with the huge serving of paella she'd eaten, along with the sweet fried bananas they'd had after, and then her mind had started turning over everything she knew so far, all the little pieces of the puzzle that was her grandmother's past.

She'd come to Cuba to discover her grandmother's heritage, but somewhere along the way her heart had been captured by Mateo, which was starting to make it feel more like her own journey of discovery. And it had also influenced her decision to extend her stay by a few days.

The way she felt about him had taken her by surprise, she'd never been swept off her feet by a romance before, but she'd chosen to embrace the way she was feeling. Besides, if Mateo's mother was going to help her, then what difference did it make if she stayed a little longer? It would be rude not to stay and see what she discovered, not to mention the fact she was meeting the former Diaz maid today, and if she wasn't lucid they might have to visit another time. And with her scheduled flight in less than forty-eight hours, time wasn't something she had a lot of without making the change.

The flights came up and she saw there was one at the end of the week. She looked at the prices and times. She could just stay for another week; maybe until the end of next weekend. That would give her an extra five days in Cuba.

Before she could second-guess herself, much like when she'd booked the tickets in the first place, she confirmed the change in schedule and entered her credit card details to pay the changeover fare, before sitting back with a sigh of relief. Her jitters had disappeared immediately once she'd made the decision.

Next she logged in to her emails and glanced through them, smiling when she saw a new one from Charlotte as well as her father. But it was one she'd missed from a day ago that she quickly clicked on, seeing that her estate agent had been in touch. It appeared that someone was already interested in her flat and wanted to know if she'd consider selling before any of the advertising began, so she quickly replied and said yes, excited that someone had liked it so quickly. Then she went to the one from Charlotte.

I cannot believe you mentioned a man and then didn't give me details! Please tell me you've found a way to make your phone work? I'm dying to talk to you! I know we promised each other we'd live in the moment, and I'm so bloody pleased you are, but being six months pregnant is so boring and I need to live vicariously through you. All I can seize right now is the toilet bowl, because for some reason my darling unborn child didn't get the memo about only making Mummy sick for the first few months. I think I'm going to be unwell until the very end. Oh, and while I remember, we've decided that we want you to be the godmother, so you can spoil our little one and be her special person in the world. Please say yes! Now, go and kiss that prince again, would you? And don't forget any of the juicy details, I want to hear it all! Every. Single. Detail.

Claudia laughed out loud, finding it impossible not to picture her friend with her enormous stomach, feeling terribly unwell but at the same time desperate to hear about her holiday fling. She sent her a quick reply back, apologising for the lack of communication and reiterating that Mateo was every bit as delicious as she'd made him sound, and with a promise to share everything as soon as she was home. Then she went to the one from her father.

Hello darling, how are you? I've uncovered something here, from a much older colleague of mine who was something of a mentor to me early in my career. He actually met this Christopher Dutton, would you believe? Although he was most connected to the older Dutton who started the firm. But most interestingly, he said that he recalls with clarity that Christopher negotiated the biggest sugar deal ever made at the time from his London office, with a sugar baron from Cuba. Apparently Christopher was tipped to take over the company after that, which he did for a short time, but something happened that year, which led to him standing down as director. I don't know any more, but what I do know is that business card has to be a link to the Diaz family, and my gut feeling is that it has something to do with that sugar deal that was made all those years ago. I don't know how it's all linked to your grandmother, and I've racked my brain all day trying to piece the puzzle together, but this is the link between the business card and the crest, I'm certain of it.

I hope you're having a wonderful time away and finding time to relax. See you in a few days. Dad xx

Claudia pondered over his email, her eyes skimming back over the words as she considered what he'd said. It meant something. Just when she'd become disheartened, this was definitely something.

Depending on what she found out from the maid, and what Mateo's mother discovered about the family's whereabouts in Florida, she might just have a chance at solving the mystery, after all.

She quickly typed a reply, telling her dad she'd extended her trip and thanking him for all his detective work, before logging out. Claudia smiled to herself as she walked out of the café and back into the balmy Cuban sunshine, wondering how she was ever going to go back to the cloudy skies of London.

22

HAVANA, CUBA, EARLY 1951

Esmeralda cowered in the corner of her room, her father's face was so red he looked like he might burst. Never in her life had she been scared of him before, never had she held her hand to her face for fear he might strike her or even raise his voice.

But today, she was terrified.

'This is what I get for showering you with affection? For letting you accompany me to London? For indulging your every whim?' he bellowed. 'This is how you treat your papá!'

'Papá, I'm sorry,' she whispered through her tears. 'I'm so sorry, I didn't—'

'Silence!'

He held the letters, her precious, beautiful letters from Christopher, and crushed them in his hand, the paper crumpling as he balled his fist. She wanted to run and snatch them from him, to beg him to let them go, but she knew it wasn't a battle she would win. She could see her maid hovering outside the door in the hall, pressed to the wall as she peered in. Her last letter from Christopher must have been intercepted, someone had discovered her secret and divulged it to her father, but one thing she knew for certain was that it wasn't the woman cowering outside her door.

She knew it with absolute conviction, because Sofia looked as visibly pained as Esmeralda herself was. She'd have trusted Sofia with her life, and she still would. But someone had betrayed her, someone in their household, which had led her father to turn her room upside down and find the letters she'd so carefully hidden away.

'I thought I'd raised you to live with honour, to show your family respect at all times?' He shook his head. 'To not disrespect your father. And look what you've done to me? To our family!'

The way he spoke, his words cloaked with disappointment, filled with a bitter taste of disgust, made her fall to her knees.

'Papá, what can I do?' she begged. 'Please, tell me what I have to do to show you how sorry I am. I never meant to disrespect you, I'm sorry, I never intended for this to happen.'

She kept her head bowed, shaking as she stared at the ground, trying to show him her loyalty, her submission.

'If your mother were alive, this would never have happened,' he said, his voice cold now whereas before it had been full of emotion. He stepped away when she reached out to touch him. 'You should be married by now. I should never have indulged my own desire to keep you close. This is as much my fault as it is yours, but you will be the one to pay the price. I will not make a mistake again when it comes to my daughters.' He shook his head. 'You've always been my weakness, all of you girls, but never again.'

'Papá, it's not your fault,' she whispered, rising and rushing to him as he started to walk away, reaching for his hands. He didn't move and hope lifted within her as she wrapped her fingers around his. 'I have never disrespected you, I've always done everything I can to honour you and our family, but, Papà, surely you can understand that we can't help who we fall in love with. I never meant for this to happen! Please!'

The slap sent her reeling, it was so entirely unexpected. Her father had always been so gentle with his daughters, she'd never once feared he might strike her or her sisters, never, even though he was capable of such violence.

She cupped her face as he glowered down at her, hurting as much from the betrayal of his usual nature as the pain. What had happened to her lovely papá? Was she truly to blame for his rage, for the way he'd struck her?

'You will be married as soon as I can find a suitable husband for you, and Gisele soon after,' he said. 'You'd be best to forget all about this love you talk of, for you will never see this man again. You've made a fool of me, Esmeralda, and no one makes a fool of Julio Diaz! You're just lucky no one outside of this household knows what shame you've brought upon yourself.'

'Papá, please!' she begged. 'Please don't do this! I love him! He's to ask for my hand!'

'Enough!' he roared. 'You more than anyone in this household should understand the importance of a marriage alliance. You will marry a good Cuban boy and I won't hear another word about it.'

'But Papá, he wants to marry me, how can you not understand that! You can't make me marry anyone else, you can't, I won't! My heart belongs to Christopher.'

'Sofia!' he barked, ignoring Esmeralda and roughly pushing her aside when she tried to grab hold of him.

Her maid came scurrying in, her head bent. Esmeralda could see that her poor maid was shaking, as terrified of her father as she herself was. They both knew that he wouldn't turn his own flesh and blood out onto the street, but he wouldn't hesitate to do so to a maid if he felt betrayed.

'My daughter is not to be let out of this room,' he said, turning sharply on his heel before pausing at the door. 'And you'd do best to understand where your loyalties lie, otherwise you will find yourself looking for a new job with no references from this household. Am I clear?'

'Yes sir,' Sofia whispered.

'Papá!' Esmeralda screamed as her father started to walk away, raising her voice to a pitch she'd never done before in her quiet, proper life. But he never stopped, his boots heavy on the wooden floor as he walked away from the daughter who'd once been his favourite, his pride and joy. The daughter he'd always told meant everything in the world to him, the reminder of his wife that he still held so dearly in his heart. 'Papá, please!'

'I'm so sorry, Es,' Sofia said, her eyes brimming with tears as she held up the key to the door. 'I don't want to do this, I—'

'Shh, you don't have to say anything.' Esmeralda rushed forward and enveloped her in a hug, wetting her beloved maid's shoulder with her tears. 'I should never have drawn you into this. It's me who's sorry, this is not your fault.' She paused, still holding her in her arms as she leaned back. 'You do whatever he tells you to do, I don't want to be responsible for you losing your job.'

'It was Margo,' Sofia whispered, drawing her closer to whisper in her ear, speaking of the old woman who ran their household and had done for over two decades. 'She saw the letter addressed to me from London, she snatched it away and took it to your father before I could do anything, dragging me with her. They questioned me and I couldn't lie, I need this money for my family. I'm so sorry for betraying you, Miss Esmeralda, I tried to get here before him but he was too quick.'

Of course it had been Margo. The old woman had been in the household since her father was a boy, and he'd let her take over running the household when his wife had died. If only she'd been more careful somehow, if only she'd told Christopher not to write to her again, if only he'd spoken to her father before he'd left, maybe things could have been different. Her only regret was drawing Sofia into her deception; her own maid had risked her livelihood to protect her, and she never would have forgiven herself if her father dismissed her.

'You haven't betrayed me, Sofia,' she said, holding her even tighter. 'You're the only person other than my own sisters whom I trust, and nothing has changed. I will never forget your loyalty.'

'I'm sorry, Miss Esmeralda.'

When Sofia finally let go, they both stared at each other for a long moment, before her maid backed away, her eyes swimming, before she gently closed the door. And when she heard the key turn in the lock, leaving her alone in her room, Esmeralda sunk to the floor, her dress falling around her in a cloud of silk as she cried like she'd never in her life cried before.

That's when she saw the business card on the floor. It must have fallen from between the letters.

She crawled on her hands and knees, reaching out for it and staring at his name, before tucking it into her dress. Her father could keep her locked like a bird in a gilded cage and burn all Christopher's letters, but she was never going to let him find this.

Never.

23

HAVANA, CUBA, PRESENT DAY

'Her family were happy for us to visit her, but they said we're to stop questioning her if she gets upset or confused,' Mateo's mother said, looping her arm through Claudia's as they walked past the reception, following a nurse. 'She has good days and bad days, and we're not to bother her if it's a bad one.'

Claudia nodded, her excitement rising the closer they got to the room. The nurse knocked, and she couldn't help but notice the peeling paint and threadbare carpet of the old building as they stood and waited. But her attention was diverted the moment they stepped into the room and saw an old, white-haired woman sitting near the window, a warm blanket draped around her shoulders.

'Sofia, there are some ladies here to see you,' the nurse said, going over to her and patting her arm. 'Old friends of yours, I think.'

The old woman turned, her eyes cloudy, and Claudia wondered if she could even see them, but within seconds her frail arm lifted and she pointed with her finger for them to sit in the chairs.

'Friends, you say?' Her voice quavered as if she hadn't had

use of it for some time. 'Have I met you before? Are you friends of my daughter?'

'I'm Beatriz,' Mateo's mother said. 'I do know your daughter, very well in fact, but I also believe you knew my parents. My father worked as the chef at the Diaz household many, many years ago, when you were there.'

'Diego?' the old woman said, her face lighting up as she said his name. 'You're Diego's girl?'

Beatriz nodded. 'Sí, Sofia. I'm Diego's girl. Unfortunately he passed some years ago, but I have wonderful memories of all the years we spent together.'

The old woman's face dropped, her mouth bracketed by a frown. The nurse said goodbye then, she'd been hovering in the doorway, and said to call if they needed her, and Claudia sat on the edge of the bed and watched as Beatriz took the chair closest to Sofia.

'Diego,' the old woman said, with a faraway lilt to her voice. 'We could never walk past the kitchen without our stomachs growling. He was the best cook in town, and he always saved the best for us. So many households, the staff ate separate meals, but not at the Diaz home. We ate what the family ate, no matter what.'

'He was a very good cook,' Beatriz agreed. 'And my son is almost as good. He has the most popular food truck in Havana, so I'm very, very proud of him.'

They sat a moment, before Sofia lifted her hand and waved it at her. 'Who is this girl? Is she your daughter?'

Beatriz smiled. 'This is Claudia. She is a friend of my son's, and she wanted to visit you today. She's actually come all the way from London to visit Cuba.'

'London?' The old woman looked confused. 'Do I know you?' She leaned forward as if to peer at Claudia. 'You don't look familiar.'

Claudia took her chance, smiling as she spoke, hoping the

older woman would warm to her. 'I'm here to learn about the Diaz family, and Beatriz was kind enough to offer to bring me here, to you. She tells me that you were a maid to the eldest daughter, Esmeralda?'

Claudia knew she was holding her breath as she waited for a response, but she couldn't help it. But instead of replying, the woman's eyes filled with tears and she clutched her hands to her chest, shaking her head, as if she'd just brought up a disturbing memory.

'Sofia?' Beatriz said. 'Please, we can stop if you're upset. I'm sorry, we shouldn't have—'

Just as Beatriz looked around at Claudia, her eyes wide, Sofia spoke, her voice barely more than a whisper.

'The letters. If only I'd hidden all the letters, if only I'd been more careful to check the mail before anyone else each day,' she said as she started to softly cry. 'If he hadn't found them, none of this would have happened.'

'What letters?' Claudia asked, leaving the bed and crouching down low next to Sofia. She took her hand and held it, noticing how paper thin and cold the woman's skin was despite the warmth of the room. 'What did he find? What letters are you talking about?'

Sofia shook her head and moved back into the chair as if she were afraid, looking more like a scared young girl than an old lady.

'Miss Esmeralda should never have forgiven me. He should never have found the letters. I should have been more careful.'

Claudia glanced at Beatriz, who looked as puzzled as she felt. Was the old woman lucid or imagining things? And what letters could she be talking about?

'I think we should go and let Sofia rest,' Beatriz said, starting to rise, but Claudia wasn't going to leave before at least trying to find out more. Surely they didn't have to go just yet? She'd come all this way and if she could only get another clue to help her...

Sofia suddenly clasped Claudia's hand tightly, her milky eyes trained on her. Claudia had thought she might be blind or almost blind from the look of her eyes, but she seemed to stare right at her now as if her vision was crystal clear.

'Do you know where Miss Esmeralda is? Can you tell her I'm sorry. Tell her I never should have locked that door. Please, ask if she'll forgive me?'

Claudia clasped her hand back as tears slowly started to fall down Sofia's sunken cheeks.

'I don't know where Esmeralda is,' Claudia said softly. 'That's why I came here, because I thought you might know what happened to her? I'm trying to find out why her family never looked for her to see if something more sinister happened. Do you know what happened the day she went missing?'

Sofia looked out the window then, her fingers loosening and eventually letting go of Claudia's hand, as if she were lost in thought.

'I think we should go, this is probably enough for one day,' Mateo's mother said, before lowering her voice. 'I don't think she knows anything, and for all we know Esmeralda may have died and her family could have covered it up. Perhaps that's why she's so upset?'

Claudia couldn't have been more surprised. 'You think they covered up Esmeralda's death?' She swallowed. 'You think it could be *murder*?'

'They certainly had enough money to cover something like that up,' Beatriz whispered, 'and there were certainly rumours over the years.'

Claudia opened her mouth again, wondering why no one had said anything to her before about the rumours, but before she could speak, Sofia beat her to it.

'Miss Esmeralda didn't die, nobody killed her,' Sofia said, rocking back and forth in her chair as she started to laugh. 'Miss Esmeralda's family knew where she was all that time, but we were paid to not tell anyone. We knew to keep our mouths shut, otherwise we'd be out on the street and Mr Diaz would make sure no one ever hired us again.'

'So you know what happened to her?' Claudia asked, barely able to breathe as she stared at the old woman. 'Do you know what happened the night she disappeared?'

'Esmeralda was with Christopher,' she said. 'When her father found the letters, she had to run away. He couldn't keep her locked up forever, people were starting to ask questions.'

'Christopher?' Claudia repeated, quickly picking up her handbag and taking out the business card she'd been carrying with her ever since she'd been given the little box. She stared at it and then looked up, her hand shaking as she held it. 'Christopher Dutton, from London?'

Sofia's smile turned to tears then, as she curled back into the chair again, staring out the window, withdrawn from the world.

'Tell Miss Esmeralda I'm sorry,' she said, before starting to repeat it over and over again. 'Tell Miss Esmeralda it's all my fault. Tell Miss Esmeralda I never should have locked the door.'

This time when Beatriz wanted to leave, Claudia rose and went willingly, but not before taking the blanket that had slipped from the chair and tucking it carefully around Sofia's shoulders. The old woman was like a frail little bird, and Claudia couldn't tell whether she was present or away with the fairies now, but in the end she'd come away with something and for that she would be forever grateful.

'Do you think she's just a confused old lady?' Beatriz asked as they waved to the nurse and told her to check in on Sofia, before walking down the hall to the car park.

Claudia held out the business card that she was still clutching, letting Beatriz see it. 'This is the only other clue I was given, so I truly believe she's telling the truth,' she said. 'All this time we've had no connection between the Diaz crest and the business card, but if Sofia is correct and Esmeralda was with this Christopher?' She stared at the card. 'It has to be this man, doesn't it? I mean, it all seems to finally make sense now.'

'I know she wasn't making sense in there, but I agree, it's too much of a coincidence that she mentioned a man named Christopher. I'm inclined to think you're right.'

Claudia's heart skipped a beat. 'If this is the connection, then it means that perhaps I've come all the way to Cuba, when in fact what I was looking for was in London all this time? I think maybe I should have focused all my energies on this Christopher Dutton.' Although her dad had been doing that and he'd come up with little so far that could help them. Not to mention that Christopher was deceased and had no children. But now that she knew this, would her search send her back to London?

'Do you think there's any chance that Esmeralda could still be alive, and in London?' Claudia asked.

Beatriz shook her head. 'I think someone would have heard from her, if she was. But I think you're right that all your clues could be pointing you back to London.'

They reached the car and Claudia's eyes met Beatriz's across the roof. 'Thank you for bringing me here today,' she said. 'I was honestly starting to think that I'd never find out anything useful, and the more I think about it, the more I want to discover the truth, for my grandmother's sake. This is by far the best lead I've had, so thank you.'

Beatriz's smile was warm as they got into the car, but her touch was even warmer when she pressed something into Claudia's palm.

'What's this?' she asked.

'Remember I told you I'd ask around, to see if anyone knew the whereabouts of the Diaz family in Florida, after Ana mentioned them that night?'

Claudia felt her eyes widen as she nodded.

'This might help you. It's the address of Marisol Diaz.'

Her fingers closed over the piece of paper. '*Marisol?* You've found the youngest Diaz sister?' Beatriz had had this information with her all day, and she was only disclosing it to her now?

Beatriz started up the engine. 'Sí, Claudia. I wanted to wait, until after the meeting, but I certainly wasn't expecting much from dear old Sofia. It truly seems as if your journey has only just begun.'

Claudia sat back and looked at the piece of paper, reading the name and the address over in her mind, wishing she could find a way to show Mateo's mother just how grateful she was. But Florida *and* London? She was surprised there were now leads that pointed her in completely different directions, to completely different countries.

'Claudia,' Beatriz suddenly said, as if she could read her mind. Claudia noticed that she kept both hands on the steering wheel and her eyes on the road, not glancing at her once as she spoke this time. 'Promise me you won't break my son's heart? I know you can't stay forever, that you have to go soon, but he's had enough pain to last him a lifetime. I can't stand to see him hurt again.'

She looked out the window, biting down on her lip as she stared out the window. 'I promise,' she murmured. What she didn't say was that she was far more in danger of breaking her own heart than she was of breaking his.

They might have only known each other a handful of days, but nothing about saying goodbye to the first man who'd ever made her feel truly alive was going to be easy.

'I actually extended my stay for an extra five days, until Sunday,' she heard herself saying. 'I was going to tell Mateo tonight.'

What she wanted to tell the woman seated beside her was that she wanted to spend as much time as possible with her son, that it was one of the reasons she'd chosen to stay longer; that even though she was desperate to find out more about her grandmother's heritage, she was even more interested in soaking up more hours with Mateo.

'Good,' was all Beatriz said, but Claudia saw the way her shoulders softened, one hand falling away from the wheel to rest on her leg as if had been something she'd been wanting to say for some time.

Claudia touched her forehead to the cool window glass as Havana passed by in a blur. *I'm going to miss this place.* Something about Cuba had gotten under her skin, and as her departure date neared, it only made her want to find a reason to come back again. And soon. 'Claudia, do you have anywhere to be tonight?' Beatriz asked.

She turned and shook her head. 'No, I don't.'

'How about I cook my huevos habaneros for you,' she said. 'Mateo said you were interested in Cuban cooking? You might like to cook alongside me?'

She laughed. *More like I'm interested in your son and he's irresistible in the kitchen.* 'I have to confess that I'm a terrible cook, but Mateo has been very patient with me. I'm afraid you'll have to expect very little when it comes to my cooking skills.'

'Then my gift to you when you leave Havana will be a recipe,' she said, tapping her fingers against the steering wheel as an upbeat song came on the radio. 'You can go home and cook your family one of our favourite meals, so you never forget your time here. What do you think of that?'

Unexpected tears pooled in Claudia's eyes. Everyone had been so kind to her, but none more so than Beatriz and Rosa; both older women who seemed so generous with their time and limited supplies.

'I would love that. Thank you.'

Beatriz took one hand off the steering wheel to pat Claudia's hand. 'My Mateo, he smiles at everyone, but his eyes, now *they* don't smile for everyone.'

Claudia watched her, her heart skipping a beat.

'But with you?' Beatriz chuckled. 'His eyes are smiling, every time he looks at you. It's good for him.' She patted her hand again. 'It's good for his mamá, too, to see him like that. To know that he's still capable of such happiness.'

'Your family,' Claudia said, trying to disguise the choke in her throat. 'You've all been through so much, you've *lost* so much, but you still seem to have such open hearts.'

Beatriz was silent a long moment before finally speaking. 'My sons, they were best friends. From the moment Mateo's brother was born, he loved him with all his heart, and he took such responsibility for looking after him. They were inseparable as children, and they were best friends even as adults, it was like nothing I'd ever seen before, the relationship they had. They would do anything for each other.'

Claudia didn't know what to say, so she stayed silent.

'When they fought they would come to blows, tumbling through my house with their fiery tempers even as grown men, but within hours they would be sitting out in the courtyard having a beer. Nothing could keep them apart,' she sighed. 'My husband and I, we used to pray that nothing would ever divide them, because the relationship they had was so special.'

'Mateo must have taken his brother's death very hard,' Claudia said.

'He did, but he never let us see,' she said. 'He became little José's father overnight, and everything he's done since has been for that boy. He truly loves him as much as his brother did, which at least means José will grow up with a second father equally as good as the first.'

Claudia nodded and went back to gazing out the window again. She'd be lying to herself if she didn't admit to a fantasy where Mateo followed her and came to London, or perhaps travelled with her. But that would mean leaving his family behind, and she knew that he would never do that, nor would

she want him to. His place was here, just like her place was in
London.

Claudia bit down on her lip and tried not to think about
leaving. She had a beautiful evening to look forward to and a
recipe to learn—there wasn't time to dwell on what couldn't be.

24

'So I hear you're not leaving tomorrow after all?' Mateo's voice took her by surprise. She expected that perhaps *she'd* taken *him* by surprise, standing in his mother's kitchen washing dishes, but if she had, then he didn't show it. His arms looped around her from behind, and his lips touched her neck, almost making her drop the soapy dish she was holding.

'You're right, I'm not,' she said, leaning back a little into him. 'It seems I'm now the queen of changing flights.'

'How much longer?'

'Almost another week,' she said. 'But I'm actually flying out to Miami, not London.'

He moved away from her then, and she watched as he went to the stovetop and took the lid off a pot, reaching for a spoon and taking a mouthful.

'Hungry?' she asked, resuming her dishwashing.

'Yes. I'm terrible at remembering to keep something for myself, but thankfully someone always leaves enough for me.'

'Your mother taught me how to cook,' Claudia said. 'Would you like to taste what we made?'

'You cooked this with my mother?' He was holding the spoon with the most comical look on his face.

'Don't look so surprised!'

'Well, she doesn't share her recipe with just anyone, or have just anyone in her kitchen for that matter.' Mateo walked back towards her with a grin on his face that made her laugh. 'You must be something special.'

'Really?'

He put his arm around her and nudged into her. 'Really,' he whispered as he kissed her.

Claudia sighed as she leaned back in his arms, reaching for the tea towel so she could dry her hands, before placing them on his chest.

'I want to show you my country properly before you leave,' he said, suddenly appearing more serious, earnest even as he stared into her eyes. 'Will you come away with me for a few days?'

'What about the food truck?'

He shrugged. 'You let me worry about the food truck.'

'Then yes,' she said. 'There's nothing I'd like more than to spend a few days travelling with you.'

He grinned and let go of her, taking down a bowl and filling it with the leftovers. He stood back then, watching her as he ate. She went back to doing the dishes, more comfortable with his gaze on her now than she'd have been even a few days ago.

'Where will we go, on this trip?' she asked.

'First I'm going to walk with you all through Old Havana, so you've seen every bit of it and tried all the very best food, and then we'll take a road trip,' he said. 'I want you to see the true beauty of Cuba, the Viñales National Park, maybe even Cayo Jutías. Can you snorkel?'

'I can swim?' she said hopefully.

He gave her a wink that sent her heart thudding to her toes.

'You're going to fall in love with Cuba, Claudia.'

She gave him a shy smile. *Perhaps I've fallen in love with Cuba already?*

'Maybe, if we have time, we could even go to Cayo Largo,' he said. 'It's been a long time since I've been there, I dived it once with my brother, and it's like nothing you've ever seen before.'

'You're sure you want to go back? I mean—'

'It's time for some new memories,' he said. 'Give me a day, and I'll have everything organised.'

Claudia folded the towel she'd been holding. 'I'll let Rosa know I'm leaving then.'

They stared at each other for a long moment, before Claudia dropped her gaze.

'Would you like to stay?' he asked, the timbre of his voice lower than usual, his eyes still on hers when she looked up.

'In your mother's house?' she shook her head, going to him and standing on tiptoe to press a kiss to his cheek. 'No. Tonight I'm going back to my room, but I'll see you tomorrow, okay?'

'Tomorrow,' he replied, catching her around the waist and stealing a kiss on the lips. 'And your paella wasn't half bad, either.'

She tipped her head back and laughed. It was a half-hearted compliment, but she'd take it.

'I'm going to miss you, Rosa,' Claudia said the next day when it was time to leave. Mateo had organised their trip in record time, and although he was cooking all day he wanted to leave by midafternoon. Ana was going to take over the food truck for the night, and then it was going to be closed for three days while he vacationed with her. It was almost surreal how quickly it had all happened.

'Come here, my beautiful girl,' Rosa said, opening her arms and embracing her. 'We're going to miss you, too.'

'I appreciate your lovely hospitality. It's been so wonderful staying here with you.'

'Don't forget to write and tell me what you discover about your grandmother,' Rosa said. 'You've drawn us all in with your clues, it would be nice to know how the story ends.'

'I will. I promise.'

She turned and found Carlos standing there, dressed in his standard uniform of white pants and shirt, and she grinned the moment she laid eyes upon him.

'Here he is,' she said. 'How lucky was I to cross paths with you the day I arrived?'

He took off his hat and gave her a warm hug. 'Have fun on your travels, Claudia.'

'Thank you.' She stood back and beamed at Rosa and Carlos, wishing she could have had longer with them. She'd left Rosa a generous tip in her room, wanting her to find it after she'd left so there was no embarrassment on Rosa's behalf, but she still wished she could have done more for her.

There was a rumble of an engine behind her and she instinctively knew it was Mateo. When she turned and saw him, her stomach fluttered.

'Adiós, Claudia!' Rosa and Carlos both called as she walked to the car and Mateo jumped out, one hand to her waist as he dipped his head for a quick kiss before putting her luggage in the back.

She got in, giddy from the anticipation of what was to come as he reached for her hand.

'Ready?' he asked.

She laughed. 'As I'll ever be.'

Early that evening, after exploring Old Havana and eating too much pizza and ice cream, they took a short flight to Cayo Largo; the place that had been last on Mateo's list when he'd pitched the idea of travelling together. They'd arrived just before dark and she'd already fallen in love, although she couldn't wait to explore in the morning when the sun came up. A beach holiday was exactly what she'd needed, and the moment her toes had touched the sand, she'd known she was precisely where she was supposed to be.

After they'd checked in to the beachfront hotel Mateo had booked for them, they'd left their bags in their room, taken their shoes off and walked straight out onto the beach. There was something about feeling the sand beneath her feet, hearing the roar of the ocean—it reminded her of the very first time she'd walked the boardwalk of the Malecón.

Mateo reached for her hand and they started to walk, slowly, not in a hurry to be anywhere. 'When day breaks, you're going to have your breath taken away.'

'I can imagine.' She inhaled, the sea air filling her nostrils.

'The water is the most pristine, vivid blue you've ever seen, and the sea life is incredible.'

'Oh that's right, I'm going to take up snorkelling, right?'

'You are,' he said, letting go of her hand and slipping his arm around her waist instead, hugging her closer. 'You're going to see the most beautiful coral reef, it's amazing, and we might be lucky enough to see dolphins or even sea turtles. I can't wait to share it with you.'

'In full disclosure, I haven't even been swimming in years, but I'm sure it's just like riding a bicycle, right?'

Mateo just laughed and murmured something that she didn't catch, his lips against her hair as he drew her even closer.

'Last time I came here, it was the most magical time of year. Hundreds of sea turtles had come to shore to lay their eggs in this beautiful white sand, it was incredible.'

Her fingers splayed around his hip as she nudged even closer. 'That's when you came here with your brother.'

They stopped walking then, and she studied Mateo's side profile in the moonlight, as he stared out towards the water.

'It was,' he finally said. 'It was our last trip together. Before José came along, we took every chance we could to snorkel or dive together, but that trip, when we came here, it was the first time we'd spent time just the two of us in a while.'

She gave him a moment, alone with his thoughts. Claudia sat down on the sand, and eventually Mateo sat with her.

'I miss him so damn much,' he said, drawing his knees up as she huddled closer, mirroring the way he was sitting. 'Sometimes I expect him to walk through a door or when I'm cooking in the truck I expect him to call out or turn up the music and sing.'

'It doesn't get any easier,' she said. 'Everyone says time heals everything, but I call bullshit.'

He interlaced their fingers, his gaze still out on the dark ocean.

'We sat here one day, in the sunshine after diving for hours and exploring the reef, and we talked about what we would do, if we could dream.'

'And what did you dream of?' she asked.

'Years ago, we were both working as chefs in hotels and decided to open the food truck.' He laughed. 'Well I should say I opened it, and then Ana finally agreed that he should join me. But I'd already called it Mateo's so we never changed the name, and then my father joined us, too.'

She could picture him, side by side with his brother, as they worked.

'But we had this crazy idea to make a business of our sauces,' he said. 'We'd read about people paying for meal deliveries in other countries, but that just wouldn't work here, but our sauces?' he shook his head. 'Crazy, I know. But we can dream, can't we?'

'I don't think it's crazy,' she said. 'Some of the best ideas we have come from dreaming big like that.'

He turned to her. 'It was a lifetime ago, and it's just me now anyway,' he said.

She wanted to ask him more, but it seemed that Mateo was no longer interested in the past. He touched her cheek, cupping it in his palm, as he gently touched her lips with his. And as she slowly lowered herself to the soft sand below, she forgot all the questions she was going to ask him and lost herself to his kisses.

The next day they rose early, eating a breakfast of fruit and pastries before heading out to the water. Mateo hadn't been overpromising when he'd said the white sandy beach and blue ocean would be like nothing she'd ever seen before—it was so beautiful it took her breath away.

'Look,' Mateo said as they stood, her toes curling into the soft sand as they looked out at the water.

She shielded her eyes from the sun and followed his gaze. There was a pod of dolphins swimming past, nudging up and down through the water. She couldn't believe it.

'You weren't lying when you said how much I'd love it here.'

'Let's just hope we don't see a crocodile.'

'When we're snorkelling?' she yelped.

He grinned. 'I'm told there's never been a tourist eaten before, so you should be safe.'

As she froze in terror, he winked and began to laugh

She would have punched him for teasing her like that, only he ran off towards the water, his towel and hotel key card discarded as he jogged. Claudia peered out, trying to focus on the dolphins and not think about anything in the ocean that could eat her.

But the moment she was in the water, the temperature

balmy, like nothing she'd ever experienced before, she forgot all about crocodiles.

'It feels so good, doesn't it?'

Mateo swam up behind her and she floated on her back, staring up at the cloudless blue sky. She wished she could bottle the feeling Cuba gave her and take it home with her; to draw on when she needed a lift or just to bring the memories back to her. But when Mateo's hands touched her shoulders, blocking the sun from her eyes as he stood over her in the waist-deep water, she wished that she could bottle him, too.

'We forgot to get our masks and snorkels,' he said. 'I'll be back soon.'

Claudia watched him go, admiring his wide shoulders and golden skin as he jogged back up the beach to the little shack that rented snorkels. Within minutes he returned, helping to fix hers on her face and getting the snorkel set up so she could breathe. It took a bit of practice, but eventually her mouth was filling with air instead of water.

Mateo took her hand and they swam side by side as she got the hang of breathing, not taking notice of how far out they were as she admired the flawless coral and colourful sea life. They didn't lift their heads for what felt like hours, and when they finally did she couldn't believe how far they were from the beach. They'd swum a long way.

'I think it's time for margaritas and something good to eat,' Mateo said.

She moved closer to him, treading water as she looked around before looping her arms around his neck. 'I was thinking of a siesta, but margaritas definitely sound good to me.'

'Siesta?' he said, looking comical with his mask pushed up to his forehead, which rose with his eyebrows.

She swatted at him, knowing exactly what he was thinking. 'I was thinking we needed the *rest* after all this swimming.'

'We do need to rest,' he said, splashing water at her and leaving her eyelashes dripping. She blinked as he started to swim away, on his back, doing a lazy kind of kick that barely propelled him. 'Because tonight we're going to eat too much food, drink too much alcohol and dance on the beach in the dark.'

She liked the sound of that. Claudia pulled her mask back down and put her snorkel in her mouth, catching up to Mateo and then going back to admiring the reef. Exploring the ocean hadn't been something she'd even thought of when she'd booked her trip to Cuba; she'd simply wanted to piece together the clues she had and figure out what it all meant.

The clues can wait a few days. Grandma would have wholeheartedly approved of me taking time to enjoy the sights. If her grandmother had been alive, she'd have wanted to hear every detail of her travels, and she'd certainly have wanted to hear about Mateo. Her grandmother always soaked up Claudia's tales as if she were living vicariously through her; and strangely enough she'd been the only one in her family who hadn't fawned over her ex-fiancé. Perhaps she'd known all along that he wasn't right for her.

'How are you feeling about that siesta?' Mateo asked when they both lifted their heads, the water shallow enough to walk on the sand.

She took off her mask and snorkel and handed them to him with a grin. 'Race you back to the room?'

Mateo ran through the water ahead of her, grabbing both their towels and jogging backwards, staying just far enough ahead of her that she couldn't grab them from his hands.

'I can't go back to our room dripping wet!' she cried.

'Cariño, this is Cuba,' he said, spreading his arms wide. 'No one cares!'

She laughed and started to walk, her hair wet down her back, droplets still on her skin as she smiled up at the sun.

Mateo was right; what did anyone care if she was wet from the ocean?

With a sudden burst of energy she sprinted past him, grabbing her towel and laughing as she ran. Cuba was good for the soul; or at least it had certainly been good for hers.

It was finally time to leave Havana; after all these days, all the hours of wanting her time to drag on as long as possible, it was time to go, and there was nothing she could do to delay the inevitable. They'd relaxed on the pristine white beaches, swum in turquoise oceans and explored a lush, tropical national park together, their final four days together crammed full of adventure and holidaying, and she'd done everything she could not to think about the end, but it was finally there.

'It sounds silly saying I'm going to miss you.'

Claudia was long past hiding her feelings for Mateo. If this was to be the last time she kissed him, then she wasn't going to miss it, even if they were in an airport surrounded by bustling crowds of people.

'I'm going to miss you, too,' she whispered, looping her arms around his neck and drawing him down for a kiss. He didn't need encouraging, his arms scooping around her waist and drawing her forward and into his body. It was a kiss that should have been shared in private, but Claudia was long past caring.

When he finally pulled away, he shook his head. 'My hermosa chica,' he said, bending and pressing one final, slow kiss to her lips. 'My beautiful girl.'

'I guess this is goodbye,' she murmured, as tears started to fall from her lashes and wet her cheeks.

Mateo was smiling, but his eyes were damp too as he carefully wiped her cheeks with the back of his knuckles. 'Don't cry, Claudia. We were so lucky to cross paths, even for such a short time.'

She nodded, taking a step back and clutching her ticket and passport in one hand. She needed to go now, before she changed her mind about leaving.

'Goodbye Mateo,' she said, swallowing and starting to turn.

'I'll see you again,' he called after her.

And as she walked to her gate, towards the plane that would take her to Florida and hopefully to uncover once and for all the mystery of her grandmother's adoption, she hoped that Mateo was right, because she couldn't stand to think she'd never see him again. The thought was almost enough to break her heart.

25

HAVANA, CUBA, 1951

Every day when it was time for Marisol to come and visit her, something lifted within Esmeralda. She'd been a prisoner since her father had discovered her betrayal; months of being kept largely in her bedroom, confined to her quarters within the house. She was fortunate—she had her own sitting room off her bedroom and a bathroom—but it was like being a bird in a gilded cage, and she was starting to go mad. Her maid was allowed to tend to her as required, and she brought Esmeralda food throughout the day, but mostly it was with a lowered gaze, placing the tray and then scurrying out.

Like clockwork she heard the gentle knock at the door and she knew it was Sofia come to deliver Marisol. She found herself holding her breath until the moment the door opened and her little sister came running, her arms wide as she threw herself at Esmeralda's legs.

'Hello my darling,' she said, bending to hug her. 'It's so good to see you.'

Marisol giggled and pressed her hand to Esmeralda's stomach. 'Is the baby kicking?' she asked.

Esmeralda smiled down at her before glancing up at Sofia.

Her maid was the only other person in on her secret; what if her father found out there was a baby on the way? She didn't even want to think about it, imagining being tossed out onto the street. She hoped it wouldn't come to that, but at some point she was going to have to tell him, otherwise the baby would arrive and then it would come as even more of a shock to everyone.

Unless, of course, she was gone by then.

'Was there word from my cousin?' she asked in a low voice when Marisol had let go of her and was climbing up onto her bed. 'From Alejandro?'

Sofia turned and softly shut the door, before scurrying back. 'Yes, he sent this.'

Esmeralda opened her palm as her maid reached into the pockets of her apron and passed her a folded square of paper. She knew how much danger she was putting her in after the last letter debacle, but she'd had no one else to ask. Her sisters would have done anything for her, but the moment they discovered her secret, it would be almost impossible for them to keep it from Papá. If he thought they were complicit in what she was planning, he would make life difficult for them as well, and that was not something she wanted to be responsible for.

She looked down at the note in her hand and quickly unfolded it, breathing a sigh of relief when she saw what he'd written. He was coming. Alejandro wasn't her favourite cousin for nothing.

'He will come?' Sofia asked.

'He will come,' she replied, giving her maid a quick hug while Marisol was still entertained. 'How will I ever thank you for everything you've done for me?'

Sofia held her tightly. 'I will never forgive myself for not protecting you. I don't need thanks.'

'What happened with the letters, it was my fault, not yours,' Esmeralda insisted. 'You have nothing to feel guilty for.'

'I'm supposed to look after you, Miss Esmeralda. It's my job.'

With tears in her eyes, her maid started to back away. 'I'll come back in an hour for Miss Marisol.'

'Thank you,' she replied. 'Oh, and Sofia? Would you ask my sisters if they might be able to come in and visit me tomorrow morning? It's my twentieth birthday and I'd very much like to see them both.'

Sofia nodded. 'Of course.'

'It's your birthday tomorrow?' Marisol asked from behind her, sitting atop the big bed like a little princess. 'Can we have cake?'

Esmeralda laughed, going to join her and putting her arm around her little sister. 'Yes, my love, I'm sure if you ask María and Gisele, they will make sure there's cake.'

'May I touch the baby again?'

Esmeralda lay back on the pillows, as Marisol placed first her hand to her stomach and then her ear, giggling as she declared she could hear the baby snoring, which was of course Esmeralda's stomach grumbling for a snack.

She watched Marisol, imagining a life without her baby sister in it, wondering if she could truly walk away from it all, from her family. They'd always been the most important thing in the world to her, but if her father was going to exile her for her pregnancy, then what choice did she have?

'Papá said you're getting married soon,' Marisol suddenly said, jumping down from the bed and tugging at Esmeralda's hand. 'Will I get to wear a pretty dress?'

Esmeralda went still. 'When did Papá tell you this?'

Marisol skipped away to the other side of the room, where Esmeralda always kept some toys and drawing pencils for her. 'This morning at breakfast,' she called over her shoulder. 'He said everything's organised, and that you'll be married by the end of the month.'

Esmeralda looked down at her stomach, placing her hand there as she tried to stay calm and breathe, not wanting her sister to know that anything was wrong.

'And did Papá say whom I was marrying?' Esmeralda asked. 'He's keeping all of this a surprise from me, just like you've kept my baby a special surprise.'

Marisol shook her head, holding up two dolls and passing one to Esmeralda. She took it, forcing a smile as her mind started to race. Time was running out; she needed to leave Cuba, and she needed to leave now.

26

Esmeralda sat on the window seat in her bedroom, her body turned slightly away from the door. She had an embroidered shawl around her shoulders and draped slightly over her midsection to disguise her stomach, on the off chance that her father came into the room. She doubted it, but she wanted to be careful. Her maid had run up a few moments earlier to tell her that her cousin, Alejandro, had arrived, and within minutes she heard a scuffle outside the door. She waited, listening to the key being turned in the lock, but it wasn't Alejandro who entered.

It was Gisele and María.

She leapt to her feet, forgetting her shawl as she hurried towards them. They'd sat outside her door often, talking to her through the wall, but to see both of them like this? It was all she'd wanted.

'It's so good to see you!' she cried as the door shut behind them. Clearly it had been Sofia who'd let them in, she was one of the only members of the household with a key after all, and she would make certain to thank her later.

Gisele had thrown her arms around her and was crying as she hugged her, but María was standing back.

'Esmeralda, you're...'

Gisele let go of her, wiping her eyes, before they widened in surprise. She'd clearly been in such a hurry to rush across the room that she hadn't immediately noticed.

'Pregnant,' Esmeralda whispered, finally saying the word out aloud. 'I'm pregnant.'

María enveloped her in her arms then, holding her as Esmeralda tried not to cry. All these months of keeping a secret, not wanting to implicate her sisters, and now they finally knew. She had no idea how little Marisol had kept her secret.

'What are you going to do?' Maria asked, leading her back to the window seat so they could all sit together. 'When will you tell Papá? I've been loath to tell you, but he's said he's found a husband for you. That you'll soon be married.'

Esmeralda swallowed. 'I'm going to leave Havana,' she said, seeing the horror on each of her sisters' faces. 'I don't see that I have any other choice.'

'Is that why Alejandro is here?' Gisele asked. 'You're going to ask him to help you, aren't you?'

She nodded, folding her hands in her lap. 'I am.'

María let out a loud sigh. 'He's the reason we were able to sneak up here,' she said. 'Papá invited him for a drink and we knew he wouldn't notice.'

'I almost forgot,' Gisele said, taking something from her pocket. 'Happy birthday, darling sister.'

'Oh yes, Esmeralda! Happy birthday!'

Both of her sisters embraced her, holding on just a little longer than usual, wondering how many hugs they would share.

'Thank you,' she said, opening the gift and seeing it was a small box of her favourite chocolates. 'I cannot wait to eat these. This baby is hungry all the time!'

Her sisters laughed with her, both of them touching her stomach and smiling. She knew they were happy for her, but there would also be worry there, for how could there not be? It wasn't as if she were married and they could celebrate her impending arrival.

'Has there been any word from Christopher?' she asked. 'Have you heard anything at all?'

Gisele shook her head, but it was María who spoke. 'The deal is still going ahead, that's all I was able to find out, but things haven't been the same since...' her voice drifted away.

'Since I was locked in here?' she asked.

María nodded. 'Papá has changed, he's not the same as he used to be.'

'He said you broke his heart,' Gisele said, for which she received a sharp glare from María.

Esmeralda reached for their hands and smiled. 'You'd best go, I don't want either of you getting in trouble on my behalf.'

They both hugged her again and they all stood, but Esmeralda kept hold of their hands.

'There is one thing though,' she said. 'If Alejandro agrees to help.'

Her sisters stood, waiting, their eyes on her.

'I need you to take a key and open my door for me, so I can leave,' she said, her voice low. 'I wouldn't ask if it wasn't absolutely necessary, if there was another way—'

'We can do that for you,' María said. 'When we get word, we will do it. Of course we will.'

'We're never going to see you again, are we?' Gisele asked, as silent tears ran down her cheeks.

Esmeralda kissed her sister's damp cheek and squeezed her hand. 'Of course you will! Don't speak like that. One day I'll be back here visiting you all with Christopher and our child. Papá will have no choice but to forgive me, surely you know that?'

But as her sisters left and the door locked behind her, fear started to cloud her mind. Because as much as she wanted to believe that he would forgive her, she wasn't so convinced he would.

Falling in love with Christopher was one thing, but carrying his baby and running away to London? She swallowed and stared out the window, repositioning herself as she waited for her visitor.

What she was doing was unforgiveable. She knew in her heart that she was never coming back here.

When the knock at the door finally came, Esmeralda's head was touching the glass and she was staring out at Marisol splashing in the swimming pool below. She'd been remembering all the long, hot summer days she'd spent swimming and sunbathing with her sisters and friends, wishing she could have just a moment of dipping her toes into the water. It was one of the many things she was going to miss when she left.

Part of her had started to wonder how miserable her life would actually be if she married a man of her father's choosing, whether it would be better to stay close to her family, but then she'd felt her baby shift inside of her. No matter what her thoughts, she no longer had any options. Her baby was going to be coming within the next month or so, which meant that she was all out of options.

'Esmeralda?'

Her name was spoken as if by surprise, and she turned her head to find Alejandro standing in the open doorway.

'Come in,' she said. 'Please.'

'Shall I shut the door?'

She nodded and he did so, before crossing the room and standing before her.

'Thank you for coming.'

'When my favourite cousin sends word that she needs me, how could I say no?' he grinned. 'Now tell me, where have you been? I've missed you. Your father said you're to be married?'

Esmeralda cleared her throat, before standing and slowly

letting the silk shawl drop to the ground, her dress straining around the middle from her rounded stomach.

Alejandro didn't utter a word, but his eyes widened as he looked at her waist.

'I'm pregnant,' she said.

'I can see that,' he frowned. 'And this is the reason you're locked in your bedroom?'

She shook her head. 'Papá doesn't know about the pregnancy, but he found out about Christopher.'

'Your Englishman?' Alejandro sighed. 'I'm so sorry, Es. All those times we joked about not marrying, about loving our lives and not wanting our parents to meddle with our future...'

They stood silently, but when Alejandro opened his arms she walked straight into them, letting him hold her as she cried tears she'd held inside for so long. His shirt was wet when she finally let go of him, taking a step back and looking up into his eyes.

'I made a mistake, Ale. I ruined everything.'

He guided her back to the window seat and sat down with her, holding her hand. 'What do you need me to do?'

She looked at their hands folded together. Alejandro hadn't just been her fun dance partner at parties; they'd grown up together, both the eldest children in their families, and it had been Alejandro who'd supported her when her mother had died and she'd had to become the matriarch of her family. He'd always been there for her, and now he was the only person in the world who knew about Christopher other than her sisters, and also about her pregnancy.

'I need to travel to London,' she said.

He let out a whistle. 'London?' he said. 'Wouldn't it be easier for me to find your Christopher and get him to come here?'

She shook her head and touched her middle. 'I don't have time for that. Christopher promised me he would ask for my hand and I have no reason to think he hasn't tried, but Papá is arranging a marriage for me. I need to leave, before it's too late.'

'When?' he asked. 'How long do I have to organise this?'

'This week,' she said, swallowing away her fears as they rose in her throat. 'I need to leave this week.'

'You know your father will never forgive me if he finds out I was involved,' he said. 'I'd lose my job; my family would be furious with me—'

'I wouldn't ask you if there was another way.'

He nodded. 'I always told you I'd do anything for you, Es, and I meant it. If I have to risk my neck, then so be it.'

'Thank you,' she whispered as she clutched his hand. 'You're the only person I trust enough to ask.'

'Do your sisters know? Can they be of any assistance?'

'They will unlock the door for me. I can only leave at night or in the early hours of the morning, when everyone is asleep.'

'Then I will send word to them when your flight is organised.'

Alejandro stood to leave and she rose too.

'I'm sorry, Es. You deserved better than this.'

She shrugged, but in her heart she knew his words rang true. She did deserve better than banishment in her bedroom, being shunned by her father for simply falling in love. But life wasn't fair, she'd learnt that the hard way when her mother had died.

'I'll see you soon, I promise,' he said, before turning for the door.

And as she stood there, in the middle of the room, watching him leave, she hoped she could trust him. Because if she couldn't, then there was no telling what was going to happen to her and the baby.

. . .

It had been four days since Alejandro had visited, and Esmeralda had become increasingly anxious with every evening that came and went. But when her dinner had been delivered tonight, her sister Gisele had accompanied the maid who'd brought it up. It was a Sunday, which was her usual maid Sofia's one day off, and she'd known something was happening when Gisele had been the one to place the tray, her eyes flitting to the covered dish before meeting Esmeralda's.

Once they'd gone and the key had turned in the lock, Esmeralda placed the tray on her bedside table and lifted the lid, eyes darting to find what Gisele might have hidden. There was nothing obvious she could see, and after lifting the plate, she was dumbfounded about what could be there. Until she picked up the napkin and unfolded it and a piece of paper fluttered to the floor. It was so small she could easily have missed it if she weren't looking for it. And there, in her sister's handwriting, was the news she'd been waiting for.

You're leaving, 4 a.m.

She let out a breath, her food forgotten as she started to pace back and forth, the little piece of paper held tightly in her palm. Tonight, she would be leaving everything she knew behind, not knowing when she'd be back.

Tears welled in her eyes but she held her jaw tightly and refused to let them fall, going instead to her writing desk and taking out a piece of paper. She reached for her fountain pen, her back straight as she wrote the words 'Dear Papá' at the top of the page, but her hand stopped then.

What was she going to say? Did she owe him an explanation after the way he'd treated her? How could she commit her feelings to paper when the way she felt towards him had changed so dramatically since he'd locked her in her bedroom like a prisoner?

For the first few days and then weeks, she'd expected him to come and unlock the door at any moment, apologising profusely and begging her forgiveness for the way he'd treated her. But when he hadn't, her love for the man who'd once meant the world to her had turned to a deep-seated anger that she wondered if she'd ever forget.

She mourned the man he'd been, the father she'd grown up with, but she no longer had warmth in her heart for him.

She balled the piece of paper and dropped it into the bin, turning her attention instead to the note from Gisele. She promptly placed the tiny piece of paper in her mouth and forced herself to swallow it, knowing it was imperative that her father never found out that her sisters had helped her and not wanting to leave so much as a trace of evidence behind.

Esmeralda stood then, deciding to eat as much of her dinner as she could, since she didn't know how long it might be before she ate again, and not wanting the maid to report back to her father that her food had gone untouched. She wouldn't do anything that could cause even the smallest suspicion that something was wrong. Then she went into her wardrobe and took down two smaller suitcases to pack her luggage into, which she would hide under the bed until later.

She stared at the rows of dresses, the beautiful gowns she'd worn over the years. Her life had been one of opulence and happiness until now, but that life was gone. What she needed to do was pack what she might need to tide her over, and more important what she could fit into, until Christopher could take her shopping for what she needed in London.

Esmeralda made her way through her clothes to pack a few different outfits, shoes, cosmetics and toiletries, checking the cases weren't too heavy since she was going to have to carry them on her own. Then she planned what she'd wear that night, when Alejandro came for her, not daring to get changed yet. A maid would check on her before bed, and she'd need to be tucked under the covers in her usual night attire to ensure everything appeared as usual. Once the house was quiet, once everyone was asleep, was when she'd prepare to leave. And then she'd wait until the early hours and hope that everything went to plan.

It had been the longest hours of Esmeralda's life when she finally heard a noise in the dark. The turn of the key was slow and deliberate, barely making a sound, but she didn't move until she saw who it was. *María.*

Her sister was in her nightgown, with her long hair falling over her shoulders, illuminated by the moonlight coming through the window from the hall, and emotion immediately choked Esmeralda's throat as she stared at her. María walked quietly in, not closing the door behind her, and they quickly embraced.

Esmeralda held her sister tightly, inhaling the smell of her shampoo, the feel of arms around her, wanting to commit her to memory before she left.

'It's time,' María whispered, her arms still around her. 'Alejandro is parked down the road, he said he'll meet you the moment he sees you walk through the gate.'

Esmeralda exhaled. 'I'm going to miss you so much, María.'

'I'm going to miss you, too, Es. Life will never be the same without you.'

She couldn't help her tears now, despite how stoic she'd been earlier when she'd banished her emotion. 'Please tell Marisol that I love her, that she's my beautiful girl,' she said. 'Love her for me in my absence, María. Make her feel like the most wonderful child in the world, be the mother she needs.'

'I will, you know I will.'

Esmeralda reluctantly let go of her sister, knowing the longer they waited, the more chance they had of being caught.

She picked up one case and María picked up the other, and with that they tiptoed from the room. Esmeralda looked back once, at the door, into her opulent childhood bedroom, committing it to memory before hurrying after her sister and moving quietly down the hall and then the stairs.

Every creak of the house sent shivers through her as they moved, expecting at any moment a light to go on or a call of anger from her father to roar down the hall, but the house stayed silent as they moved through the kitchen. Until a figure moved from the shadows by the door.

'Gisele!' she gasped, when she realised it was her sister.

'I couldn't let you leave without saying goodbye.'

She set her cases down, quickly hugging her, tears wetting her sister's hair as she clung to her one last time.

'I love you, Es,' Gisele whispered.

'I love you, too,' Esmeralda cried, letting go of Gisele so she could look at both of her sisters, holding both of their hands for a long moment before finally letting go.

It was time to leave.

She bravely collected her suitcases, one in each hand, and despite her tears, her pain at leaving her sisters behind almost unbearable, she walked out the door without looking back. She hurried through the garden and to the side gate, cringing as she did so and hoping it didn't squeak. Thankfully the night air remained silent, and she shut it behind her and looked down the street, seeing a car and quickening her pace. And then Alejandro stepped from behind a tree, startling her momentarily as he ran the short distance between them.

They didn't speak to each other as he reached for her cases and walked briskly with her to the car, placing them in the back as she settled herself in the passenger seat.

As he started the engine he turned to her, his eyes searching hers.

'You're certain this is what you want to do?'

She held her head high, not daring to consider staying, for how could she?

'I'm certain.'

'Then I will take you to the airport,' he said, pulling out onto the street. 'I have a ticket for you to travel to London, but the flight doesn't depart until nine a.m., which means you will have to pray your father doesn't come looking for you before then. I can't help you if he does.'

She swallowed as nerves ran the length of her body. 'My breakfast is usually brought to my room at eight thirty,' she said, hearing the quiver in her voice. 'I should be fine.'

'Then we can only hope that your flight has left before anyone starts looking for you.' He glanced at her and she could see the fear in his eyes. 'When he finds out what you've done, if he finds out what *I've* done...'

They sat in silence for a moment, before Esmeralda finally spoke.

'Thank you, Alejandro,' she said. 'You've been a true friend to me. Other than my sisters, I trust you more than anyone in the world.'

He grunted. 'You're the only person I'd risk my neck for, Es. I hope you know that.'

She nodded. 'I do.'

'Will you come into the airport with me?' she asked.

Alejandro took one hand off the steering wheel and reached for her, his palm settling over the back of her hand. 'I will ensure everything goes smoothly when we arrive, in case there are questions about your travelling alone, but then I'll have to leave you to wait alone for your flight. I can't risk being seen.'

'I understand.'

'Until then, we'll park the car and sit, until it's light and the airport is open.'

Esmeralda stared out the window into the dark. In a few more hours, she would be on a flight headed for London; she could imagine the feel of Christopher's arms around her, the look on his face when he realised she was expecting, that they could finally be married. That they could finally be together without having to hide their love.

So long as Papá doesn't figure out what I've done and storm the airport before my plane is in the sky, that is.

27

FLORIDA, PRESENT DAY

Claudia knocked at the door, so nervous her stomach was twisting into knots. She glanced at the piece of paper in her hand for the hundredth time, checking she had the right address and wondering why she'd decided it was a good idea to simply show up on someone's doorstep without trying to make contact first. She'd only been on US soil for two hours, having cleared customs and then collected her rental car, before plugging the address Beatriz had given her into the GPS.

Before she could retreat the door opened, and a pretty, raven-haired woman blinked back at her. She looked so much like the beautiful Cuban women she'd seen in Havana, only this woman was dressed in a luxurious short-sleeved cashmere jersey and jeans, which made her look more American than Cuban.

'May I help you?'

'I'm looking for Marisol Diaz,' Claudia said.

'Then you're looking for my grandmother,' the woman said, leaning into the door as if she might close it at any moment. 'Unfortunately she no longer lives here though.'

'Oh,' Claudia said, trying to hide her disappointment. 'Is

there somewhere else I could call on her? I was told this was her most recent address.'

'You don't know her?' the woman seemed surprised, and she stepped back slightly from the door. 'Who told you where my grandmother lived?'

Claudia put her phone in her bag and took out the image of the Diaz family crest she'd carried with her since leaving London, wanting to show it to her before the door was closed in her face. 'It's hard to explain why I'm here, but my name is Claudia Mackenzie, I've travelled here from London, via Havana, and some months ago I was given this crest as a clue to my grandmother's past. She was adopted at birth, and this is one of the only clues I have.'

The woman stared at her as if she was stark raving mad, folding her arms across her chest. Claudia had expected her to reach for the crest, which she was still holding out, but she barely glanced at it.

'If you're here to make an inheritance claim, then I'll gladly give you the number of our family lawyer. Otherwise, this conversation is over.' The door began to shut and Claudia quickly stuck out her foot to block it.

'Please, if you'll just give me a moment of your time, I can explain,' Claudia said. 'I don't want anything from you other than answers, I'd simply hoped to speak to your grandmother in case she knew how *my* grandma was connected to her family, or perhaps to her sister, Esmeralda. Her eldest sister?'

The door didn't click, instead slowly reopened a little. Claudia took her chance and spoke quickly, while she still had the chance, as the woman peered out at her.

'I went to Havana looking to discover my grandmother's heritage, she was adopted as an infant and never even knew of her link to Cuba,' Claudia said. 'All I know is that somehow she's linked to your family, and I've come all this way to try to figure out how. All I want is some closure about her past, that's all.'

She was answered by silence.

'When I was in Havana, I met a man named Mateo, he's a popular chef there, and his family helped me to uncover information about your family,' Claudia said. 'He told me that his grandfather, Diego, was the Diaz family chef, before they left Cuba, and his family still have very fond memories of working in your family's household.'

'You personally know the family?' she asked.

'I do, in fact I was eating paella with them for lunch on Sunday before I left Havana.' Claudia smiled. 'Beatriz, Diego's daughter, is the one who found your address for me,' Claudia replied. 'Please, just five minutes of your time. It's all I ask.'

The other woman appeared to hesitate, before the door slowly opened and she eventually stepped back, waving her in. 'I suppose you'd better come in,' she said. 'But only for a moment so I can hear you out.'

Claudia slipped off her shoes and stepped onto the hardwood floor, following the other woman whose name she didn't yet know. *I'm one step closer, Grandma. I'm going to figure all this out, I promise you.*

It had been a long journey, but she had the feeling that the truth about her grandmother's past was finally within reaching distance, and it was all thanks to Mateo and his mother.

The woman looked uncomfortable as she walked out onto an ocean-facing deck and beckoned for her to sit. Claudia set her bag on the table and sat, searching for the right words despite the fact she'd been rehearsing them all day. Suddenly her mind was blank.

'My grandmother died a year ago, her name was Catherine Black, and my family never knew she was adopted,' Claudia began, hoping she wasn't speaking too quickly. 'My family received the most curious email recently, from a lawyer, and he gave me the crest I showed you before, as well as an address. It was all that was left behind by my grandmother's birth mother, and it's information that we've only recently become aware of.'

The woman stared at her, before lowering herself into the seat opposite Claudia. 'May I see the crest again?'

Claudia smiled and reached back into her bag, eagerly taking out the picture of the crest and sliding it across the table. 'I want you to know that the only reason I'm here is to discover my grandmother's heritage,' she said, softly. 'I truly believe that she never even knew she was adopted, but her birth mother must have left these clues for a reason, and I want to discover her story. I need to know what happened all those years ago.'

The woman shifted in her seat, but she appeared more relaxed now, her shoulders softening and her lips turning into a smile. The room was like something from a magazine, with deep sofas adorned with velvety throw cushions and stunning large artworks covering the walls.

'My family has a tendency to expect the worst when people come looking for us,' she said. 'Money brings out the worst in people, and usually there's an endgame, hence my reluctance when we met before. I'm sorry if I appeared rude.'

'I understand. I worked in finance for many years, so I've seen first-hand what money can do to people,' Claudia said. 'But I can assure you that I have no interest in the Diaz family fortune. My only interest is in discovering how my grandmother fits into your family tree, if she's part of the tree at all, and then I'll be on my way.'

'I'm Sara,' she said, holding out her hand.

Claudia sighed in relief. She had a feeling she might have longer than five minutes to ask questions now that Sara appeared to have softened towards her.

'It's so lovely to meet you, Sara,' she replied as she shook her hand. 'You have no idea what this means to me, just being able to ask you some questions.'

'You mentioned Esmeralda before,' Sara said. 'Why is it that you think the connection would be to her? From what I know, none of my aunts ever heard from Esmeralda again after she disappeared. They searched for her for many years, but it was as if she'd vanished.'

'They didn't stay in touch?' Claudia couldn't mask her surprise.

'Like I said, she disappeared without a trace, and despite reaching out to Christopher many times, they never received word from him, either.'

'Christopher?' she asked, surprised that his name had come up so quickly.

'The man she was in love with. All they knew was that she was going to be with him, but they never heard from either of them ever again.'

Claudia sat back, puzzled as Sara rose and declared she'd make them coffee, which gave her time to think. If the other Diaz sisters knew about Christopher but hadn't heard from Esmeralda again, either she was wrong about the eldest sister being the missing piece of the puzzle, or she was in the wrong place.

Sara returned with coffee and Claudia gratefully accepted, stirring in a spoonful of sugar. She'd become used to the sweet coffee in Cuba—it was going to be a hard habit to break.

'Do you mind telling me what you know about your grandmother and her family? About how she and her sisters came to leave Cuba?' Claudia asked. 'I suppose I'm trying to paint a picture to see if my grandmother could have fitted in anywhere.'

Sara's face fell, just for a moment, before her eyes met Claudia's. 'My great-grandfather, Julio, stayed for much longer than many others after the military leader Batista fled Havana one New Year's Eve for the Dominican Republic,' she said. 'The stories I've been told tell of a man who refused to give up on Cuba, who mistakenly, or perhaps optimistically, believed that there would still be a place for him under the new regime. For a time, it seemed that perhaps he was right, for right up until he left, he still had his sugar mill and his properties.'

'I thought all of the upper class in Cuba lost all their property almost immediately when Castro came to power?' Claudia asked. 'Why did your great-grandfather think it would be different for him?'

Sara nodded. 'You're right, many had left the island long before, but my great-grandfather wasn't like other upper-class men. At one point, Cuba produced six-million tonnes of sugar, and he was responsible for producing more than half of it, but even then he was unusually outspoken in his dislike for Batista.' Sara paused and took a sip of her coffee, watching Claudia over the top of it. 'Most in their social circle kept their political thoughts to themselves or at least only whispered their thoughts in close company, but not him. My mother always said he was unusually vocal about Cuba's corrupt government, despite benefiting from it in many ways. At one point, before anyone truly knew the depth of Castro's leanings towards communism, Julio supposedly helped to finance his rebels. But I don't think he could ever have imagined what would one day happen to the country he loved so, and if he did, he never would have given them his money in support.'

To say Claudia was surprised would have been an understatement. Everything she'd heard about Cuba's upper class had indicated they'd all kept their concerns about Batista largely to themselves, benefiting too much from his regime to criticise him too deeply, and most certainly anyone making their fortune in sugar. She also knew that most of Cuba's wealthy had fled the island with jewels stuffed into their underwear during or immediately after the revolution, leaving while they could. But the story she was hearing was one quite different to what she'd expected; the Diaz family were certainly cut from a different cloth, or so it seemed.

'He was unlike anyone else in that he never openly criticised Castro, in fact quite the opposite,' she said softly. 'His love of Cuba, of what he had built there, was too great. It broke his heart to know that his family wasn't with him; that he'd lost first his wife, then his eldest daughter, and then his other daughters too when they left for Florida, albeit with his blessing. He stayed until the bitter end, and I imagine his heart broke all over again to lose the country and business he'd dedicated his life to. For such a well-liked, successful man, he had a sad fall from grace.'

Claudia shut her eyes for a moment, thinking of the Cuba she'd discovered, imagining what it would have been like in those years of glamour and prosperity, of diamonds and dresses, champagne and cigars. Cuba had stayed frozen in time in so many ways, almost as if the country was waiting for all those who'd left to return and breathe life into it once more, only they'd never come back.

'So what made him finally leave? What happened in the end?'

Sara looked away, the roar of the ocean drawing Claudia's attention, too. She could see why so many Cubans had settled in Miami; it was not only close in proximity, but also the beach at least created a mimic to the island nation they'd once inhabited. Almost as if they were trying to watch the country they'd loved from afar.

'What happened is that Che Guevara gave him an ultimatum,' Sara said. 'The night that he left, he carried only a small suitcase, with two changes of clothes and a photograph of his family. The only valuables he took with him were his wife's diamond rings, carefully sewn into his jacket, with her plain wedding band worn on his little finger. It's a story I've heard so many times throughout my life, and something about him leaving like that always manages to bring a tear to my eye.'

'He left everything else behind?'

'He didn't have a choice,' Sara said, her voice gravelly, as if it pained her to recount the story that had likely been relayed to her by her mother and aunties over the years. 'His home was opulent and filled with priceless art, but it was his business that meant everything to him, and without that, he felt as if he'd already lost it all. That his life's work had been stolen from him.' She sighed. 'In the end, right before he left, he was told he could retain one of his homes in return for working for Cuba, managing the sugar production for the entire country and using his years of expertise to benefit the communist regime. He knew that if he said no, he'd receive a bullet in the back of his head, and so within hours, he disappeared and never set foot in his beloved homeland again. He could never work for Castro or Guevara.'

Claudia sat back, imagining this proud Cuban man, a man with wealth so vast his name was known around the world, reduced to someone who owned nothing, with only a single suitcase to his name and his wife's ring on his finger.

'So he was penniless?' Claudia asked. 'What did he do when he arrived in America? Where were his daughters by then?'

Sara stood, her hand hovering near the glass as she stared out at the beach. 'Tell me, *did* you know of the Diaz fortune before you travelled here? Has anything I've told you truly come as a surprise, or did you research my great-grandfather before you came here?'

Claudia took a moment, forcing herself to breathe calmly rather than answer Sara hastily. She understood the other woman's concern; she'd have felt the same if someone had turned up at her parent's house in Surrey and claimed to be related to them. She stood and reached out to the other woman, her hand warm and steady over her arm, eyes meeting hers as she turned.

'I know only what I learnt in Cuba over the past two weeks,' Claudia said, quietly. 'I am simply trying to honour my own grandmother, and find answers to all the questions I have about her past, about *my* past. All I want is to know her story. In truth, I feel an obligation to discover what she cannot, but in answer to your question, I knew nothing before I travelled to Havana.'

Sara's eyes were kind as she stared back at her, but Claudia sensed an air of hesitancy, too.

'I'm sorry, I just—'

'You have nothing to apologise for,' Claudia interrupted. 'I understand, honestly I do.'

Sara appeared to be studying her.

'Here,' Claudia said, reaching into her bag and producing a card, and scribbling the name of her hotel on the back of it. 'You can google me, find out about me on your own terms, and then we perhaps we can meet again when you're certain I'm not some penniless gold digger.'

Sara face fell. 'I don't think you're—'

Claudia pressed the card into her palm. 'The world is full of people lying their way into situations,' she said. 'Call me when you feel ready to talk, and if you don't? I do understand. I'm sure I'll discover one day how my grandmother fits into this puzzle, but I have to say that I'd much rather hear it from you.' She smiled. 'I've loved hearing about your great-grandfather, but in truth I want to discover who my grandmother's mother was. I want to know how she ended up in England, so far from the country of her heritage. I want to know more about Esmeralda's disappearance to see whether that could be the connection.'

'My grandmother,' Sara suddenly said. 'She would have loved to meet you. If you're correct, if your grandmother was in fact related to our family...' she sighed.

Claudia smiled. 'I would have loved that, too.' She cleared

her throat. 'All these years, I had no idea my family had a connection to any country outside of England. If only I'd discovered the threads of my grandmother's past earlier, if only my grandmother had been given the little box of clues, perhaps things would have been different. Perhaps I would have been arriving here with her and your grandmother would have been the one opening the door.'

Sara nodded and Claudia rose and collected her bag, slipping it over her arm. She reached out, touching Sara's forearm for a moment again and looking earnestly into her eyes. 'Thank you. Even if you don't want to tell me more and we never cross paths again, thank you for inviting me into your home.'

She turned to leave, reaching for the door at the same time Sara called out to her.

'Claudia, wait,' Sara said. 'My grandmother is still alive, but she has good days and bad days. I'm loath to put any stress on her, her memory can come and go, but perhaps we could meet for lunch tomorrow?'

Claudia couldn't help the smile that lit her face when she turned. 'I'd love that. Thank you.' *Marisol Diaz!* She was actually going to meet Marisol Diaz!

She left the house and walked quickly to her rental car, holding in her excitement until she was behind the wheel again and Sara had closed the door. And then she sat back and shut her eyes, relief coursing through her.

I'm going to find out all about your family, Grandma. I promise. Everything was finally falling into place.

28

LONDON, 1951

Esmeralda held a small case in each hand, all her possessions condensed to the luggage she'd been able to carry herself, as London seemed to whirl around her. *I'm here.* Waiting at the airport for her flight had set her nerves on edge, expecting her father to arrive and force her to return home at any moment. She'd sat, her heels tapping the ground, until her flight was ready to board, and she'd even looked over her shoulder once she reached the front of the line, but no one had come for her. Somehow, through the grace of God, she'd escaped. But it wouldn't have been possible without Alejandro; nothing would have been possible without him.

She'd left everything behind—her sisters, her home, the country she loved. But she would do it all over again if she had to. Esmeralda put one case down at her feet and touched her hand to her stomach, knowing she'd made the only decision she could, before reaching into her pocket for the business card. She'd memorised the address months ago, but she still wanted to look again, to make sure it was correct. After all these months, she couldn't wait to see him again, for him to see that she was expecting and to tell him that she was free to marry him, that she'd left everything behind so they could be together. She'd been terrified to write it in a letter in case her father intercepted it—he'd refused to see her since the day he'd locked her in her room—which meant that she'd had no way to tell Christopher that he was about to become a father. That all these months she'd been carrying his child in secret, hoping and praying that somehow she'd find her way to him. She could only imagine how many times he must have tried to contact her father, but once her papá made his mind up, nothing could change it.

Tucking the card back into her pocket, Esmeralda picked up her cases again as she tried to figure out where to go. She was used to having her father or another chaperone to organise everything for her, and seeing the traffic whizz past and the number of people hurrying about their day only made her more confused. It was overwhelming being in a strange city, alone, especially in her vulnerable state, and she wondered if perhaps it hadn't been the smartest idea to take the train from the airport into the city. Should she have used what cash she had to take a taxi straight to Christopher's office?

She took a step forward, smiling as she imagined the look on his face when he saw her, imagining the warmth of his arms around her, of his lips on hers, but her excitement was dampened by an intense wave of pain rippling through her body. Her stomach suddenly clenched, a violent wave of nausea rising within her as her eyesight became hazy, as everything started to spin around her.

Esmeralda went to set her cases down again, grimacing as another sharp pain made her stomach contract, as she staggered on her feet just to stay upright. She reached for the card, her fingers fumbling in her pocket and then clutching it tightly, knowing that all she had to do was get to Christopher, to find him so he could take care of her. But before she could cry for help or take another step, her heel slid from under her.

The last thing she heard as the ground seemed to rise to meet her was her own cry.

'Christopher,' she whimpered, as everything went black.

29

'Where am I?' Esmeralda croaked, sitting up in the bed and looking around. She had no recollection of how she'd gotten there or where she even was.

She quickly ran her hand down her stomach, relieved to splay her hand over it and feel her baby there.

'She's in here.'

Esmeralda pushed up higher, hearing voices in the hallway as she watched for the door. She was in a hospital. It was all starting to come back to her now, fragments of memories, someone helping her up from the ground, the sound of an ambulance.

She was about to swing her legs off the bed and look for her things when two women appeared in the doorway. One was wearing a white nursing uniform and a frown, and the other was dressed nicely in a skirt and blouse, and it was her smile that stopped Esmeralda from feeling completely terrified.

'So this is the young pregnant lady,' the smiling woman said as she walked towards her. 'I'm Hope.'

'Esmeralda,' she replied, taking Hope's hand when she held it out. The skin was soft and every bit as warm as her smile.

'She was found collapsed on the street,' the nurse said, picking up her chart. 'We don't have space for her type here though.'

Esmeralda bristled. Her type? 'What do you mean?' she asked. 'Isn't this a hospital?'

Hope shook her head and came to sit beside her on the bed. 'Do you have a husband?' she asked, gently. 'Or family nearby?'

'I, I—' she glanced at the nurse but decided not to look at her again, not liking the judgement in her stare, or the way she looked pointedly at her hand, as if to make clear there was no wedding ring. 'I have just arrived in London, from Cuba,' she said. 'My name is Esmeralda Diaz.'

When neither of the women in the room said anything, she experienced a sinking realisation that her name no longer meant anything. In Havana, the Diaz name would have opened any door, it *meant* something. But here she was just another unmarried woman with a baby on the way—that was why the hospital didn't want her there. She should have thought of that before she travelled and put a diamond on her ring finger.

She hung her head. 'No, I have no family here, and I'm not married. But my Christopher wants to marry me, that's why I'm here. I was on my way to—'

'She's all yours,' the nurse said abruptly, setting down her chart and starting to walk towards the door. 'I need the room for someone else, so don't take long. I want her gone before noon.'

Esmeralda bit her lip to stop the tears that were threatening to fall, her hand falling to her stomach again for comfort. It had been a very sharp, short fall from grace.

'If I'm not welcome here, then where am I expected to go? Am I to deliver this baby on the street?' she asked. Surely Christopher would know what to do, how to deal with this kind of nurse. He would get her and the baby the very best care, he wouldn't stand for the way she was being treated.

'Esmeralda, do you have anywhere to go?'

She took a deep, shaky breath. 'I can go to Christopher, I have his business address.'

Hope put an arm around her and she found herself leaning into her, as she would have her mother many years earlier.

'We'll find your Christopher, but you're in no shape to go traipsing around looking for him,' Hope said. 'It sounds to me like you might have this baby early, and that means you need someone to care for you.'

She looked up and into the kindest eyes she'd ever seen. 'Can you help me?'

'Yes, Esmeralda, it just so happens I can.'

30

FLORIDA, PRESENT DAY

The woman walking towards her moved with the kind of straight-backed confidence that made Claudia think she was used to commanding a room. She had to be in her eighties, and her white hair was pulled elegantly from her face, framed by enormous diamond earrings that reminded Claudia of the stories Mateo had told her of Cuba's old guard. Holding on to her arm was Sara, who greeted Claudia with a smile.

'Thank you so much for coming,' Claudia said, as she rose and stood back slightly from the table. 'It means so much to me.'

The older woman stopped, staring at Claudia for a long moment before nodding and taking a seat.

Claudia exchanged glances with Sara, who gestured for her to sit down.

'Claudia, this is my grandmother, Marisol,' Sara said. 'Abuela, this is Claudia.'

'It's so lovely to meet you, Marisol,' Claudia said. 'Thank you for coming, it's quite an honour to meet one of the Diaz sisters in the flesh after hearing so much about you all. It sounds like you all had quite the reputation for your beauty.'

The older woman sat silently, her eyes seeming to study

Claudia intensely, before she picked up the menu and held it out to her granddaughter, tapping at it.

'Do they have champagne? I'm in the mood for a glass.'

She spoke with the air of someone much younger, and Claudia loved how Sara just patted her grandmother's hand, not even trying to talk her out of it. Although she supposed that women like Marisol Diaz didn't take kindly to being told they couldn't have something; she'd been raised in one of the wealthiest families in Cuba, after all.

'We'll rustle you up a glass of champagne, Abuela, don't you worry,' Sara said, with a conspiratorial wink to Claudia over the table. 'We might even join you.'

'Where's your abuelo?' Marisol suddenly asked. 'Why didn't he come for lunch? Is he being difficult again?'

Claudia had learnt enough Cuban words to understand that she was asking where her husband was, why Sara's grandpa hadn't joined them, and Sara looked like she didn't know how to reply. They looked at each other over the table for a long moment, and from what Claudia could gather, her grandpa was no longer alive.

'Oh, it's my fault he's not here,' Claudia said quickly, hoping to soothe Marisol. 'I hope you can forgive me, but I thought we could have a girls lunch, just the three of us. I wouldn't like to bore your husband with all my questions.'

Marisol seemed more settled then, but she still looked at her granddaughter. 'Why are we having lunch with this lady? Do I know her?'

Sara smiled, holding her grandmother's hand now. 'Abuela, this is Claudia. I think there's a chance that she could be your great-niece.'

Claudia looked up and saw the way Sara was nodding at her, as if trying to tell her that she was right. This woman, *Marisol*, could be her great-aunt? But that would mean that...

'I thought a lot about you after you left yesterday, Claudia, and I believe that Esmeralda may in fact be your great-grand-mother,' Sara said. 'It's the only explanation for the clues you have in your possession.'

Tears filled the old woman's eyes then as she looked off into the distance, as if seeing something they couldn't. 'Esmeralda,' Marisol whispered. 'She never came home. One day she was in her room, the next she disappeared. I never saw my sister again.'

The waiter came to their table, and thankfully Sara ordered drinks for them. Claudia's pulse was racing as she watched Marisol absently finger one of the large diamonds hanging from her earlobe. *Could I truly be related to this woman? Could Esmeralda truly be my great-grandmother?*

'What happened when she disappeared?' Claudia asked. 'Do you know what happened to her?'

'Our Esmeralda was in love,' Marisol said. 'Our father adored her, she was always his favourite, but when she left we were never allowed to speak her name again.'

'So she left of her own accord? To be with Christopher?'

The waiter returned with their drinks and Marisol was preoccupied with her champagne, taking a sip and sitting back in her chair with a smile on her face that lit up the room.

'This reminds me of the good old days,' Marisol said, before blinking at them and appearing confused. 'What are we cele-brating? Did someone get married?'

'We're celebrating your sister, Esmeralda,' Sara said, holding up her glass and clinking it to first her grandmother's and then Claudia's. 'Would you like to tell us more about her? Maybe you could tell Claudia how Esmeralda came to leave your house? Did something happen to make her want to leave?'

Claudia found herself holding her breath as she waited, to see whether Marisol would indulge them or not. She half expected her to forget what they were talking about and go off on another tangent, but to her surprise, the old lady's recollec-tion seemed faultless.

'Esmeralda was like a mother to me, but when she was locked in her room I was only allowed to see her once a day,' Marisol told them. 'He said she'd disobeyed him, and the door stayed locked from the outside. No one was brave enough to defy him, not even my sisters.'

'You remember all this?' Sara said. 'You remember her being locked in there all those years ago?'

'The maid used to unlock the door in the afternoon, after my lessons, and I would go in and sit with Esmeralda. She would tell me stories and play make-believe with me, and before I left she'd always wrap me in her arms and we'd lie on her bed. I used to think of her as my mother, she was the one who always looked after me and held me when I went to sleep each night, but once she was locked in her room, she wasn't allowed to look after me anymore.'

Claudia had so many questions, but she didn't want to interrupt Marisol now that her memories were flowing so readily. To think how many years had passed since all of this had happened, it was incredible to have it all recounted so easily.

'She asked me to keep her secret, and I never told anyone, not even my sisters.'

'What was her secret?' Claudia asked, not able to help herself. 'Marisol, what was the secret she made you keep?'

Marisol took another sip of her champagne. 'The baby, of course,' she said, after a long pause. 'I wasn't allowed to tell anyone about the baby.'

Claudia leaned forward. 'She was *pregnant*?'

'Did your father find out?' Sara asked gently. 'He must have been so mad when he discovered she was expecting.'

'Papá didn't know,' Marisol said, shaking her head. 'Papá wanted her to marry a good Cuban boy, her wedding was all arranged, but Esmeralda was never going to go through with it. She wanted to be with Christopher. Papá never saw her after the day he locked her away, but if he'd found out, he'd have been so mad. She would have been in so much trouble.'

'Christopher?' Claudia grabbed her bag and rummaged through it, taking out the card as her heart started to race. 'Marisol, is this the Christopher you're talking about? Christopher Dutton from this London trading company?'

Marisol's smile grew wide. 'Oh yes, that's her Christopher.' She laughed. 'Christopher Dutton. When he was here, they were always sneaking around. They thought no one saw them, but I did. I saw the kissing. I saw her in his arms when they thought they were hidden.'

Claudia blinked away tears; finally, after all this wondering, thinking that perhaps she was crazy to think she were somehow related to the Diaz family, she had Marisol Diaz herself sitting before her, confirming that not only Esmeralda was pregnant, but also that Christopher Dutton was indeed the missing link. That she had been pregnant by this Christopher.

'You said *here*,' Claudia said, suddenly realising what Marisol had said. 'Was Christopher in Havana? Was he in your home?'

Marisol smiled in a way that reminded Claudia of a child, a naughty child with a secret. 'He came to stay, but Papá didn't find out until he'd gone. Until he found the letters.'

Part of the story was all starting to make sense, and it all tied in with what the maid had told her back in Cuba.

'You still haven't told us why she was locked in her room though?' Sara said. 'That doesn't sound like something your father would have done unless he was very angry? Was it because of the letters?'

'Oh, Papá was angry all right. He found out Esmeralda wanted to marry Christopher, and he wasn't going to let her out of his sight until she was married to someone of his choosing. He said she brought shame on our whole family,' Marisol said, reaching for her champagne. Claudia did the same, unable to take her eyes off the mesmerising woman in front of her, who may or may not be her great-aunt. She smiled to herself as she leaned forward again to listen to Marisol.

'Papá changed after Esmeralda,' Marisol said. 'He used to let me eat pastry for breakfast, sitting on his knee and not caring about my sticky fingers. He used to laugh and smile, patting me on the head and telling me that one day I'd grow up to be just like my beautiful sister, Esmeralda. Everyone always said that I looked just like her, that I was so lucky, but after she disappeared, nobody talked about her again. It was as if she'd never existed in the first place. Even her bedroom door stayed shut after she left, never to be opened again.'

Claudia swallowed. 'You weren't even allowed to speak of her at home? With your sisters?'

Marisol's eyes filled with tears. 'In our rooms, we would lock the door and whisper about her, wondering where she was. I used to crawl into Gisele's lap and listen to my sisters talk, wondering where she was and when she would come home. But they always told me that she was gone, that Esmeralda was never coming back, and they were right. Esmeralda was gone and she never returned.'

They all sat in silence a moment, leaving Marisol to her memories as she stared off into the distance, as if she was perhaps reliving that moment in time, seeing the sister she'd missed for so many years.

'Marisol, may I ask how Esmeralda left? Did your father know where she'd gone?'

Marisol shook her head and seemed to shrink before her, as if the memories were too painful. 'Our father knew someone had helped her escape, and he was never the same after that. We hardly ever saw him, he spent all his time at the sugar mill, and once María was married I went to live with her. Gisele was married soon after.' Marisol laughed. 'He wasn't going to make the same mistake with them, and it wasn't long before we all had to leave anyhow. We left with his blessing, but our family was never the same again, even when he came to Florida.'

'Who helped her?' Sara asked, seeming as captivated by the story as Claudia was. 'Do you know how she left Cuba?'

Marisol just shook her head, looking down at her hands. 'I don't know. I was so young and they kept everything from me. I never even got the chance to say goodbye.'

'I'm so sorry, Marisol,' Claudia said, staring into her eyes and hoping she could see how genuine she was in her sentiment. 'I'm sorry you lost your sister. That must have been so hard on you.'

'We wrote to her,' Marisol said, her hand shaking as she reached for her glass again. 'My sisters even let me draw pictures and write little letters that they put with theirs, and one of the maids smuggled them out of the house and sent them for us to Christopher's office.'

'Is that how you knew she was alive? Because she wrote back to you?'

Marisol sighed. 'We never heard back from her. Esmeralda may as well have disappeared into thin air.'

Claudia swallowed and glanced at Sara, who looked at alarmed as she felt.

'You don't think something dreadful happened to her, do you? You don't think your father...' The question hung in the air between them for a long moment and Claudia found herself instinctively holding her breath.

'Papá never forgave her, he believed that she betrayed him, but he would never hurt her. He never laid a hand on any of us girls, he loved us more than anything, even when he was angry.'

Claudia had so much to ask still, so many things she wanted to know, but she could also sense that they'd perhaps pushed Marisol too far already. And the mention of her father had her eyes filling with tears; the last thing she wanted was to upset her.

'Shall we order lunch?' Claudia asked brightly. 'I think it's time for us all to have something to eat, and perhaps you can tell us about the days before you left Cuba? I would love to hear more about your childhood and what it was like growing up in that beautiful home in Havana.'

Marisol's eyes softened then, and once they'd ordered, Claudia sat back and listened to her reminisce about her childhood, about days that were filled with laughter and sunshine, parties and beautiful dresses.

And having been in Havana, and having seen its beauty herself, Claudia found herself transported to another time that she wished she could have glimpsed for herself, even for just a day. But even as she listened, she couldn't help but wonder what had happened to Esmeralda, and why she hadn't stayed in touch with her family. The Diaz sisters had been as close as family could be from the sounds of it, so something must have gone terribly wrong for her to lose contact all together. Not to mention that her father's email had stated Christopher Dutton had died without any heirs.

Claudia strolled down the beach, her jeans rolled up to her ankles, her feet bare. The day had been incredible, but now that she was alone, she couldn't stop thinking about everything that had happened since she'd first left London. And as she stared out at the sea and listened to the constant back-and-forth roar of the waves, she wished that she were back in Havana. What she wouldn't have given to go home to Mateo, or to meet him at his food truck and go for a walk along the Malecón one last time. She could almost smell the wafting aromas of his cooking on the air, standing beside him as he talked to her about the fresh ingredients he was using in his recipes.

She headed back the way she'd come and within minutes she was back at her hotel, brushing the sand from her feet before putting her sandals back on to enter the lobby. But she wasn't halfway to the elevator before the concierge was waving to her.

'There's a message for you,' he called out, before returning with a note.

Claudia thanked him and took it, opening the piece of paper as she stepped into the elevator. It was a message to call Sara, with her number attached.

She waited until she was in her room and dialled, smiling when she heard the other woman's voice. They may not have had the best first introduction, but they'd certainly had a pleasant afternoon together.

'Hi Sara, it's Claudia,' she said.

'Thanks for calling me back so soon. I just, well, I haven't been able to stop thinking about what my grandmother said today.'

'It was certainly a lot for one afternoon.'

'I just can't believe that all these years, nothing was ever said. I mean, as a child I remember they used to talk about it all sometimes at family get-togethers, about Esmeralda and how much they still missed her, but it was more just reminiscing.' Sara went silent for a moment. 'I have this awful feeling that something dreadful happened to Esmeralda, but that her sisters all imagined her living this wonderful life, leaving them all behind. It doesn't sit right with me.'

'What do you think could have happened to her?' Claudia asked.

'I don't know, but do you believe that a young woman who adored her sisters would truly disappear of her own accord and never contact them ever again? Even if she were desperately in love, why wouldn't she have reached out to them? Why would she had disappeared like that?'

Claudia gripped the phone more tightly as she stared out

the window. 'No, I don't believe it. But I don't know where else we can look to find out the truth.'

'My grandmother was so young then, it's perfectly understandable that she doesn't know all the details about how she left, but there has to be a way to find out, don't you think?'

Claudia sat on the bed, still looking out the window at the ocean. 'I've tried to find out more about this Christopher Dutton, but...' she hesitated. 'Sara, there's something I have to tell you, something I withheld today.'

She was greeted with silence at the other end of the line.

'I understand that Christopher didn't have any children,' she said. 'Or at least that's what I've been led to believe.'

Sara was quiet for a long moment, before finally speaking. 'Do you think Esmeralda never made it to him? If she even ran away at all?'

Claudia shut her eyes, not wanting to believe that something terrible could have happened to her. 'If she made it to him, wouldn't he have greeted her with open arms? And if he didn't want her, wouldn't that be even more reason to contact her family? To send her home?'

Sara sighed again. 'It's a mystery I never even knew existed, not like this.'

'That makes two of us.'

'How much longer are you here?' she asked.

'A few days.'

'Let me go and see my aunties, I'll ask around and see what I can discover. Someone must know something.'

'Thank you.'

'No, thank you. If you hadn't arrived on my doorstep, I would never have known all this, and who knows? My grandmother might not be here much longer, so we need to find out everything we can before the secret is lost with her generation.'

After saying goodbye, Claudia lay on the bed, staring up at the ceiling as she tried to piece the information she had together. But it was no use. She'd learnt two key pieces of information today: Esmeralda had been pregnant, and her intention had been to travel to London. Only it was still a stretch to believe that the unborn child was her grandmother. Wasn't it?

She glanced at the little wooden box she'd left on the bedside table. *Who would have thought something so little could have turned my life upside down.*

31

LONDON, 1951

Esmeralda felt as if her body was on fire, twisting one way and then the other as a pain like nothing she'd ever felt before ravaged her body. She cried out, but it sounded more animal than human, not a sound she'd ever made before as she clutched frantically at the bed, the sheets fisted in her palms as she rode the contraction, as she prayed that everything was all right. Because it didn't feel all right, nothing about what was happening to her felt all right.

It's too soon. This can't be happening. It's too soon! Why is this happening to me?!

Her eyes were squeezed tightly shut when something cool touched her forehead, followed by the soothing words of a woman who already meant as much to her as her own family did. Without her, she would surely have been lying on the street, with no one to care for her or assist her in her time of need. Without Hope, she'd have been kicked out of the hospital with nowhere to go.

'Please, I need Christopher,' she whispered, groaning as the pain clenched in her stomach again. '*Christopher*,' she cried.

'There, there, love,' Hope said, moving the cloth around her face, before dipping it into the cool dish of water beside the bed, wringing it out, and then going through the process all over again. 'Your Christopher will be here soon enough, don't you worry.'

'Did you find him?' she gasped, grabbing hold of Hope's wrist.

'I have one of the girls calling him again now,' she said. 'And someone else has been dispatched to his office to see if they can't find him there.'

Esmeralda let go and sunk back down onto the bed. 'You still haven't found him?' she whispered. 'He still doesn't even know I'm here?'

Hope kept pressing the cloth against her skin. 'We'll find him, don't you worry. Your job is to deliver this baby safe and sound, you hear me? That's all you need to be thinking about.'

Esmeralda shut her eyes and cried as a pain ripped through her abdomen, so severe she thought it would slice her in half. *I can't do this. I can't do this without Christopher.*

'Gisele,' she sobbed, clutching the sheets again. 'María!' *I need my sisters! I can't do this without them, I can't go through this. I can't.*

'Shh, my love,' Hope murmured. 'You can do this. Everything's going to be fine.'

I'm sorry, Papá. I'm so sorry I let you down. I'm so sorry I did this to our family.

She bit down on her lip as tears streamed down her cheeks, as the pain started to build again, as the reality of what she'd done came crashing down on her. Just like her pain came in waves, so did her memories, taking her back to Havana, to the life she'd had, to the life she'd walked away from as if it meant nothing to her.

To meeting Christopher, to the way his eyes had danced with hers, the way he'd made her feel inside. Of being in his arms, of loving him in a way she'd never known was possible.

To her baby growing inside of her, those first flutters, the life they'd created.

Her eyes opened then and she cleared her throat. As if knowing what she needed, Hope reached for water and passed her the glass. Her throat still felt like sandpaper, but at least she could swallow now. But when she looked at Hope, she wished she hadn't, because she could tell from her face that something was wrong. Something was very wrong.

'I need paper,' she said, her voice husky as if she hadn't slept. 'And a pen.'

Hope nodded. 'Of course. May I do something for you though? Could I write for you?'

'Just the paper and pen, please,' Esmeralda managed through gritted teeth, as if through willpower alone she could end the pain as it rippled through her again. 'Please.'

Hope left her side and she immediately missed the cool cloth. She called on all her strength to sit up, refusing to allow the pain to entirely cripple her as she watched Hope leave the room. She must have only been gone minutes, but they stretched on as she gripped the sheets once more, knowing what she needed to do, knowing she had the strength to cope with the pain; understanding the truth of what was happening to her body, that nothing was going to go to plan.

'Are you certain I can't do this for you?' Hope asked as she hurried back in.

'No,' Esmeralda ground out. 'Please, just—' she tried not to cry as the pain intensified, worse than earlier, worse than only moments before. 'Please, just pass it to me.'

Hope did as she asked, passing Hope the pen and paper, as well as a book to lean on, and when she saw how much she was struggling Hope propped an extra cushion behind her, hovering as if she didn't want Esmeralda to be doing anything other than resting.

Esmeralda held the pen between her shaking fingers and

tried to steady her hand as she carefully sketched an image that would be forever etched into her mind. She began with the outline and then, carefully inhaling and exhaling, pausing between contractions, she started to draw the rest of the coat of arms. It needed colour to bring it to life, but there was no time. Even in black and white, even with her unsteady hand, when she looked down at the paper it was unmistakably her family crest.

'Please,' she gasped. 'If something happens to me, if I don't make it, you need to keep this for my baby. I need her to know who her family is, who she can go to. They won't let her be an orphan.'

Hope nodded and took the paper when she extended it to her. 'I'll keep this safe for your baby, Esmeralda,' she promised. 'You can trust me to do that for you.'

'Tell her that my papá, her abuelo, will take her in. Tell her that even though he is angry with me, even though I disgraced him and my family, he will never turn away blood. He will never turn her away.'

'Her?' Hope asked, her voice kindly. 'You believe you're having a little girl?'

Esmeralda managed a smile—perhaps her first smile since she'd arrived in London. 'My family always has girls. She will be a girl.'

Hope nodded, but when she went to turn away, Esmeralda reached for her, fingers closing around her arm.

'I need you to keep something else for her, too,' she whispered as tears filled her eyes. She reached into her blouse and pulled out the business card she'd held the entire way to London, and had been holding when Hope had found her on the street. She lifted it to her lips and kissed it, closing her eyes for a beat as she wished things could have been different, wished that Christopher had been waiting for her. 'I need you to put this with the crest. I need her to know who her father is, in case he doesn't—'

Hope's hand closed over hers. 'Your Christopher will be here soon.'

'But if he's not,' Esmeralda whispered. 'If I don't make it, if he doesn't—'

Hope's eyes reflected the tears in her own as she squeezed her fingers tightly. 'Your Christopher will make it,' Hope repeated, as if to convince herself as much as Esmeralda. 'But if he doesn't, you have my word. These two things will be kept for the baby. You can trust me, Esmeralda, I will fight for you and your baby as if you were my own flesh and blood.'

Esmeralda pressed the card into Hope's palm, grateful beyond belief to the woman beside her, sinking back down as her skin suddenly became burning hot. She felt as if she were on fire from the inside, sweat breaking across her brow as she squirmed in pain. But it was different this time, something had changed. It was almost as if she were outside of her own body, as if she were starting to float away from the agony of her labour, the torture her body was enduring.

'Esmeralda?' Hope's voice seemed to swim around her. 'Esmeralda! You stay strong, I'm not going to lose you.'

Esmeralda blinked, her vision coming back as she looked sideways and saw the paper fluttering to the ground, the card falling with it as Hope pressed the cloth back to her forehead, as water that should have felt cold trickled down her temple and onto her cheek and instead felt as if it were burning her.

'This is the young lady?'

She heard a voice, a male voice, and she smiled, reaching out, her eyes still shut. 'Christopher? Is that my Christopher?' But even as she said the words she felt as if her mouth wasn't moving properly, as if she were slowly drifting to sleep.

'Esmeralda, you stay with me, you hear! You stay with me! You have a baby to meet, your daughter is ready to meet you!'

Hope's voice sounded loud and she turned her head away as something cold was pressed to her chest. She blinked again, her vision blurry as she squinted at the figure before her, trying to follow Hope's voice and do as she said.

'Christopher?'

'I'm Doctor Wilkins,' the figure said. 'Hope called on me to help deliver the baby.'

The pain she'd experienced earlier came back with a vengeance, and she cried out as the doctor took the sheet from over her and placed a hand on her stomach. She was in a night-dress so damp that it clung to her body, as if she'd been plunged in water, but her modesty was long gone. She needed help getting the baby out, and she needed it now, otherwise she knew she wasn't going to make it.

'How long has she been like this?' she heard the doctor ask.

'Too long,' Hope said, reaching for her hand and holding it tightly. 'She collapsed yesterday but the hospital refused to admit her, and I've had her here since. But the obvious signs of labour only began in the past few hours.'

A hot sensation between her legs made her cry out then, but it was the gasp from Hope that surprised her.

'We don't have long,' the doctor muttered. 'There's no chance of saving them both.'

Saving us both? She wanted to tell the doctor to save her baby, that her child was all that mattered, but if Christopher never came then who would look after her baby? Who would raise her?

'She's losing too much blood,' the doctor said as Hope placed towels beneath her and pressed them between her legs.

'I'm bleeding?' Esmeralda croaked.

'Shh, my love, everything will be fine,' Hope whispered. 'We're going to do everything we can for you and the baby.'

But the towels she took away were stained a bright red; Esmeralda saw them when she looked down, even through her hazy eyes. She didn't know much about babies and childbearing, but she was certain there wasn't supposed to be so much blood, that a doctor and a woman who assisted deliveries wouldn't be so shocked by the sight of it if it were normal.

'Where is she?' the loud yell from somewhere in the house was impossible not to hear, and it brought Esmeralda crashing back to the present, her heart pounding at the sound of his voice. *Christopher?* 'Tell me where she is!'

The yelling was followed by loud thudding that she guessed were footsteps, and as the doctor pressed painfully on her stomach, as she lost her breath, she heard him calling her name.

Christopher. It was Christopher. He's found me.

'Esmeralda!' he cried, rushing to her side, past Hope who was trying to block his way, who was starting to tell him that he shouldn't be in the room.

'Christopher,' she whispered. 'Christopher, is that you?'

Christopher took hold of Esmeralda's hand and held it so tightly she knew he wouldn't let go no matter how hard Hope tried to move him. His lips were against her forehead now, as she shut her eyes, relieved that he was finally by her side, that she wasn't going to have to do this alone.

'I came as soon as I heard, my brave, beautiful Esmeralda, I —' Christopher's voice trailed off, as if he'd finally taken stock of the situation, as if he'd finally realised what was happening and the predicament she was in. Perhaps he'd seen the blood, or perhaps the drawn faces of the other two people in the room.

'Christopher, I need to—' she was interrupted by the doctor. 'You're the father, I take it?'

'I am,' she heard Christopher say as she shut her eyes again, as a sharp pain like nothing before began to build inside of her. 'This woman is to be my wife.'

'There's no chance of both mother and child surviving this labour, she's losing too much blood and I fear—'

'We must take her to St Mary's Hospital,' Christopher

announced, his arms scooping around her as if he were going to lift her and carry her to the hospital himself. 'I shall ensure her the very best care, anything Esmeralda needs—'

'Sir, I'm sorry but it's far too late for that,' the doctor interrupted as Esmeralda began to cry, tears slipping down her cheeks as her vision started to blur again. He was too late. If only she'd found him the day before, if only he'd come sooner, if only they'd had time to be married first. 'You need to decide, the mother or the child.'

There was silence for a moment, as she tried to scream to him that he must choose their child, but the words seemed stuck in her throat as her skin began to burn, as if her entire body was on fire.

'Esmeralda,' Christopher said quickly. 'I choose Esmeralda. You must do everything you can to save the mother, she's all that matters.'

'No,' she choked, her hand flailing as she tried but failed to connect with him. 'No, Christopher, no you mustn't—'

'My darling, please,' he whispered, bent over her, his arms around her and his lips to her hand. 'We can have another baby, but I can't lose you. I *won't* lose you, not now that we're finally together.'

But in that moment she knew it didn't matter what his decision, because her body started to shudder, as if it was making the decision for them all. She inhaled the smell of him, absorbed the feel of his hand in hers, tried valiantly to lift her arms to hold him back even though it was fruitless.

She felt the moment her body went limp, all of her energy pulled into a wave of pain that felt as if it might tear her in half, that sent a searing hot knife through her and then left her spent.

The doctor began yelling, she could hear his raised voice at the same time as Hope's soothing one. Christopher's hands cradled her head, it was all she could feel, all she could think about.

Someone was crying, and she wasn't sure if it was her or Christopher, but when he grabbed at her hand and pressed it to his lips, she felt wetness and knew that the sobs had come from him.

'I love you, Esmeralda,' he cried. 'I'm so sorry I failed you. I'm so sorry.'

She wanted to reassure him, to tell him that he could hold the baby first, that everything was going to be all right, only she knew that it would be a lie. Nothing was ever going to be all right about what was happening to her body, and she could no longer utter a word, anyhow.

Everything went numb then as the room became a blur, as her eyes shut, unable to keep them open any longer. She could still feel Christopher's touch, could still hear the cries of someone, perhaps her own again, and with a burst of hope she wondered if it were the cries of her child.

'We're losing her,' the doctor cried.

'Come on, love. Stay here for your baby, you hear me?'

But Hope's words only washed over her, as if they weren't even intended for her. There was a warmth building inside of her at the same time as everything else went dark, as everything started to fade away, the voices sounding as if they were far away instead of beside her. As if she'd already left the room.

I love you, my daughter. My beautiful, strong baby girl.

Esmeralda's only wish was that she'd been strong enough to cling to life a few minutes longer; strong enough to stay alive to cradle her baby and kiss Christopher one last time.

Only she couldn't fight against the overwhelming desire to fall asleep.

'Esmeralda, please! Esmeralda, come back to me!'

But it was too late. Even as she heard his words, as they seemed to slip past her, trying desperately to keep her alive, she was gone.

32

FLORIDA, PRESENT DAY

When Claudia received another call from Sara, the morning before she was due to fly out, she certainly hadn't expected to be invited to meet more members of the Diaz family. But when she walked into the living room of Sara's house, there were four other women there, all with the same raven dark hair and beautiful brown eyes. It seemed the Diaz genes ran strong—she could only imagine how beautiful Esmeralda, María, Gisele and Marisol had been as young women.

'Hi,' Claudia said as they all looked back at her.

She was worried they might give her a frosty reception, but one by one the women rose and introduced themselves, embracing her warmly.

'I'm Sophie,' one of the women said before kissing her cheek. 'María was my grandmother.'

'Adele,' said another, hugging her tightly. 'María was my grandmother, too.'

She went on to meet Saskia and Helene, who were the granddaughters of Gisele, before Sara waved her over to sit on the sofa beside her.

'I certainly wasn't expecting all this!' she said, looking

around in surprise at the other women gathered. 'I can't believe you all came.'

'It might make sense when you look through these,' Sara said. 'We've all spent a lot of time talking these past couple of days, and going through all the old boxes of things from our grandmothers. You could say we became obsessed with solving this family mystery once and for all.'

'Not to mention talking to our own mothers,' Adele said. 'It seems they knew more than they'd told us. I think they spent much of their childhoods whispering about what might have happened to their mysterious aunt, but then never really talked about it to us.'

Claudia looked back at Sara. 'You've heard more about Esmeralda?'

'Yes, we have,' Sara said. 'And look what we found.'

She watched as Sara lifted a rectangular cardboard box from the coffee table and lifted the lid, taking out what appeared to be bundles of letters.

'Do you remember Marisol saying the other day that she'd sent Esmeralda drawings and letters all those years ago, when she was just a girl?' Sara asked, as she passed some papers to her.

Claudia gasped. There, as clear as day, were the letters Marisol had spoken of, signed with the wobbly hand of a child at the bottom.

'They were returned to her?' Claudia asked. 'Did she never know this?'

'They were returned. Everything was returned to them, in fact, it's all here,' she said. 'Untouched, but still tied altogether with string in the same way they were sent. If Esmeralda ever received them, then she certainly didn't open them.'

Claudia reached for the box and looked through it, carefully sifting through the pages and imagining the Diaz sisters carefully writing their letters, at risk of being discovered by their father, but doing it anyway, only to have them returned and never opened. It must have broken all of their hearts.

'My mother was led to believe that Esmeralda's baby had died,' Helene said, her smile kind when Claudia lifted her gaze. 'She also believed that Esmeralda herself must have met a sad end. From the stories she was told, the sisters were as close as siblings could be.'

'What do you think now?' Claudia asked. 'And why would she think her sister's baby had died?'

'Well to start with, I think that our mothers were wrong,' Helene said.

'Claudia, we all think that your grandmother must have been Esmeralda's baby,' Sara said gently. 'There's so much to sort through here, so many letters and other correspondence from such a long time ago, but something went terribly wrong with Esmeralda's plans. The only thing that seems to make sense is that she left behind clues for her baby, the clues that you now have.'

'We know she was taken to the airport in Havana,' Helene added. 'Our grandmothers were instrumental in helping her to escape, along with a cousin. They risked everything so she could travel to her Christopher. But the plan was that she would send a letter as soon as she arrived, begging for her father's forgiveness and telling them that she was safe.'

'Here,' Sara said. 'Read this.'

Darling Esmeralda,

You've been gone twelve weeks now, and our sorrow at not having you here grows by the day. I thought we'd become used to not having you here, but it's like losing Mamá all over again. What we wouldn't do to hear your voice and see your beautiful face, even just to sit at breakfast with you one last time.

I know you must be busy, but please write to us. We are so worried about you, even though I try to tell the others how busy you must be. With your beloved Christopher and your little baby, living the life you wanted. We are all convinced you had a boy! Please, let us know how motherhood is treating you. I'm certain you'll be the most wonderful mother, just as you were a second mother to our little Marisol. She misses you terribly, by the way, although Gisele and I have tried to step into your shoes and look after her the way you always did.

Papá still won't mention your name, which pains us all greatly, however, we all believe that with news of your marriage and baby, he will have to forgive you. And how could he not? Papá has always adored you. I think his pain is as much because you've made a life elsewhere, that he no longer has you at his side. Please would you write to him? It would mean so much if one day we could all be together again, at least for a vacation here in Cuba so we can see you and your little one. Oh, and how wonderful would it be if we could visit you in London! Imagine the adventures we could have, and I still remember the stories you told of Harrods and the afternoon tea there.

I love you, Esmeralda, with all my heart. My brave, loving, wonderful sister, who will always be in my heart no matter how long we are parted.

María xx

Claudia stared down at the paper in her hands. It was dated 1951.

'Why would Esmeralda not have answered this if she'd received it?' she asked. 'Why would she have returned it to the sender? Why wouldn't she have wanted to exchange letters with her beloved sisters?'

'I suppose we'll never truly know,' Sara said. 'But the reason we're all here today, is because we all believe that your connection to us is our great-aunt, Esmeralda. The only thing we all agree on is that her baby must have survived, and somehow she ended up in the home you told me about. There's no other explanation for the clues you were given.'

'We'd actually like to do a DNA test with you, to see if you're the missing link to our family,' Adele added, as her cousins all nodded at her suggestion. 'It seems only fair after you've come all this way.'

'A DNA test?' Claudia asked. 'I, well—'

'There's no pressure at all,' Sara interrupted. 'Just know that the offer is there, if you'd like to know for sure.'

Before she could reply there was a thud outside, followed by a shuffling noise, but before anyone had time to investigate a head of coiffed white-grey hair appeared in the window. *Marisol.*

'Abuela!' Sara was on her feet, with her cousins close behind, opening the door and ushering Marisol inside. 'What are you doing here? How did you even get here?'

Marisol waved her hand in the air as if to dismiss her granddaughter. 'My driver. I insisted he bring me here. It's my house, after all.'

Claudia stood back as they settled Marisol onto the sofa, and Adele disappeared and returned with a glass of water.

'Do you have anything stronger?' Marisol asked, which made them all laugh.

'No champagne, sorry,' Sara muttered. 'How about coffee?'

'I'd prefer gin.'

Claudia had to turn her face away so Marisol didn't see her smile. The old lady was hilarious. *And somehow just like my grandmother.* The thought struck her unawares, creeping up on her as she thought of her own grandmother cooking up a storm, always with a strong gin and tonic within reach. She'd always told them it was what kept her healthy, as if the slice of lemon she added somehow contained enough vitamin C to stop her from catching any passing illness.

'Abuela, why did you come today? You know you're not supposed to just leave whenever you feel like it.'

'Because I remembered part of the story,' Marisol replied, her eyes twinkling like a woman half her age, as if she possessed some great secret. 'Don't you want to hear it?'

Claudia cleared her throat as Sara replied. 'Of course, please, go on.'

Marisol sat back with her arms crossed until Sara eventually relented and went to make her a drink, returning with what Claudia guessed was gin, as the cousins all giggled to themselves. Clearly this was not unexpected behaviour.

'Once María was married, she made her husband take us to London,' Marisol said. 'It was supposed to be their honeymoon abroad, but she took me with her. I still remember arriving there, it looked so different to home, but it was the smell that told me I was in another country. It's all come back to me, the excitement of that trip. I haven't been able to stop thinking about it.'

'You were there to see Esmeralda?'

She nodded. 'We were there to find her. But when we went to the place Christopher worked, the firm his father owned, he wasn't there. Or if he was, he certainly wasn't going to see us.'

'So you never found her?'

Marisol shook her head. 'We looked and looked, but it was as if our Esmeralda had never even been there. Christopher's father knew nothing of their relationship, even when María's husband pressed him for information.'

Claudia wondered how the mystery could deepen, when she seemed so close to discovering everything she'd come searching for.

'Did you return home after that?' Sara asked, now seated beside Claudia.

Marisol shook her head. 'María marched up to that office every day looking for her, she stayed the entire week, but it was as if Esmeralda had never arrived in London at all. It was as if she'd vanished somewhere between Havana and there.'

'What do you think happened to her, Marisol?' Claudia asked, keeping her voice soft, not wanting to push her for memories that were no doubt very painful.

Marisol took a sip of her drink. 'I think something happened to our Esmeralda. I think our Esmeralda died, but no one wanted to tell us.'

'Why do you think that, Abuela?' Sara asked.

'Because of this.'

They all sat back and watched as Marisol set her drink down and reached into her jacket pocket, producing a yellowed piece of paper that was folded into a little square. Her arthritic hands shook as she opened it, and Claudia couldn't help but notice the enormous sapphire surrounded by diamonds on her finger. It was perhaps a reminder of her younger years, a gift from her husband or maybe even her father.

'I asked Papá when we got home from that trip if he knew what had happened to Esmeralda, and I was only a girl but I could see it in his eyes, I knew that he was lying to me. He couldn't look at me when he told me he'd never heard from her.'

'But he had?' Claudia asked. 'Heard from her, I mean?'

'That was the part he wasn't lying about,' Marisol said, her hand shaking as she held out the letter. 'But he did know what had happened to her.'

Sara took it and Claudia shuffled closer to her, the cousins leaving their seats to crowd around her, too.

Dear Mr Diaz,

I feel it my duty to write and tell you that your daughter, Esmeralda, gave birth to a daughter last night. The baby is

healthy, but Esmeralda is no longer with us. I am not in a posi-
tion to raise a child alone, I cannot even consider it, however, if
you should wish to adopt her, you may make arrangements
with the facility where she delivered the baby, named Hope's
House. I enclose the address below.

This will be my final correspondence on the matter. I
regret to inform you that I will no longer be conducting busi-
ness through my father's firm, however my father will
continue to honour the deal we brokered. I can assure you
that I have conducted this matter with absolute discretion,
and no one else knows about the birth or my relationship to
your daughter, so your family's good name will remain
intact.

Yours, Christopher Dutton.

'She died in London?' Sara whispered. 'All this time, you knew what had happened to her?'

Marisol was staring out the window now, as if lost to her own thoughts, nursing her drink as she sat.

'Abuela!' Sara said. 'Did your sisters know the truth? Did you all keep it hidden all these years, or was it only you?'

When Marisol looked back, her eyes were swimming. 'No one knew the truth, but me and Papá. I stole the letter from him and never showed it to anyone. I wanted them all to believe that she was alive, that she was living the life she dreamed of.' She let out a shaky-sounding sigh. 'I think perhaps I even convinced myself it was true, until you started asking me questions and it all began to come back to me.'

Claudia understood, of course she did, but when Sara stood and left the room, clearly upset, she went after her. She found her in the kitchen, her fingers pressing so tightly into the stone countertop that Claudia could see the whites of her knuckles. The cold tone of Christopher's letter was almost impossible to digest. How could he have left his baby behind so callously if he'd been in love with Esmeralda?

'I'm sorry for the part I've played in all this, bringing up painful memories,' Claudia said, touching her hand gently to Sara's back.

'She let her sisters believe that Esmeralda had turned her back on them, as if she cared so little about them that she could cut them from her life so easily,' Sara said. 'How could she do that to them?'

'It was cruel,' Claudia agreed. 'But perhaps she felt she couldn't tell them? She was only a girl at the time after all, and once she was old enough to understand, perhaps she'd kept the secret too long to share?'

'She's right.' Marisol was standing behind them now, and Sara's face softened the moment she saw her grandmother there.

'Did you want to tell them?' Sara asked. 'Did you at least feel guilty for keeping them in the dark?'

'Of course I did. But how could I admit that I'd known all those years? How could I tell them that I'd lied, just like Papá had? That their sister had died, alone in London, and that the man she'd loved, who we'd all fallen in love with when he'd visited us, had turned his back on Esmeralda's child? When she died the same way our mamá did?'

Sara stepped forward and Claudia watched as she hugged her grandmother, carefully as if she were holding something so precious. And when their embrace ended she could see why; Marisol's hands were shaking, and she wiped at her eyes.

'These are things I haven't thought of for many years,' Marisol whispered. 'Things I wanted to forget. Sometimes I tell myself that Esmeralda is still alive, that it was all a mistake. That the man she loved didn't turn out to be a coward.'

'What I don't understand,' Sara said, leaving her grandmother for a moment and taking down glasses for them all, which she filled with sparkling water, 'is why Christopher left the baby. Why wouldn't he have raised her? Or at least found family to raise her? If he truly loved Esmeralda, why would he abandon their child?'

'And why didn't my father travel to London immediately?' Marisol asked. 'It's something I've thought about for many years, something I wish I knew the answer to. He loved Esmeralda so very much, both the men in her life did, and I never understood why our papá didn't forgive her and rush to take her baby into the fold of our family. My sisters would have raised the child without hesitation.'

'Times were different then,' Claudia said, imagining her grandmother as an infant, left by the man Esmeralda had been so desperately in love with. 'Perhaps the shame of it all was too much for either man to bear?'

Sara passed them each the glass of water she'd poured, as they stood and stared at one another.

'I think you're right about my grandmother,' Claudia said. 'I think she was Esmeralda's child. I think she was the baby who Christopher walked away from. She has to be, doesn't she?'

Sara smiled. 'She does.'

Marisol looked confused then, as if she suddenly couldn't piece together what was happening, and Claudia watched as Sara led her grandmother from the room, guiding her back to the living room and setting her back in her chair. The other women had all been chatting in their absence but a hush fell over the room when they entered, and Claudia looked at each of them.

They may not know one another, but they were family to her. A family she'd never even known had existed until now, and it was all she could do to hold back her emotion. She only wished her grandmother was with her, because she would have loved to meet all the women before her.

Sara gestured for her to sit down and she did, her hand

shaking almost as much as Marisol's had as she lifted her glass to her lips and took a sip. It was then that Sara placed a hand on her knee, her touch warm as she leaned in to her.

'I don't think we need a DNA test to know that you're one of us,' she said. 'Truly, don't feel obligated to—'

'I'd actually like to do it, for all our sakes,' Claudia said, knowing in her heart it was the right thing to do. 'I feel that if I don't, there will always be this doubt over whether I am in fact Esmeralda's great-granddaughter. Seeing the result might give us all some closure.'

Sara smiled and held up her water glass, clinking it to Claudia's. 'To solving the mystery once and for all.'

Claudia grinned back. 'To solving the mystery.'

Her journey had taken her from London to Cuba to Miami, but it had been worth it. She'd managed to solve the mystery of her grandmother's birth, to give closure to a chapter of her family's past that had deserved to be discovered, and it was a journey she'd never, ever forget.

Now she just had to find a way back to Cuba, because the one chapter she didn't feel was closed was the one with Mateo.

'Come on, let's go out for lunch to celebrate,' Helene said, jumping to her feet as she indicated for them all to rise.

'What are we celebrating?' Marisol asked, looking confused.

'Family,' Sara said, helping her grandmother to her feet. 'We're celebrating our family, Abuela.'

Claudia took Marisol's other arm, linking hers through it. If only her own grandmother had still been alive; she could only imagine the stories she and Marisol could have shared.

Once she was back in her hotel room, Claudia put on her pyjamas and got into bed, exhausted from her day. She plumped up the pillows behind her and reached for her phone, realising she hadn't checked her emails since the night before.

She had so much to tell her parents, but it was too early to call them in Surrey—she'd have to wait until morning to ring with the news.

She scrolled through some emails she'd address later, stopping at one from her estate agent, that was marked as urgent.

We've had an offer on your flat! Call me as soon as you can, I think you'll be very happy with it.

Claudia smiled to herself. She'd done it. The first time she'd renovated and sold a property, she'd wondered if it was a fluke, whether she'd ever be able to do it again. But now she'd proven to herself that it was a viable business for her, that she'd been right to follow her instincts and back herself.

The next email was from her dad. But her smile quickly turned to sadness when she read his message.

Darling, I thought you'd like to see this. I don't know what you've discovered in Miami, but I found this newspaper clipping from the *Telegraph* in 1951.

DIAZ, ESMERALDA, PASSED AWAY DURING CHILDBIRTH, AGED 20 YEARS. DEARLY LOVED BY HER FAMILY, AND REMEMBERED ALWAYS.

She stared at the news clipping. So Julio had chosen to acknowledge his daughter's passing, after all? It must have been him, for who else would have had the notice printed on behalf of the family? Seeing it like that made it all the more real, too. Even though she'd already discovered Esmeralda had died, to see her name printed in black and white, to know that she'd been such a vibrant, beautiful young woman, who'd made the ultimate sacrifice in leaving her family, only to pass away before she had the chance to fully live her life. It was heartbreaking.

Claudia blinked through her tears, going back to her inbox and deciding not to reply to her father. She'd rather wait to speak to him in the morning than try to explain her day in an email.

But as she absently looked through her inbox, her finger stopped, hovering over an unexpected name. *Mateo.*

She nestled back farther into the pillows, almost too scared to tap on the message. They'd left things open between them, but in truth her feelings for him ran so much deeper than just a holiday fling, and she'd been hoping to hear from him ever since she'd left Havana.

Claudia,

I miss my sous chef. Come back to Havana before you return to London? I want to hear all about Miami. It's not the same here without you. Also, creo que te amo.

Mateo.

She smiled to herself as she read his message a second time, committing the Spanish to memory and opening Google Translate. When she read what it meant, her heart skipped a beat. *I think I love you.*

She laughed to herself as she typed him back an email, her pulse racing as she replied, as she thought of returning to Havana one more time to see him. She had to, didn't she? There was no way she could return to London and not take him up on his invitation.

Mateo,

I think I might just love you, too. I'll see you soon.

Claudia xx

And as she sunk back into the pillows, closing her laptop and pulling the covers up to her chin, her mind was filled with memories of Cuba. She might only have days with Mateo, and it may well break her heart, but if she didn't go back to him she knew she'd never forgive herself.

Somehow, just like her great-grandmother before her, she'd fallen for a man from another country, a man who didn't make sense, but who made her feel alive. Everything was stacked against them, but somehow, it didn't seem to matter. And the difference was that she had the power to make her own decisions, to choose her own destiny. Something about Havana had imprinted itself on her soul, it had taken hold of her and made her feel like the country was a part of her.

I'll see you soon, Mateo. And in her mind, she was already walking the Malecón with him, arm in arm, his lips pressing a gentle kiss to her hair as he whispered the words he'd written in his email.

Creo que te amo.
I think I love you, too.

33

'You know we'll never forget you,' Sara said, holding Claudia tight as they hugged at the airport.

'I know,' Claudia said, squeezing her back. 'Although I don't think you'll have time to forget me, my mum's already looking at flights to come over and meet you all. She's unbelievably excited.'

'Well, just remember that we're family. There's always a place for you here.'

'And the same for you in London,' Claudia replied, as her flight was called.

'American Airlines Flight 837 to Havana is now inviting passengers to board.'

'Enjoy your time there,' Sara said. 'I've been wanting to travel there for so many years, and now that Castro has gone, well, I suppose I don't have any excuses, do I?'

'Trust me when I say I can recommend the best place to stay,' Claudia said as she started to walk backwards, not wanting to be the last through the security line. 'And you won't regret it. Cuba is like nowhere else in the world.'

'Funny, Marisol has told me that all my life, since I was a

little girl. I think it's why I've never been, because I don't want to ruin this image I have in my mind of how fabulous it is there.'

'It won't ruin it,' Claudia said, blowing Sara a kiss before she turned, calling over her shoulder. 'You'll probably fall in love and never want to return to Florida!'

She listened to Sara's laugh as she hurried along, seeing that she was among the last in the security line, despite her best intentions.

'Boarding pass and passport,' the attendant said.

Claudia passed her documents over to be scanned, quickly glancing back and giving Sara one last wave. Four days ago, they'd been complete strangers, and now there was a bond between them that Claudia knew would never be broken.

She slipped her hand into her bag and felt the envelope there, right beside her Kindle and the little wooden box she was still carrying. Anticipation built within her but she waited until she was seated, her bag on her knees as she fastened her seatbelt and listened to the safety briefing, grateful there was an empty seat between her and the other passenger in her row.

And when the plane was finally in the air she took out the envelope and slid her nail beneath the seal, opening the page. She realised she was holding her breath so she quickly exhaled slowly, before finally looking down at the paper. Her eyes trailed across it as her pulse began to race, ignoring the chart and searching for the words she'd been waiting to read.

You have a 99.9 percent probability when compared to the other sample.

She clamped her hand over her mouth. There it was, in black and white. Esmeralda, the eldest Diaz sister, the woman she'd heard tales about since she'd first stepped foot on Cuban soil, was her great-grandmother.

Which meant Sara had been right; they were indeed family.

Grandma, I wish you could have met them. I wish you could have learnt about your heritage from Marisol, I wish you could have met your great-nieces. I wish you could have been here with me on this adventure.

But more than anything, she wished her grandmother could have travelled with her to Cuba. To smell the air, taste the food, see the beauty of the place her mother had come from, of the heritage that formed half of her DNA. Of the legacy that had been kept from her.

Claudia's only consolation was that Cuba would forever be part of her soul now. It was a country that had gotten under skin, forever part of her identity.

She slipped the paper back into the envelope and closed her eyes. Only one hour, fifteen minutes to go and she'd be back there again.

And not a moment too soon.

Claudia stood and watched him. She was carrying her luggage still, having come straight from the airport, and she set it down so she could stand there a while longer and look at him as he worked. There was an easiness about his smile, a casual confidence in the way he called out to everyone as he worked, making it look effortless even though she knew there was a deep sadness inside of him. He was so good at keeping that part hidden.

She'd wondered if that was perhaps one of the reasons she was so drawn to him, because he understood her past in a way that so many others couldn't, or maybe it was just a coincidence that they'd both experienced such loss. She indulged in watching him a little longer, trying to decide whether to wait until he had no one left waiting in line, or go and offer to help, but something kept her rooted in place. She might have to wait for a very long time for the line of people to disappear, as new customers walked up every few minutes, but she was starting to feel a little nervous.

He asked me to come back. He told me in his letter how he felt about me.

But even knowing all that, it still didn't stop the butterflies in her stomach as she indulged in watching him some more. She knew why—her ex had always professed his love for her and then the moment she'd wobbled from the path of perfection he'd backed away as if she'd been on fire. And as much as she knew that Mateo was different, it was still hard for her to trust, to believe that someone's feelings could run as deeply as her own.

What we have is different though. We're not planning a life together, we're simply two people trying to make the most of the moments we have together.

As if hearing her thoughts, Mateo looked up. Claudia froze. His face was impassive a moment, as if he couldn't believe what he was seeing, before breaking out into a grin and stopping what he was doing. Claudia stood as he emerged from the food truck, a towel in his hands as he wiped them before walking quickly towards her. She saw all the people in line turn, no doubt wondering where he was going in such a hurry, as she took a tentative step towards him, smilling as he scooped her up into his arms and twirled her around, his lips finding hers. But their kiss quickly turned to laughter as he set her to her feet, smiling down at her, stroking her hair from her forehead.

'When did you get here?' he asked. 'I can't believe you didn't tell me!'

She glanced down at her bags. 'I came straight from the airport.'

'Come here,' he said, his voice gruff as he cupped her face and pressed a long, slow kiss to her mouth this time.

The crowd started whistling and clapping, which made her blush all the way to her toes, especially when Mateo spun around and held up her hand as if she were a prize. But she couldn't help smiling when he lifted her hand to his lips and kissed it, shaking his head as he looked into her eyes. And she could see it reflected in his gaze, the way he felt about her, the truth of the words he'd said in his email.

'Come on,' he murmured, leaning in close before collecting her bags for her. 'They're cheering for us now, but if I burn their food they'll be chasing us with pitchforks.'

She grinned and followed after him, nodding and smiling at the customers gathered.

'My sous chef returns!' Mateo announced, throwing his arm out towards her as if her presence was something to be revered.

Claudia did a little bow, thinking that she was more suited to the job of pot washer than sous chef, but she happily went along with it, climbing into the truck behind him. The smell of his cooking seemed to engulf her and she took a moment to breathe it in, to feel the heat from the gas burners, the humidity already sending moisture across her skin. This was Mateo's happy place, and somehow, it had become hers, too. All those years of struggling in the kitchen, and suddenly cooking no longer seemed like a chore. All thanks to Mateo.

He paused then, looking at her over his shoulder and shaking his head, like he couldn't believe she was there. She couldn't believe it, either.

'It's so good to see you again,' he said.

She grinned. 'The feeling's mutual.'

And just like that they fell into an easy rhythm, of her helping with orders and passing the food out to customers, smiling and trying her best to say words in Spanish, which usually resulted in plenty of laughter from those waiting. But it didn't matter, because they seemed to like that she was trying, and she liked it too.

'Mateo, about your idea, for the sauces,' she said.

He looked up, his eyes bright as he ladled his famous ropa vieja from the pot.

'I think it's a great idea,' she said. 'I think you should do it.'

He just gave her a wink and she smiled to herself as she passed another plate out to a happy customer, who gave her a beaming smile in return and even reached out to pat her hand, looking past her to Mateo, as if to tell them she approved. She didn't need to say anything for Claudia to know what she meant. Just like Mateo had brought something to life within her, she'd somehow done the same to him, and nothing had ever felt quite so good.

'Take a seat on the step,' Mateo said as Claudia finished wiping down the counter once all the customers had gone. Every night it was a case of running out of food rather than people not wanting to buy, and although she hated seeing Mateo have to turn customers away, she was grateful it was closing time. She was exhausted from the past two hours, but she was also ready for a moment alone with him.

Claudia did as he asked and went to sit, and within minutes he joined her, passing her a bottle of Cristal. She took the beer and took a long, grateful gulp. She'd never been a beer drinker before, but something about the heat in Cuba had converted her —it was the perfect cold, thirst-quenching drink after working in stifling humidity.

Remembering the heat she touched her hair and felt it damp near to forehead, and she quickly pushed it back off her face, imagining that any escaped tendrils would have started to curl.

Mateo held up his beer and clinked it to hers, before taking a few long gulps of his. He was sitting with his knees slightly parted so that one bumped into hers, and when he lowered his beer he leaned forward, arms resting on his legs.

'I still can't believe you're here,' he said.

'*I* still can't believe I'm here,' she replied, shaking her head as she took another sip.

'Did you find the answers to what you were looking for in Miami?'

She took a deep breath. 'I did, actually.'

His stare was as warm as it was intense. 'And what did you discover?'

'That my great-grandmother was Esmeralda Diaz,' she said, still in disbelief as she said the words.

'So you have Cuban blood running through your veins, huh?' he said with a grin. 'No wonder you felt such a connection when you arrived here.'

'It seems so silly, but I actually feel like I'm meant to be here. I feel like this place is a part of me.'

'It's not silly, Claudia. This is part of your heritage. Havana was the city of your great-grandmother's birth.' He took another sip of beer and shook his head. 'Esmeralda Diaz? Unbelievable.'

'I think I'm still in shock,' she said. 'And it's quite the story, how my grandmother came to be adopted.'

Mateo swapped his beer to his other hand and reached for her, interlacing their fingers. 'I'm pleased you came back,' he said. 'And I can't wait to hear all about your discovery.'

'The trouble is, I still have to leave. I feel like I'm just drawing things out and making it harder.'

His lips turned upwards. 'What if you didn't have to go?'

Claudia dropped her head to his shoulder, shutting her eyes for a moment as she absorbed the feel of him beside her, tried to commit every part of him and Havana to her memory. When his arm looped around her, drawing her even closer, she blinked away tears.

'I can't stay,' she whispered. 'I have a life in London, my family, my friends...' her voice trailed away as she wondered if she would give it all away to be with Mateo, a man she'd known for less than two weeks. Perhaps this is how people felt when they met the one, when they took a chance on giving up everything for a person they might spend the rest of their life with. Perhaps this is how her great-grandmother had felt?

His fingers squeezed her shoulder and she looked up at him. 'I'm going to miss you.'

'I'm going to miss you, too.'

Mateo kissed her gently, his lips moving slowly over hers as she sighed against his mouth, lost to his touch and wondering whether she should have told him she'd try to stay. But no matter how much her body wanted him, it wasn't enough to uproot her life, even if it were possible.

'We were ill-fated from the beginning, weren't we?' he said, his forehead coming to rest against hers.

'Or perhaps we were only ever destined to be a moment in each other's lives. To bring out the best in each other and show us what true happiness felt like?'

He smiled. 'Perhaps.'

They took a long breath at the same time, still touching, before Mateo pulled away and took a long sip of his beer, draining the bottle. 'Another?' he asked.

Claudia shook her head. 'Not for me.'

Mateo stood and disappeared then, and she stared out at the darkening sky, her heart beating fast as she second-guessed what she'd just said. *Am I making the biggest mistake in my life in walking away from him? Should I be trying to stay, for a man I've known less than a fortnight?*

'Mateo, about what I said earlier, about your business idea,' she said.

He opened his bottle and sat down beside her again.

'What if we turned it into a business?' she said. 'Together.'

His eyebrows lifted, but before he could reply she quickly spoke again.

'If you want to be business partners, that is. I mean, I don't want to step on your toes, but if we worked together, if—'

He held up his hand for her to stop, and his grin told her everything she needed to know.

'Sí, Claudia,' he said. 'I'd very much like that.'

'You would? You're not just saying that?'

'I would like that,' he said. 'I have the sauce and the passion, and you have the brains. Plus, it would mean I get to see you again, yes?'

She grinned. 'Yes, Mateo, it would mean you'd get to see me again.'

They both laughed and this time it was her clinking her bottle against his. 'So we're going into business together?' she asked.

'Yes, we're going into business together.'

She pushed back onto her elbows, her head full of ideas. 'I can already see your sauces on the shelves at Whole Foods and Sainsbury's, the way we'd package them. I feel like this is the business opportunity I've been waiting for.'

Mateo leaned back with her. 'You really think it would work?'

'I studied finance and business at university,' Claudia told him, 'but the only future I could see when I graduated was in banking and finance, and we both know how that turned out. And I love working on property, it's something I'll always do, but to work with you on this? To put my love of business into something that actually makes my heart sing? It would be such an honour to partner with you and make this happen.'

'Is it my sauces or me that makes your heart sing?' Mateo teased.

Her mouth lifted at the corners. 'Maybe both?'

Mateo slung his arm around her shoulders then and she shifted closer to him.

'I have no idea how this is going to work, what the restrictions are on us even doing business together from your country to mine, getting you to travel to London when we launch—'

'You never said anything about London. Isn't that how Esmeralda Diaz came to a grizzly end? Falling in love with an Englishman and running away to London?'

Claudia bumped her shoulder into his. 'Whoever said anything about running away?' *Or falling in love, for that matter.*

'If I didn't have José, if things were different,' Mateo began.

Claudia touched his knee and looked into his eyes. 'We both have things in our lives that we can't change, and I'd never ask you to leave your family. You're the only dad José has now, and that has to be the most important priority in your life. I get that.' She smiled. 'I would never, ever ask you to leave your family.'

'And you can't make the same mistake Esmeralda did and give everything up for the man you love, either.'

Claudia smiled. 'The man I love, huh?'

'Why is it so easy to say in an email, and so hard to say in real life?'

She tilted his face up to him. 'They're the hardest three words to say.'

His mouth moved closer to hers. 'They should be the easiest.'

She kissed him to avoid saying them, deciding to wait. He was right, they should be the easiest three words to say, not the hardest, but knowing that didn't make it any easier.

'So what are we going to call this sauce company?' he asked, pushing to his feet and reaching for her hand.

She gladly took it, sliding her arm around his waist when they were standing and slipping her fingers into his jeans pocket as they started to walk.

She wondered if Esmeralda had walked like this with Christopher, whispering their dreams to each other and planning a way to be together again. Or perhaps they'd just lived in the moment and soaked up the little time they had in each other's company, believing that fate would somehow bring them back together again.

'Where are you staying tonight?' Mateo asked.

She leaned closer into him. 'I was hoping you might have space for me.'

He laughed. 'There's always space for you. But maybe tonight we should get a hotel room. I think we need the night alone, we have a lot of business planning to do, after all.'

His gaze was wicked when she looked up at him. 'Business planning?'

'Business planning,' he repeated earnestly.

Claudia stopped walking and stepped in front of Mateo, standing on tiptoe as she touched both her hands to his face. She kissed him, not caring that they were in the middle of the pavement and that people might have to walk around them.

'Was that part of the business plan?' he asked when she lowered herself.

Claudia shrugged. 'Maybe.'

'Then I like this business venture very much.'

They both laughed and she tucked herself to his side once more as they fell into an easy step.

'There's one more thing,' she said, slowing again.

Mateo was the one to turn this time. He held her hand and she placed it over his chest. 'I think I love you,' she whispered.

'Creo que yo también te quiero,' he murmured back, lifting her hand and kissing her fingers. 'I think I love you, too.'

Somehow it sounded even more romantic in Spanish.

'I still have to go home in a week,' she said.

'I still have to stay,' he replied.

But somehow it didn't matter. For a girl who'd spent her entire life planning everything to the letter, she was okay with letting this go and seeing where fate would take them. If she was meant to be with Mateo, then somehow it would happen, and worrying about it wasn't going to change things.

'Do you believe in fate?' Mateo asked.

'Maybe.'

'Well, I do. I believe that fate brought us together for a reason, and it will somehow keep us together, too. We just have to believe.'

Then believe she would.

34

LONDON, 1951

Hope held the little baby in her arms. She was wrapped in a soft, pink woollen blanket that Hope had knitted herself many years ago, one she'd thought she would never use after all this time. Once, she'd imagined her own baby would be swaddled in it, but now it held a little orphan who was gazing up at her with the most beautiful big, dark eyes.

The child hadn't cried once, but her eyes had been wide open since birth, as if taking everything in, as if knowing the situation was already so desperate and not wanting to add to it by making a sound.

'I'll find you a wonderful family, little one,' Hope cooed, holding her tight against her body as she tried not to cry. 'You're going to be loved for the rest of your life, I promise you. I will find you a family who've been desperate for a child, a family who will love you as much as your mother would have.'

Her efforts to suppress her tears were fruitless; they ran down her cheeks and wet the blanket as she walked to the window, staring out at the beautiful day that had dawned. How sunshine could cast its light on them was a mystery to Hope— she almost wished for teeming rain to convey the sadness of what had happened in her home. So many mothers had passed through her doors, but today had been something she'd never expected would happen. Today had been a tragedy.

'Your beautiful mother is looking down on you, little one,' she murmured, lifting her in her arms and kissing the baby's downy forehead. 'She has made the sun come out today for you. She'll be your guardian angel for the rest of your life. Your mother, Esmeralda, will always be in your heart.'

Hope blinked away her tears and carried the child through the room, glancing at the card that Esmeralda had clutched until the very end, discarded on the bedside table along with a sketch of the family crest that she'd been so intent on drawing. The father had sobbed on the floor before holding his baby, clinging to her for a long moment before passing her back to Hope. She'd seen the way his eyes travelled to the bed, to the lifeless form there, and she'd also seen the way he looked with such sorrow at the baby after that, as if somehow it was the just-born child's fault. She'd known then that Esmeralda's Christopher, the man she'd left everything behind for and had begged for all those hours since arriving in London, wanted no part in raising his child. And she'd been proven right when he'd walked away, when he'd turned into a coward before her eyes and left the baby that Esmeralda had fought so valiantly to save. That Esmeralda had given her life for.

'Your mother never wanted to give you up,' she told the child as she walked into the hallway and carefully down the stairs. 'She wanted to spend her life loving you, and now I'm going to find someone special who will adore you just as she would. But there will always be something here if you come looking, something that will help you find your way back to her.'

There was a knock at her front door and Hope cradled the baby under one arm as she peered through the glass to see who was there. It was a young woman, with a familiar deer-in-headlights look in her eyes that most of the girls who came to her had; not to mention her stomach swollen and impossible to hide.

And despite the pain of losing a young mother only hours earlier, despite the baby in her arms that she would have done anything to keep herself, Hope opened the door and greeted the young woman with a smile. *This* was why she couldn't keep the baby; there were too many girls who needed her help, who would be forced onto the streets without her.

'Come in,' she said warmly. 'I'm Hope, and you're safe here.'

The young woman looked at the baby in her arms and began to cry, and Hope gently shut the door behind her before opening her free arm and drawing her close. She was used to comforting pregnant mothers in need, but this morning she needed the hug just as much as her new arrival did.

'Shh, now. Everything's going to be all right.'

Only she wasn't certain if she were trying to convince the stranger, the baby in her arms, or perhaps even herself.

EPILOGUE

LONDON, PRESENT DAY, SIX MONTHS LATER

'You're really doing this, aren't you?'

Claudia laughed, but not before enveloping her best friend in a hug. Charlotte had her hair in a topknot, wearing tracksuit bottoms and an oversized T-shirt, her baby asleep in the pram beside them.

'I'm sorry, but I'm really doing this,' she said, holding her tight.

Tears shone in Charlotte's eyes when she let her go, and Claudia wiped them away with her fingertips.

'Ugh, this is so not me,' Charlotte cried. 'The tears, the old clothes, the fact that I haven't washed my hair since,' she grimaced. 'I don't even know when I last washed my hair! I want your life! I want *my* old life back.'

Claudia held her hand and inclined her head towards the pram. 'But you made a human,' she said. 'Don't forget how wonderful your life is. It might be tough now, but this is everything you've always wanted. It'll get easier, I know it will, and then I'll be the one jealous of what you have.'

Charlotte grunted, which made them both laugh. 'What I want right this minute is a trip to Havana and a gorgeous man to whisk me off my feet when I land. I can just see him waiting for you, those swoon-worthy eyes, his arms around you...' Charlotte sighed. 'Sorry, I'm getting a little carried away. I have a lot of thinking time at the moment.'

'It's not forever,' Claudia said, but as she looked back at her flat and at all the things she had boxed up to send to her parent's house, it did feel more permanent than temporary. She had two suitcases packed to take with her to Havana, and legally she was only allowed to stay for thirty days, but she'd been told she could easily extend that to sixty days once she was there. And after that, she wasn't sure where she'd end up. Her original flat sale had fallen through and it had taken longer than expected to find a new buyer, but the deal was done now and she was more than ready to move on.

'I'm going to miss you,' Charlotte said. 'In case that wasn't obvious.'

'I'm going to miss you, too,' Claudia replied, as they sat side by side on her outdoor sofa and soaked in the view that she'd loved from the moment she'd bought the flat. London would always be her home, but right now, her heart was in Cuba. In truth it had been there from the moment she'd met Mateo, or perhaps the moment she'd landed in Havana and taken her first breath of Cuban air. She was as in love with the country and its people as she was with Mateo.

'Despite my selfish desire to keep you here, I am happy for you,' Charlotte said. 'This Mateo, he's made you glow. I only hope he knows how lucky he is.'

Claudia smiled as she thought of him; of running into his arms when she arrived, of being back in his food truck again, smiling and laughing as they stood side by side, as he taught her how to cook and they tried new sauce recipes in his mother's kitchen. Mateo had changed the way she felt about life, had made her want to open her heart to love again, and she knew that if she didn't return to Cuba, to see whether what they had was real, she'd never forgive herself. Their business was one thing, it had started to flourish as much because of his talent as her business skills at launching it into the market, but it wasn't work she was returning for.

She'd gone to Cuba to discover her grandmother's past, and instead, she'd discovered herself and a love she hadn't even known she was looking for.

She looked down at the ring he'd placed on her finger the day before she'd left, the complete opposite of the extravagant diamond she'd once worn there, and she just knew it was right. It was made of plastic and something they'd seen as they'd strolled past a little market selling knick-knack jewellery to tourists, but it meant more to her than anything she'd ever been given before. Every time she glanced at it, she knew it was time to follow her heart, that she didn't need to be scared of doing what felt right.

Everything about Mateo gave her butterflies, but as much as she'd miss London, there was nothing and no one that could stop her from getting on that plane.

I'll see you soon, Mateo.

'You're thinking about him, aren't you? I can see that faraway, goofy look in your eyes.'

Claudia just laughed. There was no point in denying it. A little wooden box tied with string, bearing her grandmother's name had turned her life upside down, but she wouldn't have had it any other way.

There was a knock at the door then, and Claudia went to open it. She found her mother standing there, tears in her eyes as she flung her arms around her.

'I'm going to miss you so much.'

'Mum, don't make me cry!' Claudia said, blinking as her eyes moistened all over again.

Her mother held her at arm's length then, her eyes searching Claudia's. 'There is nothing more important than love, Claudia. For a mother to see her daughter so happy.' She paused and squeezed her hands. 'Your grandmother would love to see you like this, to hear all about your wonderful adventures.'

'You promise you'll come and visit?' Claudia asked. 'I can't wait for you to see Cuba, and to meet Mateo and his family.'

'Nothing could stop me from booking that trip. I'm going to Havana first, and then Miami. Now come on, let's get you to the airport. Because you, my darling, have a plane to catch.'

A LETTER FROM SORAYA

Dear reader,

Thank you so much for choosing to read *The Cuban Daughter*! If you enjoyed the book and want to keep up to date with all my latest releases (including the next books in the series!), just sign up at the following link. Your email address will never be shared and you can unsubscribe at any time.

www.bookouture.com/soraya-lane

I do hope you loved reading the *The Cuban Daughter* as much as I loved writing it, and if you did, I would be very grateful if you could write a review. I can't wait to hear your thoughts on the story, and it makes such a difference in helping new readers to discover one of my books for the very first time.

This was the second book in *The Lost Daughters* series, and I'm looking forward to sharing more books with you very, very soon. If you haven't already read *The Italian Daughter*, you might like to read that book next, and enjoy being swept away to Italy and falling in love with some truly unforgettable characters.

One of my favourite things is hearing from readers – you can get in touch via my Facebook page, by joining Soraya's Reader Group on Facebook, or finding me on Goodreads or my website.

Thank you so much,

Soraya x

www.sorayalane.com

Soraya's Reader Group:
facebook.com/groups/sorayalanereadergroup

facebook.com/SorayaLaneAuthor

ACKNOWLEDGMENTS

I usually start by saying I have a very small group of people to thank, but this time I actually have quite a long list! First, I'd like to acknowledge Laura Deacon for taking a chance on this series when I first pitched the idea to her—without Laura, you wouldn't be reading this book! I would like to thank the entire Bookouture team for their support, with special mention to Peta Nightingale, Jess Readett, Saidah Graham and Melanie Price. But my biggest thanks goes to Richard King, to whom this book is dedicated. Richard, I will never forget the enthusiasm with which you pitched my books to the world! You are the reason my readership has grown to include readers all throughout Europe in so many languages, and it's no exaggeration to say that what you achieved for me was nothing short of extraordinary. Thank you. At the time of writing, *The Lost Daughters* series was being translated into fourteen languages, and Richard is to thank for most of those publishing deals.

I must make special mention and thanks to the other editors and publishers who will be publishing *The Lost Daughters* series around the world. Thank you to Hachette; to my UK editor Callum Kenny at Little, Brown (Sphere imprint); US editor Kirsiah Depp at Grand Central; Dutch editor Neeltje Smitskamp at Park Uitgevers; German editor Julia Cremer at Droemer-Knaur; and editors Päivi Syrjänen and Iina Tikanoja at Otava (Finland). I would also like to acknowledge the following publishing houses: Hachette (Australia and New Zealand), Albatros (Poland), Sextante (Brazil), Planeta (Spain),

Planeta (Portugal), City Editions (France), Garzanti (Italy), Lindbak and Lindbak (Denmark), Euromedia (Czech), Modan Publishing House (Israel), Vulkan (Serbia) and Pegasus (Estonia). Knowing that my book will be published in so many languages around the world by such well-respected publishing houses is truly a dream come true.

Now, back to my usual small group of wonderful people! Thank you to my long-time agent Laura Bradford, who I'm so proud to have in my corner. Special thanks also to Lucy Stille for reading *The Italian Daughter* and joining the team! Thank you to my incredible writing friends Yvonne Lindsay, Natalie Anderson and Nicola Marsh—what would I do without you girls? Yvonne, thank you for being so good at contacting me every day and making me set the timer to start writing—how would I ever write a book without you? To my parents, Maureen and Craig, thank you for your constant support. And finally, to my wonderful husband Hamish, and my gorgeous boys Mack and Hunter—I'm so lucky to have you all.

I should probably acknowledge my four-legged writing assistants as well... to Ted, Oscar and Slinky, thank you for keeping me company when I'm at home writing. My office wouldn't be the same without you! Actually, it would smell better and there wouldn't be hair all over the carpet or a cat on my desk, but still.

Soraya x

Made in the USA
Middletown, DE
24 May 2023

31282233R00175